THE WAGGING TAILS DOGS' HOME

SARAH HOPE

Boldwood

First published in Great Britain in 2023 by Boldwood Books Ltd.

Cover Design by Head Design Ltd

Cover Photography: Shutterstock

A CIP catalogue record for this book is available from the British Library.

Paperback ISBN 978-1-80549-052-4

Large Print ISBN 978-1-80549-048-7

Hardback ISBN 978-1-80549-047-0

Ebook ISBN 978-1-80549-045-6

Kindle ISBN 978-1-80549-046-3

Audio CD ISBN 978-1-80549-053-1

MP3 CD ISBN 978-1-80549-050-0

Digital audio download ISBN 978-1-80549-044-9

Boldwood Books Ltd
23 Bowerdean Street
London SW6 3TN
www.boldwoodbooks.com

For my children. Let's change our stars. xXx

1

Ginny looked around the small room. The overhead light flickered before plunging the room into semi-darkness, the small sliver of a window above the kettle only enough to illuminate the silhouettes of the large table and those around it.

'Didn't I tell you? I said the bulb was going to go, didn't I?' Susan, a volunteer in her mid-fifties, shook her head and made her way towards the kettle. 'Anyone for a cuppa?'

'Two minutes, Ginny, and I'll have light in here again.' Percy brushed his snowy white beard, patted Ginny's hand and stood up.

'Good idea, Susan. Tea break and then we'll get on with discussions.' Flora gave Ginny a smile before pulling Ginny's notebook towards her and squinting at the scrawled plans. 'You've done well. If we can implement everything, this should be the biggest and best Family Fun Day and Dog Show we've ever had.'

Blowing her hair out of her eyes, Ginny gripped hold of the large sheet of rolled-up paper. Every single time she headed staff meetings something happened. Last month it had been fleas –

yes, fleas. Alex had found one on Bertie, a small West Highland, and with the extent of his panic, anyone would have been forgiven for believing the world had ended. The time before, Susan's estranged ex-husband had let himself in and declared his undying – and very much not reciprocated – love for her. Maybe one day she'd actually be able to finish a staff meeting without any drama.

'I agree with Flora. Your plans sound amazing.' Susan yelped as the hot water missed the cup and splashed across her knuckles.

'Are you all right?' Flora stood up.

'Oh, it's nothing a little cold water won't fix.' Susan dismissed her concern with a wave of her hand and ran the cold tap, plunging her hand into the freezing water.

'Yes, well, it just feels as though there's more at stake than ever, so we need to try and attract more visitors, more prospective adoptees, and more cash-laden tourists.' Ginny looked around the room. She didn't need to tell the people in here how much was riding on this one event. Of course, the fundraising for Wagging Tails Dogs' Home never stopped, but their summer Family Fun Day was the one day of the year they were guaranteed to bring in more money than all of their other fundraising efforts put together. Funds they desperately needed to keep the ever-increasing number of dogs in their care homed and fed.

'We will.' Susan placed a steaming mug of tea on the table in front of Ginny.

'I hope so. I did the inventory yesterday and we've not even got enough money to cover the electricity bill next month, let alone to buy enough food and build those extra kennels we need.'

'It'll be fine, Ginny. We always find a way.' Flora took a long sip from her mug.

Looking across at Flora, Ginny could tell she was as worried as she was. Flora just had a way of covering it up, making everyone believe that everything was fine, but Ginny knew. She knew what was at stake and she wasn't about to let anyone down, least of all Flora and the dogs who relied on them.

Tim, a student volunteering as part of his college course, cheered as Percy turned the light back on.

'There you go, Ginny.' Percy binned the old light bulb and took his seat again, nodding to Susan as he picked up the mug she'd left there for him. 'Thanks.'

'Right.' Ginny slid her mug to the side and unrolled the paper she'd been clutching. 'I've sketched out the two paddocks and done a quick map of where we could position everything. So, I've got the stalls all around the outside of the bottom paddock with the agility pen in the middle, and then the food stalls, live music and pens for the dog shows up in the top paddock.' She circled the top paddock area with her finger.

'That's a good idea. Make people walk through the stalls before they get to the main area.' Wrapping a damp tea towel around her hand, Susan sat down. 'They're more likely to see something and spend if they've got to walk through it.'

'That's what I thought. Plus, the more the stallholders make, the more likely they're going to book another stall for next year.' Ginny tapped her pencil against the plans.

Flora nodded. 'Or for the Christmas market.'

'Yes, that's true.' Ginny grinned. If they could make a success of the Fun Day, particularly if they could pull in more people from the local community, the Christmas market might just attract more visitors than it did last year. Ginny shuddered as she remembered the pitiful number of visitors, not that she could blame them – the moment the last stall had finished setting up and Percy had taken residence in Santa's grotto, the heavens had opened, and within ten minutes the paddock had been turned into a flood plain. What they really needed was to hold the market inside somewhere. Maybe the answer would be to hold it in West Par village hall?

'Ginny?'

Shaking her head, Ginny tore herself from her thoughts and focused on the job in hand – the Family Fun Day and Dog Show.

'Sorry, Susan, I was miles away. Right, so we've already got some stallholders who have signed up: Elsie's bakery, Carrie's booked a stall to sell her pottery and I think she's going to have pottery painting sessions too, the lady who sells the crystals... but obviously we need a lot more vendors.'

'Terry's column in the *Trestow Telegraph* usually attracts more stallholders, and I can go through the list from last year, see if I can encourage them to sign up again.' Flora scribbled on a Post-it note.

'Good idea.' Ginny nodded. Why hadn't she thought of that?

'Has Terry been in touch yet? Shouldn't he have started writing his column already?' Twisting in his seat, Percy pulled a newspaper from a pile on the work surface behind him. He smoothed out the crumpled paper and flicked through it.

'He usually has – should have been published a couple of weeks ago. It's not in there. I've already looked.' Flora tucked a loose strand of greying hair into her bun. 'He's normally rung by now, too, to arrange a visit. I've emailed him at least four times, but I've not had an answer yet. I really should get round to calling him.'

'Good idea.' Percy folded the paper. 'Has Clarke agreed to do the dog training demonstrations?'

'Yes, I rang him a while back now and he's coming. He said...' Ginny pulled her phone from the back pocket of her jeans, the shrill ringtone distracting her. Glancing down at the name 'Jason' scrolling across the screen, she frowned and pushed it across the table.

'Everything okay?' Touching Ginny's hand, Flora nodded towards the phone.

Ginny smiled and shook her head. 'Yes, fine. Where was I? Ah, yes, Clarke told me he's planning on shortening the length of the agility course so he can fit more taster sessions in.'

'Oh, that's a good idea. I know last year there were quite a few people who didn't get to try it out.' Susan peeked beneath the tea towel covering her hand before flinging it across the room, where it landed on the pile of towels and dog bedding stacked up in front of the washing machine. 'I know little Dylan from the village was disappointed he didn't get to take his Jack Russell, Pixie, around the course.'

'Yes, so that should work well.' Ginny silenced her phone as it rang again.

'They're persistent, aren't they? Do you want me to answer it? Put on a gruff voice and scare them away? Tell them you don't need double glazing or another phone contract or whatever it is they're trying to sell?' Percy nodded towards Ginny's phone.

'You? Scare someone away? I don't think you've got a bad bone in your body.' Flora chuckled.

'Oh, for you lot I could.' Percy grinned, raising his eyebrows.

'I don't doubt it, but unfortunately, it's not someone from a call centre.' Ginny shifted in her chair. 'It's Jason. He's moved down here and now, because we're living within thirty miles of each other, he thinks we should reconnect.'

'Jason? The sap who broke your heart? Didn't you move down here to put some distance between you?' Flora wrapped her hands around her mug and frowned.

'Yes. He's just moved to Trestow.'

'Yuck. Well, don't you go letting him back into your life. Heed my advice. Look at me and Dean,' Susan said as she held her hand against her chest and grimaced. 'Me giving him a second chance was clearly the wrong decision.'

'Oh, don't worry. I have absolutely no intention of getting back with Jason. You know me, I'm happy as I am. Romance is for wimps. I certainly don't need a man to complete my life.' Blowing a loose strand of hair from her eyes, Ginny pulled her notebook towards her again. Once bitten and twice shy, as her mum would say. She'd had her heart broken once, and she would not make the same mistake again.

'Ginny, your soulmate will come into your life when you least expect it.' Percy patted her hand and leaned back in his chair, glancing across at Flora.

Ginny bit down on her bottom lip, forcing herself not to reply to him. Percy was the last person who should be giving advice on love. It was clear to everyone but Flora how Percy felt about her, but what was the point if he was never going to build up the courage to tell her how he really felt? Just because Percy had found his soulmate, even if she was none the wiser, it didn't mean there was someone out there for everyone.

'Percy's right, Ginny. Even after my experience with Dean, I refuse to stop believing I'll meet my one.' Susan scrolled through her phone and held the screen towards her. 'I can help you set up a profile on one of these dating apps, if you like? I'm sure a girl like you will be inundated with potential matches.'

'Nope, I don't need anyone. I like my life and, besides, I don't have time for anyone.' She squirmed in her chair. They needed to get back to planning the Family Fun Day. 'If there's nothing in tomorrow's paper, I'll ring and talk to Terry and see what's happening.'

'Good idea.' Flora nodded, moving the conversation on. 'He might have plans for a double-page spread at the weekend or something. I'm sure there'll be a reason why he's not put out his usual column.'

'Hello! Anyone here?' a voice called from the reception area.

'Oh drat, that will be Tim's tutor. She's meeting to discuss how he's getting on. I completely forgot.' Quickly downing the last dregs of her tea, Flora stood up. 'I'm really sorry, Ginny. I'm going to have to go and speak to her. You've got some fantastic ideas here. Maybe we can catch up again after?'

'That's okay, I think we're more or less done.' Ginny checked the clock and began to roll up the hand-drawn map. 'I need to take Jarvis to the vets', anyway.'

2

Ginny watched as Tyler, a young springer spaniel, bounded to the other end of the paddock in pursuit of a ball she'd just thrown. She glanced down at her phone – six minutes and forty-seven seconds she'd been on hold to the *Trestow Telegraph*. It was a good job she didn't have a breaking story to report, or their journalists would be the last ones to know.

'Good job, Tyler. Well done. Drop.' She fussed over his silky, floppy ears and carefully extracted the ball from his mouth. 'One day, you'll surprise me and actually drop the ball, hey?'

Smiling, she threw the ball again before wiping the sticky saliva down the front of her jeans. This was Tyler's happy place, the paddock. After living in a family home and getting all the attention in the world, he'd had a hard time settling into life at Wagging Tails, and she didn't blame him for it. She picked off a stray piece of fluff from her jumper and pocketed it. He'd ripped his bedding apart again last night.

'Again? You want me to throw it again?' She ended the call, deciding to try the newspaper offices in person instead, and tucked her mobile back into her pocket. She needed to pop into town on her lunch break to buy more treats for Tyler anyway. There was a particular brand his family had left with him which they didn't have at the home. 'You're one gorgeous pup, do you know that? And one day, very soon, the perfect family are going to come along and snatch you up.'

The spaniel pawed her knee, leaving a smudge of mud on the denim of her jeans.

'They will. And you'll go off with them and have the best life.' She wiped her eyes. It was stories like Tyler's that really got to her. She threw the ball again.

After four years working here, she knew she should be used to it by now, used to how cruel humans could be, but Tyler's story was different. He'd been loved and cared for, part of a family. And when he'd been dropped off, she'd never had to console an owner as much as she had done with Tyler's family, but with a family illness, money troubles and their home being repossessed and having to move in with friends, they'd run out of options. Ginny had seen how difficult the decision to give Tyler up had been for them.

'This is where you're hiding, then.'

Turning, Ginny saw Flora shut the gate behind her before joining her. 'Tyler trashed his pen again last night, so I thought it best to let him run off some energy.'

'Oh, did you, pet?' Flora fussed Tyler, his whole body wriggling from side to side with excitement as he wagged his tail. 'You'll find your family soon.'

'That's what I told him.' Ginny grinned. 'I couldn't get hold of anyone on the phone at the paper, so I'll pop in on my lunch break and have a word with Terry. Maybe we can ask him to feature Tyler's story first?'

'I think that's a great idea. With any luck, he'll have streams of people ready and willing to adopt him. Everyone loves a spaniel.'

'Yes, hopefully.' Ginny bent down again and fussed him behind his ears. 'Right, I'd better get this one back and then I'll take Frank and Dino on their morning walks.'

'Alex will be pleased. He's about to clean out their kennel and you know how Frank gets with him.'

Laughing, Ginny clipped Tyler's lead to his collar. 'Are you sure it's not the other way around? Poor Frank just wants a quiet life and when Alex goes in all cheerful and singing at the top of his voice, it just rubs him up the wrong way.'

'I think you may be right there.' Flora picked up the abandoned ball, turned and began to walk back with Ginny. 'And hey, I was going to say that I'm here if you need to talk, all right?'

Ginny looked down as Tyler paused to sniff at a clump of grass. 'Thank you. I know, but I'm fine.'

'That's good then. Just as long as you know I'm always here if you need me.' Flora pulled the gate closed.

'I do, but I really am okay.'

She *was* fine. Yes, her break-up with Jason had left her in pieces, but that had been four years ago now. She was over him. And once he got the message that she wanted nothing to do with him, whether he was now living in Trestow or not, the better. Biting down on her bottom lip, she paused and waited for Flora to catch up. She owed Flora so much. She hadn't just given her a job when she had moved down here, she had shown her patience and care. She'd helped her put her life back together. She was only worried because she cared. 'We had some more blankets and things dropped off this morning.'

'Oh, really? That's great.'

* * *

Patting the back pocket of her jeans, Ginny double-checked she had the photographs Susan had given her of the dogs eligible for adoption, before pushing the heavy glass door open. The foyer was bigger than she remembered; the large reception desk was positioned in the middle of the two lifts and a group of not-so-comfy-looking chairs were huddled by the window to the left. If she remembered correctly, the offices for the *Trestow Telegraph* were positioned on the top floor, level three.

There would likely be a reasonable explanation as to why Terry hadn't begun his column to promote the Family Fun Day yet. Flora might be right: he might be planning an eye-catching double-page spread to kick off his regular column. Something just didn't feel right, though, not to Ginny. No, she was glad she'd come here.

Reaching the top floor, she paused to catch her breath before shaking her hair from its messy bun and securing it again. She peered through the glass pane in the door. Grey partitions separated small cubicles, each housing someone dressed in a suit, with a computer and a coffee mug. She looked down at herself and grimaced. Maybe she should have changed out of her muddy jeans and crinkled pink T-shirt. She shrugged. She didn't need to impress anyone. Terry was lovely and had always been an advocate of Wagging Tails; he certainly wouldn't care what she was wearing.

She pulled open the door and stepped into the general hubbub of chatter, keyboards clicking and phones ringing.

'Can I help you?' A woman sitting behind a reception desk to Ginny's left waved her over.

'Hi, I've just come for a quick chat with Terry. Could you point me in the direction of his desk, please?' She frowned as the woman tilted her head before laughing.

'Terry Bennett? Short, bald, a wardrobe full of threadbare

woollen jumpers?' The woman clicked a long red fingernail against the surface of the desk.

Had his jumpers been threadbare? Ginny shrugged. 'Yes, Terry Bennett.'

'He's long gone, I'm afraid.' The woman picked up a stack of papers and stood up, the conversation apparently over.

'Gone? Where's he gone?'

'Spain? France? A remote island off the top of Scotland?' The woman sighed as the phone began ringing. She picked it up and tucked it between her shoulder and her ear before glancing back at Ginny. 'I've no idea. He retired six months ago.'

Retired? He hadn't mentioned anything when he'd visited last year. Surely he would have told them? Told Flora... 'Who's taken over his job?'

Raising her eyebrows, the woman nodded towards the back of the office. 'The one in the corner.'

'Right, thanks.'

Ginny made her way through the office and tried to ignore the stares from people on phones, from those scribbling in notebooks or tapping away on keyboards. As she neared the cubicle the receptionist had indicated, Ginny smiled. A man in a sharp grey suit was sitting hunched over his keyboard, squinting at his computer screen. He may not be Terry, but at least he looked professional. She walked up to his desk.

'Hello?'

Frowning, the man looked her up and down before turning back to his computer screen.

Clearing her throat, Ginny tried again. 'Hello, I understand you've taken over Terry Bennett's job?'

He turned slowly and looked at her again, an expression of irritation flashing across his face. 'I have.'

Ginny sighed. First impressions could definitely be deceptive.

She held out her hand. 'I'm Ginny Stevenson. I work at Wagging Tails Dogs' Home.'

Ignoring her hand, he turned back to his screen. 'Hi, Ginny. Now, if you don't mind, I'm just in the middle of something.'

Ginny narrowed her eyes. Hadn't he been taught any manners, or even basic social skills? 'I do mind, actually. I should be taking the dogs out, training them, and trying to rehome them. Instead, I've come all the way over here to ask Terry why he's not started his column about us in preparation for this summer's Family Fun Day.'

'Sorry, didn't anyone tell you? Terry's retired.' He pulled a notebook towards him and began to scribble something down, pausing every so often to scroll down the web page on his screen.

Who did he think he was? Not only talking down to her, but, more importantly, dismissing the dogs at the home with such ease? She picked up an envelope from a pile of papers on his desk and read the name.

'Darryl Thomas, huh? Has nobody explained to you that by taking over someone's job, you are actually expected to do just that? Their job? You are in charge of Terry's column now and every year, for the past decade or so, he has written about the preparations for the Family Fun Day. He's been highlighting the work we do and been featuring dogs who are ready to be adopted.'

Pushing his chair away from the desk, Darryl turned and looked at her. 'Look, Gina, I understand Terry used to cover your story. I'm sure our readers found your work at Woofing Tails Dogs' Home riveting. I'm sure it was some real nail-biting, perching-on-the-edge-of-the-sofa stuff, but things have changed. I'm doing this job now and I get to decide what to write about.'

Seriously? Didn't he understand how his decision would affect the dogs' home? Folding her arms, Ginny tapped her trainer against the cheap, grey carpet tiles. 'You can't do that. We have an understanding with the paper.'

'You had an understanding with *Terry*. Terry is no longer here.'

'We don't have an advertising budget. We hardly have enough money to cover the bills and food for the next two weeks. The column in the paper brings in donations, vendors who want to hire a stall at the Family Fun Day, visitors who spend money there and donate...'

'Okay, okay, I'll look into it.' He held his hands up, palms forward.

'Look into it? It's next month. We need to raise awareness; we need to fill the stalls.'

Shaking his head, Darryl picked up his pen. 'I'll see what I can do.'

'Do you think you can get something written in time for tomorrow's edition?'

'As I said, I'll try. That's the best I can offer, I'm afraid.'

'You'll try?' Why did she have the distinct feeling the only thing he was trying to do was to get rid of her?

'Oh, yes. I'll try. Now, if you don't mind, I really do need to get on. I have a meeting with...' he looked around the office and then used his pen to point to another journalist a few desks away '... that guy.'

Ginny nodded. 'Thank you.'

'Bye.' Darryl stood up and waved at her sarcastically.

Ginny headed towards the stairs, shaking her head as she walked. Time would tell as to how sincere he was being. She'd have to remember to tell Flora. If he really did write a column for tomorrow's paper, they'd likely get an influx of calls asking for details. They'd have to make sure someone stayed within earshot of the phone.

3

───────

Stepping outside, Ginny pulled her mobile from her back pocket and sighed as the photographs Susan had given her scattered across the ground. How had she forgotten those? She began to gather them up.

'Fancy seeing you here. Are you stalking me?'

Ginny looked up. She knew that voice. She'd recognise it anywhere.

'Jason.'

'Here, let me help.' Bending down, Jason reached for a photo. 'Oh, he's cute. You're still working at the dogs' home then?'

Ginny plucked the photograph from Jason's hand. 'How do you know where I work? In fact, how did you even know I was living down this way?'

She'd thought it odd when he'd first started ringing last week and leaving messages to say he'd moved. Someone must have told him. Who though? After their relationship had ended and she'd moved down to West Par, she'd only told a handful of people where she'd been going: Anna, one of the other estate agents she'd worked with at her previous job, her mum who had emigrated to America the month after she'd left, and her old school friend, Mary. She couldn't imagine Anna or Mary telling him where she'd gone. Why would they? And her mum had never liked Jason, had always said he wasn't right for Ginny, too controlling. She wouldn't have spoken to Jason, let alone told him where Ginny was living now. Maybe Anna or Mary had accidentally let something slip, or someone from her old job. Her old boss had always thought highly of him...

'You know, I hear things on the grapevine.' Jason grinned.

'Right.'

She didn't know anyone 'on the grapevine' as he called it. The majority of her so-called friends had been people she'd met through Jason, and they'd swiftly exited her life when they'd split up.

'I left you a voicemail. I don't know if you got it? I wondered if you wanted to catch up now I'm living down here?'

Catch up? Really? What did he expect her to say? That she'd love to spend an evening reminiscing over the old times? Would they chat over their starters about the fact he'd cheated on her for six months? Would they ponder over the way she'd had to claw back money from their wedding venue, the fact she'd had to call the bridal boutique and explain between sobs how she didn't need the wedding dress she'd taken so long to choose and that, yes, she was all too aware that she would lose her deposit? Would the topic of him basically chucking her out of their shared house so that he could move his mistress in be kept for dessert?

'I don't think that's such a good idea.'

'Really?' Jason frowned, reaching out to touch her elbow.

Ginny took a step back, gripping the photographs tighter. 'Yes, really. Surely you've not forgotten what you did to me?'

'No, but, well, that was a long time ago now, wasn't it? We're both adults. Surely we can move on?'

Both adults? Well, yes, they were, only one of them had a moral compass and one of them didn't.

'How is Natasha?'

'Natasha? She... we split up shortly after you moved out.'

Ginny opened her mouth before thinking better of it and turned around. 'I need to go.'

'Ginny, wait, please.'

Without looking back, she pushed the heavy glass door open and strode back through the foyer of the office building, heading straight towards the stairwell. The sooner she gave Darryl the photographs and could get away from Trestow, from Jason, the better. After all the hurt Jason's affair with Natasha had caused, how could he be so calm, acting as if none of it had ever happened? She swiped at her eyes, taking the stairs two at a time. She was better off without him. Him having an affair had been a blessing in disguise. It really had. If he hadn't, they would have likely been married by now, maybe even have a child or two, and she'd be living with him, sharing her life with him. She shuddered. At least she'd found out what kind of person he really was before their wedding day. Besides, she now lived in the beautiful seaside village of West Par, had a wonderful group of friends and a job she loved.

First floor. And who did he think he was to assume she'd even want to spend any time with him? In the four years they'd spent apart, his ego must have only grown. Why else would he just take it upon himself to presume she'd jump at the chance to even consider meeting up?

Second floor. She could imagine what Flora would say when she told her about running into him. And she would. She told Flora everything. Without her mum close by, Flora had stepped into that role, pretty much from the moment Ginny had turned up on her doorstep with her suitcase in one hand and the flyer advertising Wagging Tails in the other. Flora had welcomed her with open arms, and, after only a month of volunteering, she'd given her a permanent job, a focus, a way to piece together her heart and rebuild her life. Six months after that, Flora had helped her find a small cottage to rent in the village.

Third floor. Without pausing to catch her breath this time, Ginny pushed the door open and made her way back to Darryl's desk.

'Short meeting?' she asked when she saw him sitting there, still scrolling on the screen.

'Gina? You're back.' Spluttering into his coffee mug, Darryl looked at her, his eyes hooded, guarded. 'And what can I do for you this time?'

'It's Ginny, not Gina.' She threw the photographs on his desk. 'I forgot to give you these. They're photos of dogs we have ready to be rehomed. Terry featured different dogs, placing a photo of them in the paper with a brief description of their personality, history, likes and dislikes.'

'Likes and dislikes.' Darryl nodded.

'We'd like you to feature Tyler first, please. He's a springer spaniel, just over a year old, placed in our care when his family had to give him up due to circumstances out of their control. He loves to play fetch; he'd play all day given the choice. He hates confined spaces. Can be rehomed with other dogs...' Ginny frowned. 'Aren't you going to write this down?'

'It's all in here.' Darryl tapped the side of his head. 'Is that all?'

'What? No.' She shook her head. 'He's well trained and walks on the lead without pulling, which is quite a rarity for spaniels. He's neutered, up-to-date with his vaccinations and is generally healthy.'

'Right, healthy.'

'Are you sure you're going to remember all of this? Do you want me to write it down?' She reached out for his notebook.

Pulling it back away from her grasp, Darryl shook his head. 'I'll remember.'

'And you've got the date of the Family Fun Day? You'll make sure to mention the dog show too? Both the locals and the tourists love it. There'll be taster classes as well: basic dog training, agility, tracking, hoopers.' She counted them off on her fingers.

'Uh-huh.' Darryl picked up a doughnut from his desk and sank his teeth into it, sugar covering his lips.

What was it with men? They were all the same. Apart from Percy, of course, and her colleagues Alex and Tim. She shook her head. That wasn't fair. There were plenty of lovely guys in the village. It was only Jason and Darryl she had a problem with.

She watched as he set down the half-eaten doughnut on the plate at the side of his computer before wiping the sugar from his coarsely stubbled chin.

'Do you even know what hooper training is? Or tracking, for that matter?'

Grinning, he shrugged. 'I'm a journalist. Research is my middle name.'

'I can just tell you.'

'I really should get on, you know.'

'Why? Have you got another pressing two-minute meeting to attend?'

Raising his eyebrows, Darryl looked at her. 'Maybe.'

The feeling was mutual, she couldn't wait to get away from him either. The difference was she cared about the dogs and about what he included in the article, whereas he wasn't even pretending to mask the fact he was opposed to writing the article at all.

'Right, in that case, I'll let you get to your... umm... important meeting.' She took a step away, and then turned back. 'I can tell you don't think this is important, but it is. The Family Fun Day will raise more money for the dogs' home than we get through any other event, and for dogs like Tyler...' she pointed to his photo '...it could be his chance to find his forever family. He's really struggling with the upheaval and complete change of lifestyle. He needs this.'

Rolling his eyes, Darryl picked up Tyler's photo and placed it next to his keyboard. 'I'll feature Tania tomorrow.'

'Tyler. It's Tyler.' He could call Ginny by the wrong name, she didn't care, but he needed to remember Tyler's.

'Tyler.' Nodding, Darryl pushed his chair back and, once again, picked up his notebook and pen, signalling the end of the conversation.

'Thank you.' Turning, Ginny headed back towards the stairwell. All she could do was hope that he'd remembered at least some of what she'd told him.

As she walked through the foyer door and out into the sunshine, she pulled her mobile from her back pocket before scrolling through to Anna's name. She'd known Anna for years, they'd both started working at the same estate agents fresh out of college and had then moved to the next agency together too. People had always joked that they were twins. She needed to tell Anna who she'd ran into.

'Hello?' Anna's voice sounded guarded, uncertain.

'Hi, Anna. It's me, Ginny. You'll never guess who I've just had the pleasure of running into.' The sarcasm slipped into Ginny's voice.

'Oh, hi, Ginny. I don't know.'

'Jason! Would you believe it? The one person I thought, hoped, I'd never have to set eyes on again and he's here. Working and, I assume, living too, not thirty miles from where I live.' She glanced behind her, suddenly worried Jason would be trying to catch her up.

'Jason? He's moved down there?'

Ginny sidestepped around a mother and buggy. 'Yes, of all the...'

'I've got to go. Bye.' And that was it. Anna had hung up.

Frowning, Ginny looked at the screen on her mobile. She'd really hung up on her. She didn't speak to Anna very often any more, but when she did, they normally spoke for at least an hour. She must have been busy.

4

'It's okay, Tyler. I'm not cross with you.' Ginny kissed Tyler on the top of his head before grabbing another handful of fluff. That was the fourth duvet he'd ripped apart this week. 'Just you wait, when people read about you in the paper and see your gorgeous picture, you'll have queues of people all wanting to give you a loving home.'

Tyler nudged his plastic dog basket, clattering it against the wall of his kennel.

'What are you trying to tell me? Do you want another duvet? I'm not too sure that's such a good idea, sweetheart. How about I try to find you some blankets instead? Super indestructible ones?' Ginny laughed as the small springer spaniel snuffled up to her, a cloud of fluff sticking to his nose. Gently pulling it off, Ginny looked up as a loud bark seeped through the open windows. More barking and a loud screech for 'help' soon followed.

Standing up, Ginny brushed the fluff from her knees. 'I'll be back in a minute, Tyler. Let me just see what's the matter with Alex.'

After closing the door to Tyler's kennel firmly behind her, she ran down the corridor, a chorus of other dogs joining in with the excitement, their barks only seeming to antagonise whatever situation was going on outside. Running out into the sunshine, Ginny saw Alex, who was walking Ralph, a large and very nervous Staffie. Her gaze shifted to two other small dogs running, unleashed, around the training garden.

'What's going on? Where have they come from?'

'I don't know. I was just walking Ralph, and they showed up,' Alex called above the noise. 'You know how nervous Ralph gets, though. I can't promise to be able to control him if they get much closer.'

'I know. Just get him back to his kennel. I'll try to catch these two.' She waved Alex away before trying to corner one of the small dogs. 'Hey, it's okay. I'm not going to hurt you.'

'You okay out here, lovely?'

Glancing away from the dog, Ginny looked across at Flora, who had stepped out of the reception room. 'These two have just appeared from nowhere.'

'I bet someone's thrown them over the gate.' Flora shook her head. 'I'll go this way, you go that, and we'll try and encourage them to go behind the shed. We'll be able to corner them there and, with a little luck, get hold of them.'

'Good idea. Why wouldn't they have just tied them up at the gate? For all they'd known we might use this space for exercising off-lead.' Ginny changed direction and, holding her arms out wide, helped Flora to usher the dogs behind the storage shed.

'I know, love. I saw poor Alex had a hard time of it getting Ralph away as it was.' Flora bent down, barely a metre from the dogs. 'Some people just don't think though. They make the decision to dump their dogs, and once they've made up their minds, it's as though all common sense gets thrown out of the window.'

'That's it. You're going the right way.' Ginny slowly inched towards one of the dogs before sighing as it ran between her legs and back out into the courtyard, closely followed by the other one. Pausing, she placed her hands on her hips and watched as the two small dogs began following Ralph's scent towards the kennels.

'Don't worry, the first thing Alex would have done is to make sure the door is firmly shut.' Flora rubbed Ginny's shoulder. 'Come on, let's try again.'

'That's true.' He would have. Alex loved Ralph; he had a special place in all their hearts. He would have made sure he wouldn't be put in any situation where he might get scared and react. Taking a deep breath, Ginny walked towards the dogs again, Flora beside her.

'That's it. Go on, back behind the shed.' Holding her arms out, Flora ushered the dogs back the way they'd come.

'They certainly don't look fazed by this whole experience.' Ginny walked towards the dogs, keeping her eyes firmly fixed on them, ready to dart forward and stop their escape. Far from looking meek and scared, the two dogs looked as though they were having the time of their lives.

Flora chuckled. 'I have a feeling these two might liven things up around here a little. Ready?'

'Yep. Ready.'

'Right, lovely. Shall I grab the one with the pink collar and you get the one with the orange?'

'Okay. On the count of three. One, two, three.' Lunging forward, Ginny grabbed the dog. 'That's it, well done, little one.'

'They seem friendly enough.' Flora checked the tag of the one she'd gripped hold of. 'Belle. A cockapoo, by the looks of it.'

'Same here.' Ginny looked from Belle to her dog and back again. 'They may well be siblings. Let's see what your name is. Tiger.'

Flora chuckled as she looked at Belle's collar again. 'Oh, you've got to love it when people abandon their dogs and forget the tags have their phone numbers on.'

Ginny laughed. 'Now, that will be an interesting conversation.'

'You're telling me. Let's get these two settled in the empty kennel and then we'll make that phone call.' She picked up the young cockapoo. 'Come on, Belle.'

'You too, Tiger. Shall we find your new home?'

Fussing the dog behind the ears, Ginny stood up, holding him firmly in her arms. Making sure he was facing away from her, she hugged him to her. It was always a little dicey holding an unknown dog, but without a lead on her, she didn't have much choice.

'We're full now, aren't we?'

'Yes, all the inside kennels will now be taken. I was keeping this last one for a dog from the pound. Yvonne called this morning, begging us to take a Labrador.'

'Labradors are normally easy to rehome, at least.'

'I do hope so.' Flora held the door open for Ginny.

'We could set up the outside kennel. I know it's not perfect, but it'll be better than turning her away.'

'I guess we'll have to. From what Yvonne was saying, we're her last hope. I'll get Susan on the case. I'm sure she'll work her DIY magic and be able to transform the dilapidated outside kennel into somewhere liveable and she should be fine for a while, at least. Besides, we should be getting calls about Tyler soon, so it won't be long until we have one of the regular kennels free.'

'That's true.' Ginny nodded. 'I'll pop out on my break and grab a paper. See what Darryl has written,' she said, spitting out his name. 'I still can't believe the way he spoke to me, but I guess none of that matters if he does a good job of promoting the home.'

'I've still a good mind to ring up his editor-in-chief and complain. From what you said, his attitude towards you was awful.'

'There's no point.'

Ginny pulled open the door to the kennel and carefully lowered Tiger inside.

'That's it, you go and explore. I'll get you both something to eat in a moment.'

Flora closed the door, Belle's tag in hand. 'Come on then, let's see what this so-called owner has to say. I can understand people leaving them tied up at the gate, but to chuck them over...' She shook her head.

'Some people just don't care.'

'No, some don't, but as I always try to say, it's only a few; the majority of people are good.'

'Umm.' Ginny looked across at Flora. It still surprised her that, after thirty-five years of running Wagging Tails and experiencing first-hand the cruelty some people can impose on poor innocent creatures, Flora could not only believe there was good out in the world, but could also be sure that the majority of people were kind.

'There you both are.' Percy hurried down the corridor towards them, waving a newspaper in his hand. 'I've been looking all over for you.'

'Oh, has our article been published?' Flora grinned.

'Umm, don't get too excited.' Heading back up the corridor to the reception area, Percy pulled a red and white checked handkerchief from his pocket and wiped it across his forehead.

'Let's have a look then.' Now behind the counter, Flora pushed the notebooks and pens to one side, making space for the newspaper. She tapped the surface impatiently.

'Of course.' Percy leafed through the pages before laying the newspaper open.

'Huh, where is it?' Flora balanced her reading glasses on her nose and squinted. 'Is this it?'

'Just that, I'm afraid. I've been through the whole thing twice and all we've got is Tyler's photo and a brief description. And when I say brief, I mean brief.'

Leaning across the counter, Ginny frowned. 'He hasn't written anything that I told him.'

'Tyler's described as a cocker spaniel, too.' Flora tapped the page.

'And there's definitely not another article about Wagging Tails or the Family Fun Day anywhere else in the paper?' Ginny rubbed her temples. She'd gone through everything with Darryl, given him every detail he could possibly need and that's all they got? A tiny description about Tyler stating the wrong breed? 'I can't believe he's done this. I asked him if he needed to write it down. I even tried to write it down for him myself.'

'It's not your fault, lovely.' Flora rubbed her arm.

It sure felt like her fault. If she hadn't got off on the wrong foot with him, if she'd talked him round... Had she described everything properly? Told him what the Family Fun Day would comprise of? Explained how crucial it was to the running of the home?

'It's a darn shame that Terry has retired.' Percy shook his head.

Taking her car keys from beneath the counter, Ginny looked at the two of them. 'I'm going to talk to him.'

'Do you really think that's going to convince him to do a better job?'

'If I can get him to come and visit us, he might just begin to understand how important this is to us, to the dogs.'

She had to try. She couldn't just sit back and let him get away with this.

5

At the top of the stairs, Ginny rolled her shoulders back and took a deep breath before pushing open the door to the *Trestow Telegraph*'s office.

'Can I—' the receptionist started, but Ginny ignored her, making her way between the partitioned cubicles towards the back of the vast room.

There he was. Sitting at his desk, checking his phone without a care in the world. Clenching her fists and digging her nails into the palms of her hands, she strode towards him.

'How dare you?'

'I beg your pardon?' Putting his phone down, Darryl twisted in his chair to face her.

'I said, how dare you? How dare you play with our lives, the dogs' lives, like that? You didn't write a feature about the dogs' home, you didn't promote the Family Fun Day at all, not one little sentence.'

'I wrote a description about the dog you want to get rid of.'

Ginny swallowed. Seriously?

'Want to get rid of? We don't want to get rid of Tyler, we want him to find his forever home. We want the best for him. We want him to have a family where he has a proper house to live in, is taken care of, can play fetch as often as he likes. We never want to get *rid* of dogs, but to help them find someone to care for them, to love them, to accept them as they are. It's what we do. Wagging Tails is a dogs' home. A very overstretched dogs' home.' She took a breath. 'And you called him a cocker spaniel. I told you he was a springer.'

'Cocker, springer. They're both spaniels, aren't they? At least I didn't describe him as a pug or a greyhound.'

'This is important.'

'Of course it is,' Darryl muttered under his breath, his words barely audible. 'And there was me thinking they had given me all the rubbish stories...'

'You really don't get it, do you? You really don't understand that we're a charity. We rely on donations and the goodwill of the public. We rescue dogs who would otherwise stand no chance of finding a home. Do you know how many dogs are abandoned each year? How many dogs end up in pounds or shelters up and down the country?'

'I'm sure it's a few.' He shrugged.

'A few?' Narrowing her eyes, Ginny glared at him. He really didn't care. At all. 'Not a few. A lot. Over one hundred thousand dogs, to be precise. That's how many are taken to pounds, shelters and dogs' homes each year. One hundred thousand, and that's not counting the sixty-seven thousand stray dogs living on the streets.'

Averting his eyes, Darryl raked his fingers through his dark hair. 'Well, isn't it a good job there are good people like yourself looking out for them, then?'

Stepping into his line of vision, Ginny glared at him. 'People like me, dogs' homes like Wagging Tails, don't have near enough money or capacity to look after them all.' She pinched the bridge of her nose. He didn't care. He wouldn't, not even if he knew all the stats, but she couldn't stop. She had to tell him. She had to let him know how important what they did was. How important all the dogs' home up and down the country were. She had to try to make him see. 'Twenty-one dogs are put to sleep every single day because of the lack of space to keep them before they can be rehomed. *Twenty-one a day*, and that's just in the UK.'

'What do you want me to say?'

'I don't want you to say anything. An apology from you won't mean a thing, you won't mean it. I want you to *understand*.' She shifted her feet. 'I want you to come and visit Wagging Tails. See what we do there, meet the dogs, and witness first-hand why this Family Fun Day is so important to us.'

Holding his hands up, Darryl shrugged. 'I'll rewrite the piece about Tyler, okay? I'll even write the column about your dogs' home.'

'Come to Wagging Tails. Terry always came to visit; he understood what we needed. That we needed him to promote us through the paper, that we needed him to remind people we existed, to hype up the Family Fun Day.'

'I don't think that's going to happen.' He indicated his desk and his keyboard. 'I've got so much to do here.'

Shaking her head, Ginny scoffed. 'So much to do that you can't even do your job properly.'

'I've said I'll write the darn column, haven't I?'

'And you'll include details such as the date, time, how to get in touch to hire a stall—'

'I'll include it all, yes.' He glanced behind her and shook his head. 'Oh great, just what I need.'

'What?' Ginny frowned.

'Morning, Darryl, mate,' came a familiar voice. 'Ginny, what a wonderful surprise.'

Slowly turning, Ginny narrowed her eyes. What was he doing here?

'Jason.'

'Have you come to see me? You've changed your mind about dinner?' Putting his hands in his trouser pockets, he rocked on his feet, a huge grin spreading across his face.

'No!' Looking him up and down, she shuddered. How had she ever been in love with this man? 'Why are *you* here?'

'I work here. Editor-in-chief. Run the office. Made the move from magazines to newspapers about three years ago.'

Great, that was all she needed – to have to contend with both Darryl's and Jason's inflated egos. They might as well write off the whole newspaper column idea completely. Look into other ways of getting the word out. Leaflets? Social media?

'Being as you're here, shall we grab some coffee?' Jason indicated a large glass-fronted office to their right. 'Oh, and Darryl, I've got a great lead I'd like you to work on.'

'What's that then?'

'A couple living on one of the estates on the edge of town have transformed the whole of the inside of their house into a cave. They've painted the walls, crafted boulders from papier mâché, the whole works. There are even rumours of them encouraging bats to nest inside.'

Darryl's nostrils flared almost imperceptibly.

'Great, I knew you'd love it. A real human interest piece.' Jason tapped the edge of his desk. 'You can head over there now. Take some photos, interview them.'

Glancing from Jason to Ginny, Darryl stood up and grabbed his jacket from the back of his chair.

'I'd love to, but I'm afraid I already have commitments today. I'm visiting the local dogs' home.'

'You are?' Ginny turned to look at Jason, changing her expression into something that looked like she already knew this fact. 'He is. It's all arranged.'

Jason nodded slowly. 'Okay.'

'Anyway, we'd better be off. Don't want the little squidgy doggies to think we've forgotten about them, do we?' And with that, Darryl turned to leave, cupping Ginny's elbow and leading her out of the office.

'Little squidgy doggies?' She coughed to disguise the laugh rising to her throat.

'Don't. Just keep walking.' His voice was low as he strode towards the lift.

'Oh, I don't—'

'Ginny doesn't use lifts,' came a voice from behind them. 'She'll go down the stairs.'

Ginny turned and looked at Jason who was now a few feet behind them. She set her jaw. 'I use lifts.'

'Really? It's just that when we were together, you couldn't. You had that awful phobia. Do you remember that time in Greece...?'

'You dated this guy?' Darryl's mouth was so close to her ear, she could feel his breath against her skin.

'Anyway, bye.' Pressing the button to call the lift, Ginny watched Jason out of the corner of her eye.

Please go, please go.

The lift pinged, announcing its arrival to the floor.

After a quick glance back at Jason, who was now standing and watching, his hands still in his pockets, she took a deep breath and stepped inside. Standing in the middle of the tiny space, she forced herself to grin as the thick metal doors sealed them inside.

'You used to date him? *Him?* What did you ever see in a guy like that? You don't even look as though you'd be friends, let alone date each other.'

'We were going to get married.' Ginny swallowed, her eyes fixed on a fleck of white on the stark metal flooring. Had someone dropped a bit of tissue?

'Married? You were going to marry him?' Darryl sneered.

Crossing her arms, Ginny gripped her elbows and began to count her breaths. In one, two, three. Out one, two, three. She could feel the space reducing, their reflections in the mirrors surrounding the metal walls closing in on her.

'I really can't imagine that. Married.' Darryl turned to face her, his chuckling finished. 'Are you okay? You're shaking.'

'I don't do lifts. I *can't* do lifts.' Ginny could hear her heart pounding, feel her breath quickening. She covered her eyes with her hands.

She really shouldn't have got in here.

'You don't do lifts and yet you got in one. Okay, we'll get off at the next floor.' He jabbed the button. 'Just keep breathing nice and slow. In one, two, three. Out one, two, three. Come on, you know this will work.'

She could feel his hands cupping her elbows and the heat from his body. The warmth of his touch was comforting, grounding. She tried to match his breathing, her heart rate slowly decreasing with every breath.

'That's it. Almost there.'

As the lift juddered to a stop, she shot her arms out, gripping Darryl's jacket. 'It's broken down, hasn't it? That's it. Over. We'll be stuck in here for hours.'

'It hasn't broken down. Look, see, the doors are opening. We've just arrived at the second floor, that's all. Fancy taking the stairs the rest of the way?'

Looking from Darryl to the door, she breathed a quick sigh of relief and as soon as the gap was wide enough, she stepped outside, thankful to be free. Walking through another office, they made their way towards the stairwell.

'You literally just put yourself through that to impress your ex?' Darryl said as he jogged down beside her.

'Not to impress, no. To prove to him that he doesn't know me any more.'

Although, in reality, nothing had changed regarding her phobia of lifts. She shook her head. It had made sense at the time.

'Right. Can I make a small suggestion?' Darryl held his hand in front of her, his thumb and index finger a centimetre apart.

'What?' She shook her head.

'Don't try to prove him wrong by putting yourself in a position like that again. No one's worth putting yourself through that.'

Keeping her eyes focused in front of her, Ginny slumped her shoulders. 'You're enjoying yourself, aren't you?'

'Not at all. I just know that no one's worth feeling like that for.'

Pausing, she looked across at him, waiting for him to stop and look back at her. 'You've got a phobia, too. That's why you knew what to do, how to calm me.'

Running his fingers through his hair, Darryl continued down the stairs.

'Go on, tell me. You know what mine is now.'

Jogging down, she caught him up and matched his pace.

'We really don't have time to chat. We've wasted enough time with your dramas in the lift.' Increasing his speed, Darryl raced to the bottom of the stairs.

Frowning, Ginny watched as he pushed open the door into the foyer.

6

Tapping her mobile against the steering wheel, Ginny thought about the situation. Had Flora received her message warning her that she was bringing Darryl back? Or Susan? Or Alex? She checked her messages again. Nothing.

Taking a deep breath, she shook her head. There was nothing she could do. Not now. She'd just have to hope they'd seen the messages but were too busy rushing around making the necessary preparations to reply.

She watched Darryl's sleek BMW pull into the small car park and had to stifle a laugh as he tried to manoeuvre his car around the potholes. The look of horror on his face was hilarious. What had he expected?

She stepped out of her car and waited for him to join her.

'Thanks for coming.'

'Huh. Let's just get this over and done with,' he said, looking down at the mud beneath his feet.

Why did she have the distinct feeling he'd only agreed to visit to get away from Jason? Not that she'd blame anyone for trying to get away from him. Whatever the reason, he was here now and

Ginny just needed to make sure that by the time he left he had a bit more empathy with their plight. She could do this. She began to lead the way towards the reception.

At the door, she nodded for him to go ahead.

Darryl glanced at her before stepping inside, immediately covering his mouth with the sleeve of his suit jacket.

Inside, the strong undeniable whiff of dogs muck filled her nostrils. Great. This was all she needed. All *they* needed.

'Flora? Susan? Alex?' Where was everyone? She'd at least expected someone to be around to greet them and yet the reception area was empty, quiet. She really didn't think she could cope with showing Darryl around on her own. Hadn't she done enough getting him here in the first place? The thought of spending any more time alone with him... Looking across at him, she shuddered. She peered into the kitchen. Nope. That was empty too. Just as she thought everyone had abandoned the place and she really was stuck with Darryl on her own, the door from the kennels opened and out came Flora.

'Come on, Belle, let's go and get you cleaned up.' Pausing, Flora looked from Ginny to Darryl and back again.

'Flora, this is Darryl, the journalist who's taken over Terry's job. Darryl, Flora founded Wagging Tails Dogs' Home thirty-five years ago with her late husband.'

'Oh, Darryl? Afternoon.' Flora gripped hold of the small dog as she writhed around in her arms. 'I... I'll just pass this little one to Tim and then I'll come and introduce myself properly.'

Flora rushed past and into the dogs' washroom, leaving the door to swing shut behind her. Ginny plastered a smile on her face and rolled her shoulders back. Yes, Flora rushing through with a soiled Belle might not have been the best first impression she could have given Darryl, but...

'Seriously? What's wrong with some people?' Her thoughts

were interrupted by another person rushing in, the kennel door flinging open again. This time it was Alex, holding a bundle of towels in his arms. 'I mean, as if abandoning two little dogs isn't enough, to also be incapable of feeding them something fit for consumption...' He shook his head as he slowed to a stop in front of Ginny and Darryl.

Clearing her throat, Ginny gave Alex a pointed look.

'Alex, this is Darryl from the *Trestow Telegraph*...'

Alex opened and closed his mouth before bundling the towels into one arm so he could hold his other hand out. 'You've come to have a look around?'

Darryl glanced down at Alex's proffered hand and then to the soiled towels. He set his jaw and returned the handshake. 'Afternoon.'

'It's so great you've come to visit. Terry always came every single year.' Alex grinned. 'He loved this place, Terry did.'

'So I hear.'

Looking down at his armful of soiled towels, Alex nodded towards the washroom. 'I'd better get on. Catch you later.' The whiff of dogs' muck lingered as Alex followed in Flora's footsteps.

Ginny watched as Darryl inspected his hand intensely. She quickly stepped forward and offered him the hand sanitiser bottle from on the counter. 'I'm sorry. This isn't quite the first impression I'd planned to give you.'

Darryl nodded, pumping out some sanitiser for himself and rubbing it between his fingers.

Ginny frowned. This was it then. He'd leave thinking they couldn't cope, and not wanting to ever step foot inside the place again. What article would he write, if he even did so? Maybe it would be better if he didn't bother at all. She pinched the bridge of her nose, feeling a headache coming on.

'Right, I'm so sorry about that, Darryl,' Flora said as she burst through the door from the washroom. She dried her hands on a tea towel before laying it on the counter and holding her hand out for a handshake. 'We had a couple of pups thrown over the fence earlier and they both have upset tummies.'

'Are they okay?' Ginny asked. 'Do you know what caused it?'

'They'll be fine, Ginny, lovely. Their previous owners must have given them something.' Flora shook her head before looking back towards Darryl. 'Maybe we can start again?'

Looking down at her hand, Darryl accepted it before jumping back as the door to the kennels opened again.

'Coming through.' Hurrying through the reception area, Susan carried Tiger in a huge, dirty towel.

Averting his eyes, Darryl looked at his shoes and mumbled, his voice barely audible over the chatter from the washroom. 'Jeez, got any more in there?'

Narrowing her eyes, Ginny shook her head. Why did he have to be so rude? These were dogs who had been abandoned, possibly mistreated too. It wasn't their fault if they'd eaten something they shouldn't have and it certainly wasn't their fault if their so-called owners had fed them rubbish food. Why couldn't he understand?

Flora placed a hand on Ginny's forearm and turned to Darryl. 'Shall we grab a nice cuppa and we can discuss the upcoming Family Fun Day, before Ginny introduces you to our residents?'

Ginny took a deep breath and placed her hand over Flora's. She always knew when Ginny needed that little extra bit of reassurance. 'That's a good idea.'

Shifting on his feet, Darryl hitched up the sleeve of his jacket and looked pointedly at his watch. 'Actually, I have a meeting coming up soon, so...'

Nope, there was no way he was going to come all this way to Wagging Tails and pull a stunt like that, not with her, not again.

Forcing herself to smile and suppressing the urge to tell him exactly what she thought of him and his 'meetings', she yanked open the door to the kennels and nodded towards him.

'Don't worry, we can discuss the Family Fun Day and meet the dogs at the same time.'

'Well, I...' Looking towards the door, Darryl slumped his shoulders. 'I suppose I can spare a few minutes.'

What did he want? A medal? For doing his job?

As soon as Darryl stepped through the door, excitement swept through the kennels as the dogs felt the presence of a new person. The sound of barking filled the room. Ginny swallowed. The way the dogs reacted to an unfamiliar person always made her heart skip a beat. She could almost feel the anticipation in the air.

Bending down, she placed her palm flat against the bars of the first kennel. 'Hey, Ralph. How's it going?'

The large Staffie shuffled towards her, rubbing his cheek against her palm before licking her.

'That good, hey?' She glanced at the small whiteboard attached to the outside of the door. 'I see Tim has already taken you out today, but I tell you what, shall I take you out again in a bit?'

'They're smaller than I imagined.' Darryl stepped closer towards the kennel door.

Ginny watched Ralph as he stared up at Darryl, his ears pinned back, concern etched at the corners of his mouth.

'It's okay,' she said. 'This is Darryl.'

She rubbed his nose, and then continued down the corridor.

'We get that a lot. The truth is, if we make the kennels bigger, the less dogs we can take in, and even as it is, we're forced to turn some away.'

'Right.'

'We're lucky to have a group of loyal volunteers who come and help us walk them. We've got a couple of secure paddocks out the back too, so we can offer them off-lead time.' She led the way towards the end of the corridor and paused outside the last kennel. 'This is Tyler.'

'Tyler?'

'Yes, the cocker spaniel you were supposed to write a piece about? To entice potential adopters to get in touch?' She frowned. Did he really not remember?

'Tyler. Of course.' He nodded and pulled his mobile from his jacket pocket.

Tyler was pawing at the bars, a strangled squeaking noise gurgling from his throat as he desperately tried to seek Darryl's attention.

'Look at him. Please. Just for a second.'

'Uh-huh.' Darryl nodded, yet continued to scroll through his phone.

Nostrils flared, Ginny shoved her hands in her pockets, not trusting herself not to fling his precious phone from his hand.

'Darryl, please? This is Tyler's life. The piece you wrote about him was his chance to find his forever home, to find someone who would love him and could offer him somewhere safe and secure to live. To offer him a home.' Pausing, she took a breath. 'You let him down.'

Pocketing his mobile, Darryl glanced down at Tyler before looking at Ginny. 'I need to go.'

* * *

'Come on, lovely. Let's get a cuppa and warm these two up.' Flora placed her hand on Ginny's shoulder and nodded towards Tiger and Belle where they were wandering around the reception area.

But Ginny was looking out of the window, watching as Darryl inspected his shoes before opening his car door.

'I just don't understand how someone can be so uncaring. I mean, we were literally right there outside Tyler's kennel, and he was too busy with that darn phone of his to take notice of the poor thing. And you know how he gets when someone comes within a few feet of his kennel...'

'Oh, was he doing his impression of a strangled cat?'

Ginny nodded. 'Darryl has the power to tell Tyler's story, and he just doesn't care.'

Following Ginny's gaze, Flora tilted her head and frowned. 'Don't write him off just yet.'

'Huh? Really? I think he's already written *us* off.' Ginny watched as Darryl's BMW weaved around the potholes before disappearing out onto the main road.

'He might surprise you.'

'I doubt it.' Grabbing one of the bath towels Susan had left on the counter, Ginny bent and scooped Belle up from the floor. 'Let's get you warm and toasty, shall we?'

7

'Are you sure you're okay, Susan? You look shattered.' Balancing on the stepladder and holding the roofing felt in place, Ginny looked down at Susan as she shifted the ladder closer and joined her.

'I am. Dean turned up at my house last night.' Susan held a nail in place before bringing the hammer down.

'Again?'

'Yep. You would have thought he'd have moved on by now, but you know, I suppose I am quite fabulous!' Chuckling, Susan hammered the nail in further and then began to climb back down the ladder. 'Seriously, though, I don't really know what else I can say to him to put him off. Maybe I should just start setting him up on blind dates.'

'Now that might be an idea.'

Susan stifled a yawn. 'It would be if it wasn't for the fact I actually like my friends and wouldn't wish Dean on any of them.'

'Umm, maybe it's not such a good idea then.' Ginny climbed down and looked at the battered outside kennel in front of them. Even a complete novice at DIY like Ginny could tell that there was a long way to go before it would be habitable. 'What are you going to do?'

'Don't worry, I'll think of something.' Susan wiped her hands down her jeans before moving her ladder across and picking up another strip of roofing felt. 'It's my own fault. I shouldn't have taken him back, given him another chance.'

'That's not your fault.'

Susan grimaced. 'I knew what he was like, and we've all heard the saying that leopards can't change their spots.' She passed the felt to Ginny before picking out some more nails from the tool-box. 'Anyway, if last time we split is anything to go by, then I've only five months of him begging for my forgiveness before he gives up.'

Ginny shuddered. 'I don't know how you do it, seeing him around all the time. I moved down here so I could walk down the street without having to see Jason.' Folding the felt over her arm, she started to climb back up the ladder. 'Though it seems I was destined to run into him again anyway.'

'Oh, yes, I heard you saw him at the newspaper office.'

'Yep.' She rolled her eyes.

'That's looking good.' Alex paused in front of them, a tennis ball in his hand and Tyler standing next to him, his head tilted back and his eyes on the ball.

'Forever the optimistic, Alex.' Susan grinned. 'There's a long way to go but we'll get there.'

'How long until Yvonne drops off our newest resident?' Alex swapped the ball into his other hand, Tyler immediately weaving behind his legs to keep his prize in sight.

'The day after tomorrow.' Ginny stepped down from the ladder and laid the felt over the toolbox before bending down to fuss Tyler. 'You look a happy lad today.'

'He should be. We've been playing fetch for the past hour. This boy has the energy of a kangaroo on caffeine.'

'Aw, he's lovely though, aren't you, Tyler?' She laughed as Tyler twisted his neck to lick her, his tongue rough on the back of her hand.

'He sure is.' Susan pulled a dog treat from her pocket and knelt next to Ginny.

'Susan, I've got these,' called Percy, walking across the courtyard to join them, holding up a bag of nails. 'Are they any good for you?'

'Thanks. I found some in the end, but those will come in handy if we run out.' Taking the bag of nails from Percy's hand, Susan nodded towards the rolled-up paper under his arm. 'Is that the *Trestow Telegraph*?'

'Yes, don't get your hopes up though. Another poorly written article about this place, hidden at the back again.' Shaking his head, he took the paper from under his arm and flicked it with his finger. 'I'm hoping Flora hasn't seen it. The home was described as "chaotic" and "needing all the help we can get".'

'What?' Standing up, Ginny reached out for the paper. 'Chaotic?'

'Is it that Darryl bloke who wrote that? The one who visited?' Alex narrowed his eyes.

'That's the one.' Percy nodded. 'I'm just sorry I wasn't here when he visited. I would have given him a piece of my mind, I would.'

Ginny knelt down and laid the paper on the ground, flicking through until she found the article. Yep, it was short and tucked beneath an advert for antibacterial spray. As she skimmed the article, she could feel her heart pounding, her hands shaking. How dare he? How could he have written a piece like this? He'd basically slammed Wagging Tails, calling it chaotic and busy, stopping short of calling them unprofessional – but only just. The only saving grace was that the article was difficult to find.

'Is it as bad as Percy says?' Susan leaned over Ginny's shoulder, squinting at the paper.

'It sure is.' Sitting back on her haunches, Ginny untied her hair before bundling it up into a messy bun.

'I mean, I know it was a little crazy when he came – Belle and Tiger had just had an accident – but does he really believe that it's like that all the time? Not to mention that it was an unpreventable incident. We can't control a dog's health or what state they're in when they get here.' Susan sighed. 'This will break Flora's heart.'

'Which is why I'd rather you kept it to yourselves.' Percy picked up the paper, rolled it back up and placed it under his arm again. 'The only place for this is the bin.'

'We won't say anything,' Susan said as she picked up the hammer again.

'It's Tyler I feel sorry for. We all know how quickly he'd have been snapped up if his information had been put in the paper.' Percy sighed. 'Properly, I mean. Not the quick hashed paragraph Darryl gave. Mistakes and all.'

'That's just it. If Terry was still at the paper...' Susan shook her head.

Standing up, Ginny looked from Tyler to the reception area and back again. This wouldn't just affect Tyler, it would be all of the dogs. All of them. Without funds coming in from the Family Fun Day, who knew how much longer they could keep afloat.

'You okay, Ginny?' Percy rubbed her arm.

'Yes... No.' She squinted her eyes against the morning sun. 'Can I take that?'

'The paper? Yes, of course.' Percy passed it over to her. 'What are you going to do?'

'I'm going to go down there.' She ran her fingers across the paper.

'Again? Is there any point? He's obviously not interested in covering the story.' Alex shook his head. 'Even after visiting, he's clearly not put any effort in at all.'

'Maybe not, but it'll make me feel better.'

Or not.

'Do you want me to go instead?' Susan leaned in closer. 'So, you don't have the risk of running into Jason?'

'It's Jason I want to see. Obviously, Darryl doesn't care about drumming up interest for the Family Fun Day, or the dogs for that matter, so I'm going to try and get someone else to cover it.' She waved the paper in front of her. As sick as the thought of speaking to Jason made her feel, she had to do something. Darryl wasn't a good fit for them, and they needed a reporter who cared or the whole home could go under.

'Okay. Well, good luck then. We'll keep our fingers crossed for you,' Percy said.

* * *

Ginny locked the car door and shoved her car keys in her pocket, before opening the paper and finding the article again. Not that you could call it that. It hardly constituted for a paragraph. Who had signed off on it anyway? Didn't they have editors at the paper? Wasn't everything passed by Jason before printing? Surely his job was to check everything? That obviously meant he didn't care either. Or was this more of a personal attack? He'd always hated dogs when they'd been together, insisted he was allergic, with no symptoms of course. Was this some sick way of making her agree to meet up with him? Was he banking on her complaining to him?

She ran across the road, weaving between the oncoming traffic. Well, it wouldn't work. If anything, it was doing the complete opposite, putting her off him for life. Not that she'd ever think about giving him a second chance, not after the way he'd treated her. She shuddered. No, she was far happier on her own, thank you very much.

This though. Letting this so-called article through to be published... She tugged at a loose strand of hair, slipping it through her hairband. It wasn't right. It just wasn't. It was damaging. It was offensive. It was... Keeping her eyes focused on the door to the offices, she sidestepped around the person in front of her.

'Gina?'

She turned around, eyes narrowed. There was only one person who couldn't be bothered to call her by her actual name. She glared at Darryl.

'Hey, Gina. Can I help you?'

'No.' As she walked towards the door, she could feel him following her, a few short steps behind.

'Gina, wait. What can I help you with?' He spoke urgently, touching her arm.

Pausing, she brushed his hand away and turned back to face him. 'It's Ginny. My name is Ginny, not Gina, or anything else. It's Ginny.'

'Okay.' Holding his hands up, palms forward, he stepped back in submission, though that inane grin was still on his face. 'What can I help you with, *Ginny*?'

'Nothing. Absolutely nothing.' She spoke through gritted teeth.

'Who have you come to see then? Jason?'

Her nostrils flared, she looked him in the eye. 'Yes, now, please step out of my way.'

'Why have you come to see Jason?'

Tapping her foot against the tarmac, she took a deep breath in. Was he being serious? 'Isn't it obvious?'

'No. I didn't think you liked him.' With a shrug, Darryl stepped aside. 'I guess you've changed your mind.'

'Changed my mind?' She held up the paper, tapping the piece he'd written. 'I've come to see him about this... this article, if that's what you can even call it.'

'There's no need for that. It has nothing to do with Jason.'

'Is that right?' She pulled open the door to the office building before turning around one last time. 'You really don't care at all, do you? You don't realise how much power you have. You don't realise how something like this can do so much damage to us – to our reputation, to our funding, to the dogs who rely on us.' She glanced down at the door handle. 'Or maybe you do. And that's even worse.'

'Wait. Hold on. You don't need to see Jason. What's he going to do? It wasn't him who wrote the piece.'

'No, it was you, and I've tried speaking to you. I've tried explaining, showing you what we do so now's the time to go above your head.'

'Whoa, there's no need for that. Talk to me.' He placed his hand over hers.

Who did he think he was?

'As I said, I've tried that.' She looked down at his hand covering hers. 'Please let go of me.'

'Of course. Sorry.'

She pushed the door open and held it wide for a group of people dressed in suits who were passing through.

'Let me come and visit again. Let me see what good you do.'

Ginny frowned. 'I've tried that. Remember?'

'I know, but let me visit again.'

'What's the point? Just so you can write another damaging piece about us?' He clearly didn't care, he'd made that pretty obvious to her, so why the change of heart? Why would he suddenly want to visit again? 'With every day that passes we're missing out on stalls being booked up, dogs missing out on their forever home. I've not got time to waste on you again.'

'It'll be different this time.' Darryl shifted from foot to foot, looking from Ginny to the open doorway and back again. 'Please.'

'Why?'

What was the point?

'Just give me a chance. Another chance, and then, if you still don't agree with what I've written, by all means complain to Jason.'

Ginny bit down on her bottom lip. Why was he so worried about her speaking to Jason? What hold did he have over him? Was she being daft by even contemplating giving him another chance?

'I can run the article past you if you'd prefer? You can read it before I submit it even.'

She rolled her eyes. She must be daft even contemplating giving him another chance. 'Okay, okay. One more chance, after that I'm demanding another reporter is allocated to cover the story.'

Darryl nodded slowly. 'Fair enough.'

8

'And these two are the ones who had the upset stomachs? I recognise them.' Leaning down, Darryl fussed Belle and Tiger through the bars of their kennel. 'What happens to them now?'

'We'll assess them and then, all being well, they'll be put up for adoption.' Ginny looked down the row of kennels. Darryl had stopped at each one in turn, spending a few minutes with each dog, either stroking them through the bars or talking softly to them. He was like a completely different person. Unrecognisable from the man she'd first met.

'Will they get rehomed together?'

Ginny shrugged. 'We'll do our utmost to find a home where they can stay together, but if it comes to it, they'll have to be split up.'

'Oh, that'd be a real shame.'

'Yes, but unfortunately, adopters happy to take on two new dogs are few and far between so if it's a case of finding them a home separately or them staying here, obviously two forever homes are better than none. We'll try our best though.'

'Maybe we could feature them in the paper? When they're

ready of course.' Darryl made his way to the final kennel. 'And this is Tyler, right?'

'That's him.' Ginny paused as Darryl knelt down again. Tyler rushed towards him at breakneck speed, sticking his nose through the bars, desperate for attention.

'He's really struggling settling in here. He came from a lovely family who unfortunately just couldn't look after him any more and he's really been missing his home comforts and the attention he used to get.' Ginny crossed her arms. 'We've had to give him blankets because he kept destroying the duvets.'

'Boredom?' Darryl glanced back at her.

'Possibly. Or because he's scared. According to his previous owners, he's fully housetrained and never used to destroy anything. They ring up every couple of days to ask if he's been rehomed.'

Darryl hung his head before fussing Tyler behind the ears. 'Sorry.'

Ginny unfolded her arms and clasped her hands in front of her. 'Why didn't you bother before? With the articles? If you'd written about Tyler properly, given him a glowing report, then he'd have likely been matched with someone by now.'

Sighing, Darryl nodded. 'I'll write another piece about him.'

She'd heard that before.

'I will.' Darryl stood up and looked at her. 'Can I take him for a walk? Get to know him a little better?'

'I guess so.' She nodded. 'The top paddock is free. We could take him up there, play fetch for a while. He loves that.'

'Great.' He pulled a small notebook from his pocket and jotted something down before looking across at the artwork that ran along the wall opposite the kennels. 'This mural is amazing. Do you mind if I take a photo for the paper?'

'I guess not.'

Standing back, Ginny watched as he used his phone to take a picture. She remembered painting the words 'Wagging Tails Dogs' Home' across the wall like it was yesterday. The dogs she'd painted surrounding it each a memory of the dogs they'd had in the home at that time. Dottie the greyhound, her tongue lolling to the side after a lap around the paddock, the tiny fluffball Yorkshire terrier who had terrorised the other dogs with his yapping, and, of course, Ralph, who had been a resident then as he was now. She remembered how he'd watched her every move, every paint stroke and smudge, his face pushed up against the door to his kennel.

'It's really uplifting, isn't it? Something nice for the dogs to look at.'

'That was the plan.'

'Did you get a local artist in to do it?' He traced the tips of his fingers along the features of a greyhound. 'It's real, isn't it? Been painted from scratch, I mean, rather than one of those wall murals bought online.'

'Yes, it's real.'

'And who's the artist.'

'It wasn't an artist; it was just me.' She looked down at her trainers. Jason had always described her painting a time-sap, a hobby she hadn't needed. He'd always said her spare time would be better used working on her career or focusing on their relationship. He'd made her feel guilty for spending time on herself, doing something she enjoyed. Huh, it wasn't as though the few hours a month she'd actually been able to spend painting would have saved their relationship – not when he'd been having an affair. Still, she hated people focusing on it.

'Wow, seriously? You painted it?' He smiled.

'Yes.' She looked away. She'd painted the mural for the dogs, not for it to be judged. She knew Flora was right, that Jason had sapped any confidence she'd once had in her abilities, but, still, any attention the mural got made her feel uncomfortable, dredging up past feelings of hurt.

'Do you mind standing next to it and I can take a photo of you as well?' He nodded towards the wall.

'I'd rather not,' she said. 'I'll just go and get Tyler's lead.'

When she reached the door leading into the reception area, she glanced back. Darryl was kneeling in front of Tyler's kennel again. How could one person be so different from one day to the next? Shaking her head, she shut the door behind her.

'How's it going, lovely?' Flora looked up from the paperwork she was filling in at the counter. 'He's stayed longer than before, that's got to be a good sign?'

'Okay, I think. He wants to take Tyler for a walk.' Ginny leaned her elbows on the counter.

'Oh really?' Flora looked up, pen in hand.

'Yep.'

'A complete U-turn then?'

'Seems to be.' She glanced back towards the door.

'You don't sound so sure.'

'Well, no. I'm not. How can someone go from not caring at all to acting as though he loves dogs and cares about the future of this place? It doesn't make sense.'

'Give him a chance, Ginny. There might be a genuine reason for his past behaviour.' Flora laid her hand over hers.

'You think I should give him the benefit of the doubt?'

'Sometimes it's the only thing we can do. Time will tell.'

'I guess so.' Ginny sighed. 'Right, I'd better get Tyler out before Darryl changes his mind, says he has an urgent meeting or something he needs to rush off to.'

'Let me help you.' Flora reached behind her and took Tyler's lead from one of the hooks behind the counter.

'Thanks.' The lead in hand, Ginny headed towards the door, before calling over her shoulder. 'Wish me luck.'

'You'll be fine.'

* * *

'Wow, you weren't joking when you said he liked playing fetch.' Darryl took the ball from Tyler's mouth carefully, having given up telling him to drop it after the first ten goes or so. Swinging his arm back, he released the ball across the paddock.

'Nope. He loves it.' Ginny grinned as Tyler bounded across the paddock in chase of the ball, his legs pounding and his paws thudding against the worn grass, his whole being focused on the prize ahead of him. As soon as he retrieved it, he flew back to Darryl, placing his muddy paws on the knees of his suit trousers.

'Whoa, buddy.' Darryl staggered back.

'Sorry.' Ginny looked down at the splodges of mud engrained across Darryl's once pristine suit. That would be it then, he was sure to use it as an excuse to leave. That or somehow weave into the article something about them neglecting the paddocks because of a bit of mud.

'Don't worry. It's only a bit of mud. It'll brush off.'

As Darryl threw the ball again, Ginny swallowed. Maybe she was wrong, maybe he really wasn't bothered about the mud. 'Can I ask you something?'

'Ask away.'

'Why the change of heart?'

'What do you mean?'

'Well, yesterday you couldn't get out of here quick enough. You turned your nose up at us, at the dogs, and today... you seem different. Interested.'

Running his fingers through his hair, Darryl watched as Tyler ran to the end of the paddock. 'I...'

'Ginny, Susan's looking for you,' came a voice from behind. 'I think it's urgent.' Alex looked at Darryl. 'Sorry, I didn't realise you still had company.'

'Don't mind me.' Darryl shook his head.

'Okay, thanks.' Ginny turned and watched Alex approach with Jarvis, the large dog pulling him towards them. She turned back to Darryl. 'We should get back anyway. Do you mind?'

'Not at all.' Darryl clipped Tyler's lead on and took the ball from him, Tyler emitting a small whine as he realised playtime was over. 'Time for some rest, Tyler.'

'Thanks. Susan probably just needs a hand. We were fixing up one of the outside kennels when I saw the piece you'd written in the paper.'

'Outside kennels? Do you keep some of the dogs outside then?' Darryl frowned.

'Well, not outside-outside. We've just got a couple of kennels not in the main building. They're more like sheds with an outside area attached. Not the greatest, but they'll be fine for a short-term fix, especially in the summer, and better than having to turn dogs away because we've reached capacity. We've not used them for a couple of years, so they need a lot of work doing to fix them up and we've got a dog coming from the pound in a couple of days so need to get it fixed up by then.'

'Can't the pound keep them there? If you've not got room, they can wait until one of your regular kennels becomes available.'

'No, the council pound only has a certain number of spaces available, like us. Dogs taken to the pound only have seven days to be reunited with their owner before they're rehomed. Then, they need to find them a place at a shelter, like ours – or, as a last resort and in cases where that's not possible, they're euthanised. Hence why we need to make sure we can take in the dogs when the pound gets in touch.'

Darryl ran his palm across the stubble on his chin, a deep furrow forming between his eyebrows. 'Seven days. That's no time at all.'

'No, it's not, but the pound needs to keep spaces open so they can help newly found strays.' Ginny swallowed. She knew the facts; Flora had explained it all when she'd first arrived here, but whenever she had to say them out loud again, it still got to her. She looked away. 'There's Susan with Flora.'

She nodded towards where Susan and Flora were banging nails into a newly placed piece of wood covering a gaping hole in the wall of the kennel.

'Is everything okay?' she asked when they were close enough. 'Alex said you were looking for me?'

'Thank goodness you're here, Ginny. The pound just called and they're dropping Luna off in a couple of hours.' Susan wiped the back of her hand across her forehead.

'A couple of hours? What's changed? I thought they could keep hold of her for a couple more days?'

She looked at the kennel. The roof had been fixed, but apart from that and the hole in the wall, which Flora and Susan were covering now, it was nowhere near ready. The door was hanging off and, in truth, probably needed replacing, the window frame was dangerously rotten and the wood that the galvanised steel dog run panels were attached to needed reinforcing.

'They've had a house raid out past Trestow, resulting in five more dogs arriving.' Flora shook her head. 'We need to take Luna now. We can't turn her away. We just can't.'

Darryl stepped forward, gave Ginny Tyler's lead and picked up a hammer. 'Do you need a hand?'

'What?' Ginny shook her head. 'Don't you need to get back to the office?'

'I'm sure I can spare a couple of hours. My dad was always a keen DIYer, and I spent many a weekend helping him.' He smirked as he picked up a piece of wood.

'Thank you, Darryl. That's very kind of you.' Flora smiled and nodded towards Ginny.

9

'Here you go, teas all round.' Flora held up a tray of mugs as she walked towards them. 'How are you getting on? It looks about finished.'

'Almost. We've just got the window frame to strengthen now.' Susan laid her hammer down and picked up a mug. 'Thanks.'

'There's one for you too, Darryl.' Flora nodded towards him.

'Great, thanks. I'll just finish this off first,' he said, with a quick glance towards her before focusing back on the strip of wood he was sawing.

Ginny wiped her hands down the front of her jeans and picked up a mug. 'Thanks, Flora.'

'You're welcome. I can't believe how you've all transformed this place so quickly. I really thought we had at least another day's work left on it.'

'It's thanks to Darryl that we've got this far this quickly.' Susan grinned.

'Oh, it's nothing. As I said, I enjoy this sort of thing.' Pausing, he looked around.

Sipping her tea, Ginny looked across at Darryl as he picked

up another piece of wood and then brought the saw easily across it, back and forth, back and forth. He'd abandoned his suit jacket as soon as he'd started the task, hanging it over the kennel door, and with his shirtsleeves rolled up and sawdust discolouring his once pristine white shirt, he looked completely different to the emotionless reporter who had visited yesterday.

'Yes, well, this is going above and beyond,' Susan said.

Choking on her tea, Ginny scoffed. 'Not really. He has a lot to make up for, don't you think?' Had everyone forgotten what damage he'd done with his so-called articles about them?

'Ginny, I...'

'No, it's okay. She's right. I do have a bit of making up to do.' Darryl leaned the freshly cut strip of wood against the kennel and picked up his mug.

Huh, that was the understatement of the century. Not trusting herself to keep quiet, Ginny took a gulp of her tea. What was his game? And why did he keep looking around? Was he hoping to catch them out? Was he hoping for a lead to a juicy story?

'What?' Almost as if he could feel her looking at him, Darryl turned around to glare at her.

'Nothing, I was just thinking how different you are to how you were when you visited yesterday. I would never have imagined that you'd have wanted to help like this.'

He shrugged. 'Yes, well, people can change their minds, can't they?'

'I guess so.' She nodded and took a sip of her tea, letting the hot liquid hit the back of her throat. Was it as simple as that? When she'd run into him outside the office earlier, he'd been jumpy, the arrogant confidence had disappeared. Something was going on. Was it to do with Jason? Had he already had words with him? She doubted it. It wouldn't be like Jason to do her any favours – possibly if she'd agreed to meet him, but after the way she'd brushed him off she very much doubted that Darryl's change of heart had anything to do with Jason, not on her behalf anyway. But why wouldn't he tell her? She'd asked before and now again, and he still wasn't being upfront.

'You okay, Ginny, lovely?' Balancing the tray in one hand, Flora touched Ginny's forearm with her other. 'You look miles away.'

Ginny smiled and shook her head. 'I was just thinking.'

'Jason didn't badger you about meeting up again then?'

'No, I didn't see him in the end.' She looked across at Darryl who picked up the saw again, pulling it across the wood slowly and deliberately. Was he listening in?

'Oh right. That's good then.' Flora nodded.

'Is that Yvonne's car?' Susan pointed across the courtyard towards the gate, where a white van was pulling up.

'Oh drat, yes, it is. She's early, isn't she?' Flora checked her watch. 'Oh, well, nothing we can do now. I'll go and let her in.'

'I'll run and grab some bits for the kennel,' Susan called as she headed towards the reception area.

'Is the new dog here?' Darryl asked as he lowered the saw.

Ginny nodded.

There was only one thing for it – to finish off the kennel as best they could. Putting her mug down on the slabs, she grabbed a broom that was leaning against the kennel and began to sweep the sawdust.

Darryl continued to work, lining up a piece of wood against the window frame. 'Look, once I've secured this piece, it should hold for a while. Might not be particularly waterproof but we haven't got rain forecast for a few days. I can pop back, say, tomorrow, and finish off when Luna's out on a walk or something?'

'Really?' Ginny looked from Darryl to Flora, who was now opening the gate, and back again. He'd used Luna's name. What was going on with him? He hadn't even got Tyler's breed correct in his article, but now he seemed to be taking more notice. 'Yes, that would probably be the best idea. It's always good to get a newcomer settled in their new base straight away. Susan can probably finish off the window though.'

'Oh, right, of course. I'm happy to pop back though.' Darryl nodded and began to pack the tools away.

'Here, she is,' Flora said as she came towards them, a bright pink lead in hand and a large golden Labrador sniffing the ground in front of her. 'Luna, meet Ginny and Darryl.'

The dog immediately flopped onto the ground in front of Ginny, her limbs limp and her tongue hanging out.

'Oh no, is she okay?' Bending down, Ginny began to stroke her head. 'Are you okay, Luna?'

Chuckling, Flora knelt down next to her and fussed Luna behind the ears. 'This is what she does, apparently. Whenever she meets someone, she lies down and refuses to budge until they give her the attention she wants.'

'Really?' Ginny laughed. 'I've never heard of a dog doing that before.'

'Me neither, but according to Yvonne, this is what she's been doing at the pound.'

'Hello, Luna.' Darryl held out his hand for her to sniff. 'Oh, you're a lovely one, aren't you?'

Luna stood up and nudged Darryl's hand.

'You want some more fussing?' Kneeling down, he ruffled her ears, while she leaned in closer and licked his cheek. Once Luna seemed to be satisfied with the amount of attention, Darryl stood up and looked across at Ginny. 'Right, well, I'd better get back to the office.' He looked down at himself and grimaced. 'I should probably swing by home to change first though.'

'That might be a good idea, lovely.' Flora laughed. 'Thank you for all your help. We'd have never finished in time otherwise.'

'No worries. As I've said to Ginny, the window frame just needs finishing off, but it should be fine for a couple of days at least so she can settle in.'

'Thank you.' Flora reached out and patted his arm.

'Yes, thanks.' Ginny nodded. 'You've been a great help.'

'No worries. I'll get that article written this afternoon.'

As Darryl walked back to his car, pulling his suit jacket back on as he went, Ginny frowned. Was he really going to write another article? What would be in it this time around? And, possibly more to the point, what was in it for him? He hadn't wanted her to talk to Jason, instead, he'd come here and helped all he could. There must be a reason. People didn't just change like that. Not as quickly as he seemingly had.

'Give him a bit of your trust, Ginny. He might surprise you.' Flora waved to Darryl as he opened the courtyard gate.

'You can't blame me for not trusting him. Look what damage he's done so far. Thanks to him, poor Tyler is still suffering, adapting to kennel life, and we've got no more stalls agreed for the Family Fun Day than before. In fact, it wouldn't surprise me in the slightest if the few people we do have booked up pull out after the rubbish in today's paper.' She shook her head and forced herself to look away.

'Today's rubbish? Was there another article in today's paper?' Flora frowned.

'Oh, I—'

Ginny flushed, remembering that they'd agreed not to tell Flora. Looking across at Susan as she came towards them, her arms full of bedding and toys, she'd never been more thankful for a distraction.

'Here we go, Luna. Look, I've found the most puffiest duvet I could find and some brand-new toys too.' Susan threw the duvet into the kennel before bending down and fussing her as she once again flopped down onto the courtyard slabs. 'You're a cutie, aren't you?'

With Flora's attention now focused on Susan and Luna, Ginny breathed a sigh of relief.

'She sure is,' Flora said. 'We'll do our checks but hopefully we'll be able to put her up for adoption by the end of summer.'

'Oh, yes, I can imagine she'll be snapped up in no time. Won't you, beautiful little lady? Now, let me go and make your bed all comfy,' Susan said, straightening her back, before disappearing into the kennel.

'I'd better go and get on with some chores.' Ginny pointed towards the reception area, and backed away before Flora could question her any further.

How could she have almost let it slip like that? Percy was right, it would break Flora's heart to read Darryl's description of Wagging Tails. She tucked a loose strand of hair back into her messy bun. It would take more than a couple of hours spent fixing up a kennel to make up for the damage Darryl had caused.

10

'That's all the kennels cleared out.' Yawning, Ginny closed the kennels door behind her before looking across at Flora. 'Sorry,' she mouthed as Flora was speaking hastily into the phone.

'Yes, I have your contact details,' she was saying. 'We'll be in touch as soon as we can. Thank you.' She placed the phone in the holder, clapped her hands and declared, 'That's the fifth one this morning already!'

'Fifth what?' Leaning her elbows on the counter, Ginny cupped her chin in her hands.

'Phone call enquiring about Tyler!'

'Really?' Standing up straight, Ginny widened her eyes. 'Do you think Darryl actually wrote a proper adoption piece about him?'

'He must have done. There's no other logical explanation.' The shrill ringtone of the office phone filled the small reception area. 'Ooh, that might be number six.'

'I'll leave you to answer and go and start walking the dogs.' She glanced at the clock. It was half past nine already and there was still no sign of Susan. She normally arrived just after Ginny did, definitely by quarter to eight. 'Shall I give Susan a call? Check she's okay?'

Covering the mouthpiece of the phone, Flora whispered, 'Sorry, lovely, I meant to tell you but what with all the phone calls...' She tapped the phone. 'She rang in sick. Got some stomach bug or other.'

Nodding, Ginny pushed herself away from the counter. She yawned again. What was wrong with her today? She didn't dare go and have a break; the way she felt, the moment she sat down she'd likely drop off for a nap. She pushed the heels of her hands against her eyes. She must have had less than four hours' sleep last night. Between worrying about how Luna had been coping during her first night at Wagging Tails and trying to work out Darryl's game, she'd not been able to get to sleep for hours and then she'd woken at just gone four.

'And don't think you've got away with coming in at half five this morning.' Covering the mouthpiece again, Flora gave Ginny her best motherly stare. 'I'll be having words with you later. No wonder you're half asleep.'

Holding her palms up, Ginny said, 'I was worried about Luna.'

Flora shook her head and spoke into the phone again.

Ginny picked up Frank's and Dino's leads before turning to the door again. Just as she pulled it open, the barely used Wagging Tails mobile began ringing, vibrating its way across the counter from beneath a pile of papers. She leaned across the counter and picked it up.

'Morning, Wagging Tails Dogs' Home, how can I help you today?'

* * *

Hitting the 'end call' button, Ginny pushed herself up from the stool she'd perched on and grinned across at Flora. 'That's three more stalls booked for the Family Fun Day.'

Flora chuckled, scribbling in her notepad. 'That's fantastic news. We've got nine potential adopters for Tyler and one couple coming in to meet Frank and Dino! They specifically asked if we had any greyhounds.'

'Frank and Dino? Seriously?' Ginny widened her eyes. The two greyhounds had been residents at Wagging Tails long before she'd even moved down here. Flora had told her how they'd been brought in together after sharing kennels at the racecourse.

'Yes, seriously. And they're happy to consider a double adoption. Though with Dino having two failed adoptions behind him and Frank three, I'm not going to hold my breath. But how amazing is it that people are interested?' She took the yellow handkerchief she always carried in her pocket and dabbed at her eyes.

'It is amazing. Really amazing.'

'I'd given up on them ever finding their forever homes. We all had. We'd all assumed they'd just be our resident dogs here. Especially after Frank's last failed adoption. Do you remember he completely wrecked their new three-piece suite? In two hours?' Flora shook her head.

'I remember.' Ginny nodded. 'The day Frank left I think Dino went through four duvets in the space of a few hours.'

'Yes, that's right. Susan had to crochet him a blanket after that. Butter wouldn't melt when they're together though, so if we can pull this off – them both being rehomed together – it might just work.' Flora held her hand up, crossing her fingers.

'Aw, I'll miss them.'

Even after four years of waving dogs off to their new homes,

Ginny still teared up each time. It was a strange feeling watching a dog you loved being rehomed. Her stomach churned each time: unbearable sadness, because she'd miss them, mixed with pure elation that they were finally getting the second chance they deserved.

'Me too, but if they do get adopted, hopefully their new owners will pop by to visit every so often. I don't think Alex will miss Frank though, or Frank him for that matter.' Flora chuckled.

'Aw, they love each other really.' Ginny grinned, thinking of all the times Alex had marched in fuming that Frank had relieved his bladder up his new jeans or Frank had refused to come out of his kennel so Alex could clean it.

'I think you're probably right. They're too alike those two, both big characters.' Patting her eyes dry again, Flora nodded towards the door. 'Here comes Daniel and Carrie. Early as usual. I don't know what we'd do without our regular walkers.'

The bell above the front door tinkled as Daniel and Carrie stepped inside.

'Morning,' they both chorused.

'Hello, Daniel. Hello, Carrie, lovely.' Flora unhooked the clipboard from behind the counter and ran her finger down the list of dogs needing to be walked. 'Daniel, how are those little lovelies you teach?'

'Ah, they've run me ragged this week.' He chuckled. 'We've got the school's summer fayre this afternoon and we've been crafting things to sell all week. I've still got glitter in my hair, even after a shower when I got home yesterday evening and another after my morning run today.' Running his fingers through his hair, he laughed. 'If it wasn't for Carrie volunteering to teach a couple of lessons on pottery skills I'd be covered in clay too.'

'It'll all be worth it when you raise enough money to replace the playground equipment. That's what the school's raising money for at the moment, isn't it?' Flora reached across the counter and brushed at his shoulders, causing silver glitter to cascade onto the counter.

'Thanks.' Brushing the glitter off the wooden counter, Daniel nodded. 'Yes, that's right. We've been raising money all week, what with the school disco last night and a sponsored skipping marathon on Wednesday. I don't know about the kids, but I'm fit to drop and am already looking forward to crawling into bed as soon as the summer fayre's over.'

'I bet you are. I'm hoping to pop along to Penworth Bay this lunchtime to talk to Elsie about her stall, so I'll pop up to the school too. What time does the fayre start?'

'Not until two o'clock. It's two until four.'

'You can just take a late lunch then.' Ginny smiled.

'Yes, I might just do that.' Flora nodded. 'How are the pottery classes going, Carrie? When you're not volunteering at the primary school, that is.'

Looking up from the clipboard Flora had placed on the counter, Carrie grinned. 'Great, I've just signed up two more students for my one-to-one pottery sessions too.'

'That's fantastic news. I knew you'd do well over in the bay. It's lovely you've breathed new life into Adrienne's old studio.'

'I still can't believe I'm living down here doing something I've always loved, creating pottery pieces and teaching. I still pinch myself some days to make sure I'm not dreaming.' She smiled.

'You're definitely not dreaming,' Daniel said as he hugged her around the shoulders.

'And how are Scout and little Winston getting on?'

'Great.' Carrie pulled her mobile from her back pocket and scrolled through before showing Flora and Ginny a photo of the two dogs they'd adopted.

'Aw, good. You'll have to bring them in for a cuddle soon. Me and Ginny were just saying how lovely it is to have our old residents visit.'

'Yes, we will. The dogs love it too. As soon as we park up, they know exactly where they are and can't wait to come and see you folks.' Daniel ran his finger down the list on the clipboard.

'Good, good. Now, can I give you Ralph today please?'

'Yes, of course. We love him. Well, we love all of them of course, but we do have a soft spot for Ralph,' Carrie said as she pulled some poop bags from the dispenser on the counter.

'We certainly do. If he got on with other dogs, I'd adopt him in a heartbeat.' Daniel took Ralph's lead as the phone began ringing again.

Flora spoke quietly into the receiver, while Ginny quickly explained.

'We've had so many calls today. People wanting to adopt Tyler and we even had someone call up about Dino and Frank. Plus, lots of people asking about hiring stalls.' At that moment, as if to further provide proof to her words, the shrill ringtone of the mobile began to ring through the reception area. Ginny grabbed it before the noise disturbed Flora's call. Speaking quietly into the receiver, Ginny then covered the mouthpiece and whispered to Carrie and Daniel, 'Sorry.'

'Don't worry. We'll let you get on with it,' Daniel whispered back. 'Would it help if we stayed on an extra hour or so? Let you man the phones for a bit?'

'Oh, that would great, but only if you have time? Susan's off today and with it being the weekend Tim isn't in either, and Alex's working through the behavioural checks with our new dog, Luna.'

'That's decided then. We'll stay until we have to go across to the school to help set up for the summer fayre.' Daniel picked up the clipboard. 'We should be able to walk a fair few of them for you.'

'Thank you. You're both lifesavers.' Ginny smiled before turning her attention back to the phone.

11

After chucking her lunchbox on the back seat of her car, Ginny ran back to her cottage and pulled the bin out onto the street. She looked up and down the road, checking she'd got the correct bin out – yes, it was recycling day today. She glanced back towards the small row of cottages, they all had their bins out apart from the cottage at the end – Enid's. Her son normally popped around the evening before to wheel her bin out onto the street, maybe he hadn't visited yesterday.

Being as quiet as she could, Ginny pulled Enid's bin out from behind the hedge next to the front door just as the door opened and Enid stepped outside, tying the belt of her dressing gown tightly around her middle. 'Sorry, Enid. I didn't mean to wake you.'

'You didn't wake me, Ginny, dear. I'd have had to be asleep to be woken.'

'Aren't you sleeping properly again?' Ginny paused, resting the bin back on the ground.

'No, I've ran out of my medication, and I think that's what's affecting my sleep. Finley didn't visit yesterday; the grandchildren had a friend's party to go to and by the time it had finished he had to get them home to bed.' Enid walked down the path and held the gate open for her.

'Thanks.' Ginny pulled the bin through and positioned it next to the other ones on the street.

'No, thank you. It just gets too heavy for me to tug along.' Enid rubbed her wrist. 'I see it's another early morning for you then?'

'Yes. Well, in truth I don't really need to get to work this early, but...' She shrugged.

'You like to, don't you? It's your happy place up at that dogs' home, isn't it?' Enid smiled at her.

'Yes, it is.' Grinning, Ginny wiped her hands down the front of her jeans. 'I'll pop out when the pharmacy opens and pick up your prescription for you.'

'Oh, you don't have to do that. I can ring Finley and ask him to pop over this evening.'

'Don't worry, I'll grab it. That way you won't be missing this morning's as well as last night's.'

'Okay, if you're sure, that would be lovely, dear. I'd have usually got my new ones before the last ones run out but there was a mix-up.' Enid shrugged.

'That's decided then. I'll pop them by in a couple of hours. See you later.' Smiling, Ginny pulled her car keys from her pocket.

'Have a good day.' Standing by her gate, Enid waved as Ginny drove down the narrow street.

* * *

Ginny laughed as Tiger jumped onto her back while Belle weaved between her arms. 'You two are determined to stop me cleaning your kennel out today, aren't you?'

She squeezed the excess water from her cloth back into the bowl and tried to wipe down the plastic dog bed again. It was no good; Tiger had now jumped down from her back and was trying to tug the cloth from her hands, intent in adding it to his tug toy collection. 'Tiger!'

'Having fun?' Alex paused outside the kennel, mop in hand.

'These two definitely know how to brighten up someone's day, don't they?' Letting go of the cloth, she watched as Belle gripped the other end in her teeth, a tug-of-war game ensuing between the two small cockapoos.

'Ha ha. They do. Neither of them has any idea of what personal space means either.'

'Nope.' Ginny looked from Alex to the two dogs and back again. 'I don't suppose you have a spare cloth, do you? I'm wondering if I might be able to finish cleaning while they're occupied with mine.'

'I sure do.' He pulled one that was hanging from his back pocket and threw it towards her.

'Thanks.' After catching it, she plunged it into the bucket of soapy water beside her.

'In fact, I've got two. I'll give you a hand, if you like? If there's two of us we'll stand a better chance of getting it finished before they notice what we're doing. Even with Susan back in today, if these two got their way we'd be spending the whole morning trying to clean their kennel.' He dipped another cloth into the water. 'I read Darryl's latest article last night.'

'Oh, yes? What did he have to say this time?'

'You've not read it?' Resting back on his haunches, he looked at her and frowned.

'Nope. I've just not come across it.' She thought about the newspaper lying on the floor in her hallway that she'd stepped over after work yesterday and again this morning. She'd never been particularly fussed about reading the paper – it usually focused on news from Trestow and the busier villages, and she'd always wondered how they managed to find enough news to report on to fill three editions each week, but since Darryl had been printing the articles about Wagging Tails, well, she'd gone out of her way to avoid reading it. 'Well, to be honest, I haven't read it because I didn't want to be disappointed again.'

'There's definitely nothing in it to disappoint anyone this time.' From where he was scrubbing the floor, Alex glanced back at her. 'Especially you.'

'Umm, well the phones haven't stopped ringing with people enquiring about adopting dogs, renting stalls or just general queries about the Family Fun Day, so I guessed it couldn't have been as scathing as the previous piece, but... I don't know, I just can't bring myself to read it just in case.' She shook her head before pausing, remembering what he'd just said. She looked at him closely. 'What do you mean by "especially you"?'

'Oh, nothing.' With a shrug, Alex wrung his cloth out.

'No, you've said it now. Go on, what did you mean?'

As he sat down on the concrete floor, Alex sighed dramatically, holding his hands up, palms forward. 'Okay, okay. Just that he speaks highly of the staff here. And mentions you by name.'

'Oh right. Well, that's a turnaround.' She raised her eyebrows.

'It sure is. Are you sure you didn't ask Jason to have a word with him?'

'No, I ran into Darryl before I'd even stepped foot inside the office.' She shrugged. 'Maybe he just mellowed a bit after spending some time with the dogs.'

'Uh-huh, maybe.' Alex looked across at her, a slow grin lighting up his face before looking away.

'What's that supposed to mean?'

'Nothing, just that the two of you were very pally on Friday when he helped fix up Luna's kennel.'

'Pally?' Ginny rolled her eyes. 'That's one thing we aren't. One hundred per cent. After the way he's behaved I wouldn't trust him as far as I could throw him, and after Jarvis nearly pulling me over on yesterday's walk, hurting my shoulder, that's not very far at all.'

'Why wouldn't you trust him?' Leaning back on his haunches, Alex wrung out his cloth again.

'Why would I? Why would any of us? The way he's treated us, the way he's written about Wagging Tails and not been bothered with Tyler's adoption piece, why would I trust him?'

'Isn't Flora going out to see some potential matches for Tyler this afternoon?'

'Yes, but that's after Darryl has written three articles about him. Three! If Terry was still working at the *Trestow Telegraph*, Tyler would have been adopted after the first article, not the third. If anything, the first two probably put a lot of people off.'

'He came good in the end though.'

Shoulders slumped, Ginny shook her head. 'In the end? This time. This one time he wrote a half-decent piece on us. We've still got a few weeks until the Family Fun Day; just think of what damage he can do if he decides he's no longer interested.'

Why was Alex defending him so much? Didn't he remember Darryl's first visit? How Darryl had behaved? The article he'd written after? It wasn't just Alex though, was it? Darryl appeared to have won Flora over too. What were they seeing in Darryl that she wasn't? Or more accurately, why couldn't they see him as Ginny did?

Alex shrugged. 'I don't think that's going to happen.'

'What are you? His new best friend?'

'No, I just think you should give the man another chance.

That's all.' Standing up, Alex threw his cloth back into the bucket, a wide smile on his face. 'It looks as though we're all done in here now.'

'Yes, thanks for that. I think you're wrong about him though. He doesn't deserve any more chances.'

Ginny approached Tiger and Belle slowly, trying – and failing – to pick up the now-abandoned cloth before either of them noticed.

'Come on, you've got all your lovely toys to play with, you don't need this dirty scrap of a cloth.'

As she picked up the cloth, Ginny watched as Alex began to mop the corridor again, whistling some song she vaguely remembered being played on the radio earlier. She shrugged. Just because Alex trusted Darryl, it didn't mean she was going to change her mind about him.

'Shall I take Luna out for a walk around West Par?' Ginny asked after jotting another name of a confirmed stallholder into her notebook and pushing it across the table. 'Alex said she passed the behaviour assessment with flying colours. I could take her down to the cove too. See what she's like with the sea and anyone we meet.'

'That's a great idea, lovely,' Flora replied. 'Go careful though. Yvonne mentioned she had some behavioural issue or other. Shame she didn't expand but she didn't have much time when she was dropping Luna off. Had an urgent call she had to deal with. I meant to ring her and have a chat but what with all the calls over the weekend, I clean forgot.' Flora tapped her forehead.

'Unless it's just the fact she flops in front of any passer-by and won't budge until she's had a fuss?' Ginny grinned. Every time

Luna did it, Ginny had to stifle a laugh. She'd never seen a dog behave in quite such a demanding but adorable way before.

'Quite possibly.' Flora nodded as the bell on top of the counter tinkled, ending their conversation.

After placing her mug in the sink, Ginny followed Flora through to the reception area, her heart sinking as she realised who had rung the bell.

'Afternoon, Flora. Hi, Ginny.'

'Darryl.'

What was it with him? First, he refuses to visit them and now they couldn't keep him away.

'I was just passing and thought I'd pop in to see if you needed that window frame finishing?' He laid his suit jacket on the counter and began to roll up his shirtsleeves.

'No need, Darryl, lovely. Susan was back in today and finished it earlier. Thank you though.'

'Oh, that's good then.' He began to unroll his sleeves again.

'But Ginny is taking Luna down to the cove. I'm sure she'd be happy of the company.' Refusing to look Ginny's way, Flora smiled at Darryl, a twinkle in her eye.

'No, don't worry,' Ginny said, plucking Luna's lead from the hooks and walking towards the door quickly. 'I'll be fine. Thanks though.'

'I'd love that. Thank you.' Darryl glanced at Ginny and raised his eyebrow.

'Good, good.' Flora picked up her mug. 'At least it won't be a wasted trip for you.'

Who cares if Darryl had a wasted trip? He'd wasted enough of their time, why shouldn't he have a piece of his own medicine? Stepping outside into the bright sunlight, Ginny shielded her eyes as she looked back at Darryl. What was he even doing here anyway? When he'd offered to come back to finish fixing the window they'd told him Susan would be able to fix it. Did he really think they needed him interfering? Yes, with his help they'd managed to get Luna's kennel fixed in time, but they'd have managed. Somehow they would have. They could cope. They'd managed without him all this time. Was he being sincere, or was he on the hunt for another story?

'You really don't have to come.'

'I know I don't. I'd like to, though. If it's all right with you of course.' He ran his hand across the back of his neck, unsure of himself, a slight flush colouring his skin. 'Besides it would be wonderful to see Luna again. Has she settled in well?'

Ginny shook her head, only just resisting the urge to roll her eyes. 'Fine. She's settled in fine.'

There wasn't any point arguing. Someone as stubborn as he was wouldn't change their mind anyway.

12

'Where are we taking her?' Darryl said as he shut the door behind him.

'Down through West Par village and to the cove. It's just up the road. Have you ever been?' Probably not. She couldn't imagine someone like Darryl enjoying the peace of West Par and the tranquillity of the ocean. No, he'd be more at home in the hustle and bustle of Trestow, or somewhere even busier maybe.

'Know it? I live there.'

'Really?' She looked back at him before opening Luna's kennel door. Was he joking?

'Yes, really. I live with my dad up along North Street. The road up—'

'I know it.' Turning her back on him, she greeted Luna and prepared her for their walk.

Great. He lived in the next street up from her. How hadn't she noticed him about before? Yes, she spent most of her waking hours at Wagging Tails, even when she wasn't working she was down here helping out or chatting to whichever staff member was on shift. And when she wasn't here, well... she was at home. She'd never been very sociable, even before she'd moved to Cornwall. The majority of her so-called friends had been linked with Jason, his mates' partners or old school friends of his who she'd met and got along with. Of course, as soon as their relationship finished, they'd all dropped her.

She rolled her eyes at the memory, clipping Luna's bright pink lead to her collar. Some friends they'd been. That was the funny thing about relationships: as soon as one was over, everyone linked to that partner suddenly dispersed. Ginny had effectively become invisible to them, eliminated from friendship groups. His side of the family had forgotten her, regardless of the fact his mother had repeatedly told her she looked upon her as the daughter she'd never had.

'She looks as though she's settled in well.' Darryl held the kennel door open, letting Ginny and Luna through. 'Has she?'

'She seems to have.' After closing the door behind her, Ginny walked on ahead, Luna at her heels. Did he really have to come? She couldn't shake him off now, could she? Why did he even want to come? She shuddered. It was as though she was under constant surveillance, her every move being watched, monitored closely.

'Is everything okay?' Darryl paused by the gate, a crease forming between his eyes.

Ginny unlocked the gate while she thought about how to respond. This could be an opportunity to put him off coming with them; now could be the time to tell him she'd rather go on her own. She looked down at Luna who was sitting obediently at her feet, waiting for her to close the gate behind them. Gritting her teeth, she smiled. She couldn't. She needed him. Wagging Tails needed him on its side. Luna needed him. Especially now Tyler was going through the adoption process, his next piece could be on Luna. If he was happy to write another. She just had to put up with him.

'Everything's fine.'

'Are you sure?'

'Why wouldn't it be?' The gate closed with a satisfying clunk, and shielding her eyes from the summer sun, Ginny crossed the road.

'You just seem off with me.' Darryl shrugged.

She waited for him to catch up. Maybe she should just tell him the truth? Not that she should really have to; he should know why she wouldn't be over the moon to have to spend more time with him. Was he that arrogant he really couldn't see that? That how he'd treated the dogs – and Flora and her – had been wrong?

'Can you blame me?' She swallowed. There, she'd said it now. She shouldn't have, but she had.

'Sorry?' He frowned.

'Just that... Can you blame me for being off with you? You completely slated Wagging Tails. And, by the way, we haven't shown Flora that particular masterpiece of yours. It would break her heart.'

'But I helped out yesterday. I helped fix up Luna's kennel.'

'One good deed doesn't undo all of the wrong. It doesn't make up for the fact that poor Tyler had to wait longer than he should have for the loving family home he deserves. Knocking a couple of bits of wood together doesn't make up for the fact that it's only just now that stallholders are ringing up to enquire about the Family Fun Day. Fixing the hinges on the door doesn't wipe out all of the bad publicity you gave us.'

Not that many readers of the *Trestow Telegraph* would have stumbled across the small article squished between adverts but that wasn't the point. The point was that he'd done it. He'd written those words. He'd believed them.

Looking at the ground, Darryl shoved his hands in his pockets. 'I regret that now. I should have taken the story more seriously. I should have given you – Flora, all of you – the attention you deserved. Sorry.'

Turning, she looked at him. Did he mean what he was saying? Did he really feel bad about what he'd said, what he'd written? Or was he just trying to get her to trust him in the hope she'd mess up, tell him something he could use against them in the paper, like he had when he'd described Wagging Tails as chaotic? She turned away. Whether he did or not, he'd still done what he had. What was it with some people? Why did they think that one small word could erase hurt? Could transform the past? It couldn't.

'Sometimes sorry doesn't cut it.'

'I understand.' Darryl sighed before jogging to catch her up.

Shaking her head, she avoided eye contact with him, keeping her gaze focused ahead. A figure was approaching them – Mr Euston, her neighbour, and his little French bulldog, Gray. She looked down at Luna, apprehensive. She looked relaxed enough, she wasn't on high alert. How she'd react remained to be seen though, no matter how well she'd responded to the people and other dogs at Wagging Tails.

Luna was walking casually as Mr Euston and Gray neared.

'Afternoon, Ginny. Hello, Darryl.' Mr Euston tipped his cap towards them both before looking down at Luna. 'I see you have a new one here.'

'Yes, this is...' So, Mr Euston knew Darryl. It must have just been her who had been oblivious to the fact he lived in the village.

There she goes. Ginny laughed as Luna collapsed to the floor, rolling onto her back, her paws in the air.

'Oh dear. Oh dear. Is the poor thing all right?' Mr Euston stroked his greying beard, frowning.

'She's fine. Meet Luna. It's a quirk of hers. She won't let you pass by until you've stroked her.'

'Well, in that case we should do as she asks.' He began to make a fuss of her, while Gray watched on.

Ginny laughed. 'I've never seen such a puzzled expression on a Frenchie before.'

Placing his hands on his knees, Mr Euston straightened his back, glanced at Gray and chuckled. 'As long as she doesn't give him any ideas.' He looked over at Darryl. 'So, Ginny here has roped you into volunteering too then?'

'Me? No...' He shook his head quickly. 'I'm just here on work business.'

'Oh, yes, I saw your article in the paper. Very good, lad.' And with that, he tipped his cap once again. 'Right, I'd best get on. I've got a loaf in the oven.'

'Good to see you, Mr Euston.'

Now Luna had stood up, Ginny gently guided her towards the edge of the path, letting Mr Euston and Gray pass.

'You too, Ginny. Bye, Darryl.'

'See you.' Darryl lifted his hand to wave.

'Come on, Luna, let's go down onto the beach.' Ginny looked ahead towards the cove.

'Have you got Luna's backstory yet?' Darryl asked, glancing across at her. 'Do you know how she ended up at Wagging Tails?'

'Yvonne from the pound said she'd been found as a stray. You can tell she's been used only as a breeding machine. Whoever was making money off her likely abandoned her because she got too old.' Reaching down, Ginny fussed Luna's ears. 'How could anyone be so callous?'

'She's got such a beautiful temperament... Especially for a dog who's likely been locked away most of her life.'

'Yep, she has. Although we don't know for sure how long she'd been kept as a breeder. There's a chance she may have been someone's much loved pet and was stolen.'

They turned down the lane towards the cove, the cottages lining the road quiet and still in the afternoon warmth.

'Wouldn't she have a microchip? That'll have been checked, wouldn't it?'

'She hasn't got one. If she was stolen, the breeder may well have had her chip removed. Or she never had one. Or she may have just been bred to breed.' Ginny shrugged. She wasn't sure which scenario would have been worse for Luna, to have experienced the love and care of a family and then been ripped away from it or to have never known what she'd been missing out on.

'Poor thing.' Darryl watched as Luna walked, her eyes lighting up as they reached the cove. 'I suppose this might be the first time she's seen the ocean if that's the case.'

'Yes, maybe.' Ginny looked down as Luna paused, nervous of the pebbles of the beach in front of her. Darryl might just be right.

'Come on, Luna. They're just pebbles,' Darryl said, kneeling in front of her. 'Look, they're much the same as the cobbles.' He picked up a handful of pebbles and held them out to her nose.

Luna sniffed them then looked up at Darryl, before taking a tentative step forward.

'That's it. Well done, Luna.'

Ginny grinned as Darryl began to shuffle backwards, still crouching in front of her, encouraging her to move forward. He continued to pick up the pebbles, this time letting them fall gently from his hands. Whatever he was thinking, it was working.

Luna stepped forward, a little more confidence in her actions this time.

'I wonder what she'll think of the water.' Darryl glanced behind him before focusing again on Luna.

Looking out towards the ocean, Ginny smiled. This was the reason she'd moved down here. The seaside was the only place she'd ever felt at home, free. She took a deep breath, filling her lungs with the salty taste of the sea air.

'Shall we find out?' Standing up, Darryl glanced back towards Luna. 'Do you mind if I take her?'

Ginny shrugged. What harm could it do? The cove was empty. 'Why not?'

'Great.' Taking the lead, he patted the side of his leg. 'Come on, Luna, I've got something to show you. Something I think you'll love.'

Ginny found a place to settle down on the pebbles and watched as Darryl and Luna ran across the beach towards the ocean. Before reaching the water, Darryl slowed, coaxing Luna forward step by step. He was really good with her. She had to give him that. He may not have cared for the plight of the dogs at Wagging Tails when he'd begun working on the story, but now, here with Luna, he looked as though he really did. That or he was an extremely good actor. She pinched the bridge of her nose. Had she been too hard on him? Was he being genuine? He had given up his time to help them fix up Luna's kennel and he seemed to be interested in their plight now. She watched as Luna stepped gingerly into the water, Darryl right there beside her. This couldn't be a game, not the way he was acting with Luna. Why would it be? No one else was here to witness him apart from her. Maybe she should give him a chance?

She looked down at the pebbles surrounding her, picked up a small grey oval one. Running the pad of her index finger around the edge, she closed her eyes, tilting her face towards the sun. Summer was her favourite time of the year here in West Par. It hadn't always been. Not when she'd been with Jason. Back then, summer was all about meeting up with friends, pub gardens and barbecues, which should sound like fun, but she'd always been vying for his attention. Whereas he'd been like a magpie – drawn to shiny, happy people instead of Ginny who he could see at home. As soon as they'd arrive, off he'd go, mingling amongst his friends, not a thought given to her. And if he had happened to glance in her direction or she'd managed to catch his attention, he'd made her feel needy, rolling his eyes and even apologising for her social inadequacies. At the time, she'd excused his behaviour, telling herself he'd just been afraid of missing out – a social butterfly. Now though, she'd come to realise that it had been deliberate, he'd known what he had been doing and, as much as she tried, she still couldn't shake off those feelings of being discarded, forgotten, boring.

She laughed to herself. Maybe she had been. Maybe she was. She'd spoken to Flora about her fears, her worries of never being good enough and, of course, Flora had always reassured her, but here she was, still alone after being cheated on over four years ago.

She shook her head. It didn't matter. She was happy being single. She wasn't lonely. She had Flora, Susan, Alex and all of the volunteers for company, plus her neighbours. She'd never known a place could be so welcoming, so friendly.

'That's it, Luna!'

Opening her eyes, Ginny grinned as she saw that Darryl had abandoned his shoes and rolled up his trouser legs and was running through the waves, Luna at his heels, barking and following his every move. He must have a dog, she decided, or else had one while he was growing up. He was just so natural around her. Far more relaxed than he'd been when she first met him in the office, or on his first visit to Wagging Tails for that matter.

'Hey, Ginny! Come in and join us? Luna's loving it!' He was waving his hands above his head to catch her attention, his gaze only being broken by Luna jumping up at him, leaving huge wet paw marks on his pale blue shirt.

What did she have to lose? Her dignity? Well, she certainly didn't care about that in front of Darryl. With a shrug, she proceeded to slip her trainers and socks off, though when she began to tiptoe across the hot pebbles, she immediately regretted not leaving them on until she'd reached the sand. As she stepped into the water, she gasped. It was cooler than she'd imagined it would be. She let her feet sink into the wet sand and the water wash against her ankles for a moment before she made her way in deeper, towards Darryl and Luna.

'She's a true water baby, isn't she? She was a bit timid at first but as soon as she walked in, she loved it.' Darryl splashed water towards Luna, who jumped, trying to catch it all in her mouth.

Ginny laughed as Luna splashed her way towards her. 'She sure looks as though she's loving every minute.'

'She really is, isn't she?'

13

'Look! Watch this! Turn around, Luna.' With his index finger, Darryl drew a circle in the air above Luna's head. Wagging her tail, Luna turned her body, following Darryl's guidance. 'I've only shown her a couple of times.'

'That's great. She's a fast learner. Aren't you, Luna?' Ginny braced herself as the dog bounded back towards her, jumping up at her with her wet paws. Staggering back, she corrected her stance and laughed. 'Alex has already taught her sit and down, although you wouldn't believe it at the moment. Down, Luna.'

Lowering her paws, Luna glanced back at Darryl before beginning to shake her whole body, covering both Ginny and Darryl with a fine dusting of seawater and sand.

'Aw, thanks for that, Luna.' Ginny wiped her face dry with the back of her hand.

'Yes, thanks. Just what we needed,' Darryl laughed, wiping his face then rubbing his hands down his trousers leaving grainy slime across his once-pristine suit trousers. He looked up at Ginny. 'Do you fancy grabbing a coffee before we head back?'

'Umm, why not?'

'Great. There's usually a coffee van in the car park; we could get one there. I don't know if we'd be welcome at the café with Luna bringing in half the beach with her.' He chuckled.

'Good point. Come on, Luna.' Ginny waited until Luna had settled at her feet before she slipped her socks and trainers on again. She wriggled her toes and smiled, enjoying the familiar sensation of sand against her skin. West Par Cove always reminded her of the holidays of her childhood, Fridays when her mum would meet her at the school gates, suitcases packed and Floss, their dog, in the car ready and waiting for a surprise trip to the seaside. A couple of days exploring their favourite bolthole, the beautiful Lulworth Cove in Dorset, had been the perfect antidote to the stresses of life back home. Now, with the cliffs hugging West Par Cove and the calm waters, she could close her eyes and be transported back to that time. That time when her mum was by her side and the ocean breeze would blow all the cobwebs of life away. Those memories had been the draw down to West Par, the promise of the sea air and its restorative qualities. And it had worked. To a point. She'd been able to start again – until now anyway. Until Jason had decided to show up.

'Well, that was fun. I might have to pop home and change before I go back to work, or no doubt Jason will have something to say,' Darryl said with a grimace as he led the way back up the narrow street.

Just as she thought: there was no getting away from Jason. Why would he have swapped from glossy magazines to a local newspaper anyway? Surely that was a demotion rather than a promotion? If he'd been someone passionate about delivering real life stories or news then she'd have understood – living the news in a small community and all that – but not Jason; he had always been led by money and status.

'Coffee?' Darryl nodded towards the van parked at the edge of the car park.

'Yes, please.' She led Luna towards one of the small metal tables positioned on the gravel in front of the van, pulled a treat from her pocket and told her to sit.

'What is it with you two, anyway?' Darryl placed a plastic cup on the table in front of her before sitting down opposite.

'Thanks. Us two?'

'You and Jason? I mean, I mean you're completely different.'

Shaking her head, Ginny looped the lead around the leg of her chair before taking a sip of coffee. 'Because he's well dressed, career-oriented and smooth?'

'Ha, no, because he's arrogant, thinks he's better than everyone else and is generally a bit of an idiot, that's why.'

Laughing, Ginny wrapped her hands around her cup, the warmth penetrating her skin. 'I guess we were both quite different when we got together.'

Shifting in his seat, Darryl knocked his cup slightly. Ginny watched as it teetered, a stream of liquid running down the side and pooling on the table. As Darryl wiped it up with a tissue, he shook his head. 'I can't imagine he was ever different enough to make him bearable to spend time with.'

'What can I say? I was young, impressionable and... daft.' She shrugged. 'I've learned my lesson.'

'Oh really?' Darryl raised his eyebrows.

'Yes.' Nodding, she looked at him. 'I don't envy you working with him.'

'You mean working *for* him, as he likes to remind me daily.'

'Yuck. He's not changed then.'

'Apparently not.' Darryl grimaced. 'Did you used to live in London or was it a long-distance relationship?'

'We lived together. In London.'

'Ooh, now I was going to say if it had been long-distance, it would explain a few things, but you lived with the guy. You have no excuses then. You can't even pretend you didn't know him.'

'Cheers. Thanks for that. Just mock my life, why don't you?' She laughed. 'It's true though, I have no excuses, despite the fact that I was young and naive.'

'Fair enough. I guess we can't be held accountable for the decisions we make when we're younger.'

'I take it you've not been sucked into Jason's fan club then?'

'Not in a million years. He waltzes in and immediately thinks he owns the place... Yes, he may be the boss, but loads of the other staff have been there long enough to be able to run the paper standing on their heads with their eyes closed, and yet he makes out as though if it weren't for him, everyone else would be out of a job.' Darryl shook his head. 'I don't know, he dishes out all the rubbish, dead-end jobs to everyone else and gives the best jobs to his pals or even keeps them for himself. It's no way to run a paper. People are going to end up leaving.'

'Right, so you get given all the rubbish, dead-end jobs then?' She pursed her lips.

'Yes, no. I didn't mean...' He covered his face with his hand. 'I didn't mean covering Wagging Tails was dead-end. That's not what I meant.'

'Uh-huh. I believe you.' After downing her coffee, Ginny unwound Luna's lead and prepared to head back to Wagging Tails. Just when she thought he was someway decent he had to go and say something like that.

'Ginny, please don't go. Sit down and let me explain. That wasn't what I meant.'

'I think I've heard enough.' She tucked her chair under, and threw her plastic cup in the recycling bin before turning away. 'Come on, Luna, let's get back to people who appreciate us.'

'Ginny, please. Let me explain.' Jumping up, he followed her out onto the street.

What did she have to lose? Five minutes of her time? She shrugged. It might be worth it to watch him try to squirm out of this. Pausing, she turned to look at him. 'Go on then. Explain.'

'Great. Thank you. I appreciate that. Just five minutes of your time, that's all I'm asking for.'

With a sigh, she looked at her watch. 'Time's ticking.'

'Of course. Yes.' Clasping his hands in front of him, Darryl looked from Ginny to Luna and back again. 'Honestly, when Jason first assigned me to this story, I thought – assumed – it would be... I don't know... on the same par as covering the story about the couple who decorated their house like a cave.'

'Great. Thanks for that.' Ginny began to walk on. So that's what he thought of them then? She'd known he hadn't thought much of Wagging Tails but to compare the importance of finding their dogs new homes to covering some story about a house which had been painted like a cave?

Focusing on the pavement in front of her, she bit down on her bottom lip, the taste of blood quickly filling her mouth. There was so much she could say to him, wanted to say to him, but what would be the point? He'd decided before he'd even visited Wagging Tails how lowly he thought of them. She gripped Luna's lead tighter, the pink fabric digging into her palm. The thing that hurt the most was this... him dropping by, pretending to have fun with the dogs. And why had he bothered to help them fix up Luna's kennel? There was something for him to gain obviously. People like him, like Jason, only helped if they stood to gain something. Maybe she'd been right, maybe he had been looking for a story.

'I haven't finished.'

She could hear Darryl's voice cracking. Maybe he'd gone too

far even for himself. Maybe the act would drop now. 'What hurts the most, Darryl, is that you lied to me, to all of us. You've been acting as though you cared, as though you understood what we were about and how much the paper could help the Family Fun Day be the best it can be. You lied.'

'No, that's the point. I'm not lying. Yes, to begin with I wasn't grateful to be assigned the story, but I am now. You've shown me how important Wagging Tails is to the local community, to the dogs that you rescue, and I want to help.'

'Really?' She frowned. Was he actually telling the truth? He looked as though he was genuine. The creases between his eyes and the way he clasped his hands in front of him suggested he was.

'Yes, really. I'm just trying to be honest with you so that you can see I'm being sincere.' He walked towards her and took her hands in his. 'I'm sorry I didn't see the potential in writing about Wagging Tails to begin with. I'm sorry I acted like a complete idiot when I first met you.'

'You really did. You made us feel that small.' Pulling her hand away, she held her index finger and thumb millimetres apart.

'I know I did. I can only apologise and try to make it up to you.' He ran his fingers through his hair.

'Up to all of us.' Ginny indicated Luna who had given up on walking and was now sitting on her foot.

'Yes, all of you. Although I do think Luna has a bit of making up to do for herself too.' He chuckled as he wiped a sandy smear from his shirt.

'Yes, you're probably right.'

'Can we start over?'

Ginny looked at the ground. Could they? 'I don't know.'

'I understand, but I do mean it. All of it.' Taking her hands again, Darryl looked in her eyes.

Looking back at him, she noticed flecks of gold surrounding his pupils. She hadn't noticed them before. Ginny frowned.

'Your eyes have gold flecks in them,' she said.

'So I'm told.'

His face was mere inches away from hers, she could feel the heat of his breath against her mouth. She leaned forward and closed her eyes, their lips brushing. What was she doing? This wasn't right. Stepping back, she looked down at Luna. 'I have to go. Come on, Luna.' Turning, she kept her eyes focused on the path in front of her as she hurried back to Wagging Tails. She could feel Darryl behind her. Of course he would be, he had to get his car.

14

After securing the door to Luna's kennel, Ginny made her way across the courtyard towards the reception area. After Darryl had caught her up, they'd hardly said a word to each other on the way back, an awkward silence hanging in the air between them. She could hear him saying his goodbyes to Luna before he jogged to catch her up.

'Thank you for this. It's been fun.'

She nodded. It had obviously been a mistake, what had almost happened. Or else she'd imagined the whole thing, but for a moment back there she'd felt a real connection, before she'd come to her senses. Whatever had happened or been going to happen, he hadn't said anything and she wasn't about to bring it up. No, the sooner he left today the better.

'Luna should be worn out for the day too.'

'Yes, she should be.'

'I... umm... I'm sorry about earlier.'

Looking back at him, she paused, her hand on the door handle. So he'd realised it had been a mistake too. Why had he bothered? 'I...'

Slowly, she pulled the door open. Flora, Susan, Alex and Percy were huddled around the counter, a bottle of fizz and some mugs sitting proudly beside the pile of paperwork and clipboards.

'Oh, you're just in time! Come on in, you two.' Flora poured two more mugs and held them out.

'What are we celebrating?' Ginny frowned as she took a mug.

'The home checks for Frank and Dino's new family were successful and so they're going tomorrow.' She dabbed at her eyes with her yellow handkerchief. 'Six years they've been here, six years since being retired from the greyhound racing and they've finally found a home.'

'I thought they'd be our resident dogs forever.' Susan smiled. 'I'm going to miss them though.'

'Same here.' Alex laughed as everyone looked at him and he began to explain himself. 'Just because Frank and I don't get on it doesn't mean that I don't love the guy.'

'We know. We're only teasing.' Susan drew him in for a hug, rubbing the palm of her hand across his hair.

'Hey, do you know how long it took me to style it this morning?' As he pulled away, he spiked up his hair again.

'Here's to Frank and Dino.' Flora held up her mug. 'Nobody's story is over until it's over.'

Everyone clinked their cups before taking a sip.

'Yuck. That truly is disgusting.' Percy picked up the bottle of fizz, a grimace on his face. 'I guess what do we expect from something that's at least four years old and alcohol free?'

'It really is quite disgusting.' Ginny forced herself to swallow the acidic drink.

'And I think we should raise a glass to Darryl too,' Flora said, putting her arm around his shoulders. 'Without him writing about Wagging Tails, the family who are adopting Frank and Dino would never have found them.'

'To Darryl.' Percy raised his glass before putting it on the counter. 'I hope you don't mind me not taking another sip, I don't think I can stomach it.'

'I don't blame you at all.' Darryl chuckled as he placed his mug on the counter and pushed it away from him.

'To Darryl.' Susan held her mug up.

'Darryl,' Ginny mumbled, watching Darryl shift on his feet, his hands now plunged into the pockets of his trousers.

'Thank you, and I'm so pleased Dino and Frank have found their forever home. I'm humbled to think this may be because of something I wrote.' He glanced towards Ginny. 'Talking of which, I really should be getting back to work. Hope you all have a great afternoon.'

'You too, Darryl, lovely,' Flora said, patting him on the arm.

'Bye, Ginny. Thanks again for a great walk.' He smiled.

With a quick goodbye of her own, she turned away and picked up the bottle before following Flora into the kitchen.

'So, they're picking them up tomorrow?' she asked.

'That's right. You should see their house. The back garden is huge, and they've already bought so many toys and chews and things that Frank and Dino won't know what to do with them all.'

Ginny grinned. Dino loved his stuffed teddies. 'And they've got experience of greyhounds?'

'That's right. They've had rescue greyhounds for years and recently lost their most recent one. They know they'll have challenges ahead, especially with Dino and Frank having lived here for so long, but they're ready for the challenge. I can't quite believe they're going. It's going to be so strange them not being here.'

Flora blinked as she washed the mugs out in the sink.

'It really will.' Ginny swiped at her eyes. 'They've been here longer than I have. I've only known Wagging Tails with them here.'

'Oh, lovely. I know.' After wiping her hands on the tea towel, Flora pulled Ginny in for a hug. 'This is what we're all about though. We've done our job when they leave us.'

'I know. I'm happy for them. I really am.'

And she was. She'd just miss them, that's all. She'd miss the way Dino would saunter up to the door of his kennel as she passed, a blue stuffed dinosaur dangling from his mouth. She'd miss the way Frank would try to bolt on the lead as soon as he spotted a squirrel or a bird or even a leaf. The two of them were such characters; their new family would be lucky to have them.

'Right, come on. We'd best get on. Tiger and Belle haven't had their walk yet and neither has Ralph. Who do you want to take?'

* * *

'Come on, Dino. That's it, get comfy. Come and sit next to me and Frank.' Pulling the duvet up to cushion the wall behind her, Ginny shifted along so Dino and his blue dinosaur could fit onto the pile of duvets that he knew as his bed. Over the years, they'd tried giving him and Frank separate baskets, but they'd always pulled the duvets out of them and slept together in a mound of blankets, stretched out on their backs with their long legs entangled. The running joke had always been that they couldn't tell where one dog ended and the other began.

'I thought I'd find you in here.' Flora opened the door to the kennel and held it open for Ginny. 'Time for home.'

'I'm just going to stay here for a bit.' She smiled as Frank strolled across to Flora.

'I thought that might be your answer. Not too long though, lovely. You need your sleep too. Make sure you head off soon.'

'I will.' Nodding, Ginny held her arm out as Frank came back towards his bed, flopping across her legs, his bony body digging into her.

'Okay. Night then, lovely.'

'Night.'

Ginny listened as Flora made her way back down the row of kennels, her voice soft as she wished them all a good night.

She turned to Frank and Dino. 'You two are going on a big adventure tomorrow morning. Your new family are going to take you home and, if you like it there, you can stay. You can have your forever home, together.'

Dino yawned, stretching his mouth wide open, the stuffed blue dinosaur falling into her lap.

'Time for sleep.' She wrapped her free arm around him as he slumped against her. 'Just think: this time tomorrow you'll both be snuggled up in your new bed in your new home, but don't worry, you'll come and visit, so you'll see us again. Not that you'll want to of course. You won't have the time – not between running around your new big garden, going on beautiful walks in the countryside and sleeping in front of the open fire.'

Frank opened a sleepy eye, looked at her and closed it again.

Leaning her head back against the concrete wall, Ginny also closed her eyes. She could see Darryl in her mind's eye, standing in front of her, her hands in his and... She shook her head. 'Why am I even thinking about him?'

At the sound of her voice, Dino nuzzled her arm.

'Sorry, was I not giving you the attention you want?' Smiling, she rubbed his neck as he leaned back against her. 'What do *you* think of him, hey? Do you think Darryl's being genuine now or just trying to get a good story?'

Frank pawed at the duvet mound before twisting around and resettling, his back to Ginny.

'So that's what you think then? You're probably right. Besides, he works with Jason. That's enough to warn me, right?' Why was she questioning herself now? He couldn't be trusted. He'd proven that time and time again. He'd written article after article to prove what he really felt about Wagging Tails. He was just trying to worm his way in and she wasn't about to let him. She needed to remember what he was really like. She wouldn't succumb to his charms. She just wouldn't. Although judging by the way he'd acted after their near kiss, he didn't want anything like that either.

She leaned her head back against the wall again and stared at the concrete wall opposite. Life was going to be so different for this pair tomorrow. They'd have a whole house and garden to enjoy. She smiled. Flora was right: this was what it was all about – giving dogs a second chance at a happy ending. It was notoriously difficult to rehome greyhounds, and the pound got a lot of them, so it would be nothing short of a miracle to successfully rehome two of them together.

She fussed Dino's ears. What with Tyler going to his adopted home later in the week too, they'd have two free kennels to take in two more dogs from the waiting list or to save for emergencies from the pound. Two more characters to keep them busy, two more pups to try to rehome.

Closing her eyes, she tried to push away all thoughts of saying goodbye to Dino and Frank. And all thoughts of Darryl and what had almost happened earlier.

15

The sound of dogs barking interrupted Ginny's dream and suddenly she was surrounded by dogs – dogs on the beach, dogs swimming in the sea, dogs at her ankles. Darryl was there too, standing in front of her telling her something. She couldn't make it out though. What was he saying?

'Oi, Ginny! Have you been here all night?'

It was Alex's voice. He was close, but she couldn't see him – he wasn't on the beach. She couldn't pinpoint where his voice was coming from.

'Hey, sleepyhead. Time to wake up now.'

Forcing her eyes open, she blinked sleepily. It took her a few moments to remember where she was. It must be breakfast time; the dogs weren't barking any more and the aroma of canned meat filled the air. Alex was sitting on his haunches in front of her, the breakfast basket – as they called it – set on the concrete floor at his feet. Dino and Frank were munching their way through their first meal of the day, having abandoned her on the makeshift duvet bed.

'Alex.' Yawning, she stretched her arms above her head. 'I must have fallen asleep.'

'Don't tell me you've been here all night?' He laughed and shook his head.

'I didn't mean to.'

'Come on, Flora's in the kitchen. She'll have the kettle on. Go and get a coffee or something.' Standing up, he held out his hand.

'Coffee sounds good.'

* * *

Pushing open the door from the kennels into the reception area, Ginny paused. She could hear people speaking. Who was Flora talking to? She recognised the voice. It was Darryl. She knew it was. She recognised the rise and fall of his words, the tone. What was he doing here? Didn't he have work?

She looked back at the kennels behind her, where Alex was feeding the last of the dogs. She needed coffee, and a stretch. Sleeping on the mound of uneven duvets might be super comfy for Frank and Dino, but it definitely hadn't been for her. She'd just have to face Darryl.

Taking a deep breath, she opened the door fully and stepped inside.

'Morning, Ginny, lovely,' Flora said from where she was pouring a mug of coffee from the cafetière. 'I see someone didn't take my advice last night.'

'Thanks.' Taking the mug, she breathed in the hot bittersweet aroma. 'I didn't plan on falling asleep.'

'Morning.' Darryl nodded, holding his own freshly brewed cup.

Looking at him over the rim of her mug, she frowned. He

didn't look as though he'd had much sleep either, not if the dark rings beneath his eyes were anything to go by.

'You slept here?'

Shifting her position, she leaned her elbows on the counter and chewed her bottom lip. 'Yes.'

'She was told not to. I'm not one of those monster bosses.' Flora looked across at Ginny and shook her head, changing the subject. 'It's Frank and Dino's last day with us today.' She looked at the small carriage clock wedged between an array of dog training books on the shelf. 'In fact, they'll be leaving in a couple of hours.'

'You stayed all night to be with them?' Darryl raised his eyebrows.

She shrugged. 'I didn't intend to. I just fell asleep.'

'In their kennel?' He took another sip of his coffee.

'Yes.' Wrapping her hands around her mug, Ginny tried to focus on the heat penetrating her skin rather than Darryl's judgement. She'd done nothing wrong. She'd spent the past four years of her life working alongside Frank and Dino; why wouldn't she have wanted to spend some more time with them?

'Why don't you head home after your coffee, Ginny, lovely,' Flora said, wiping up a splash of coffee she'd spilt when pouring.

'No, I wouldn't be able to get back to sleep anyway.'

'We'd cope. We'll be two dogs down by the end of the morning anyway and today's always a busy day for volunteers.'

Ginny dipped a digestive into her coffee, holding it there until the submerged biscuit began to soften. And then, placing the softened biscuit into her mouth, she savoured the coffee marinated taste, the creamy texture the perfect mix with the strong coffee.

'No, I'll be fine. I've got nothing to do at home. I'd just be bored.'

'In that case, why don't you keep Darryl company on his expedition today?' Flora gestured towards him with a biscuit. 'You wouldn't mind, would you, love?'

'Me? Umm, no, that's fine.' Darryl swallowed. 'Yes, you'd be welcome to join me. I'm visiting Looe Island Nature Reserve for a piece I'm writing.'

'Oh no, I don't think so.' Ginny shook her head. 'Thank you though.' Even through the tired mugginess filling her head, she could imagine how awkward spending a whole day with Darryl would be.

'Oh, go on. You've always wanted to go, haven't you? It's always been on your list of New Year resolutions. I'm sure you wrote it on this year's, and you said you were determined to tick it off this time. You've always said you wanted to experience the untouched beauty of the island, see the wildlife, and you know how difficult it is to get on a tour. They barely run any.'

Ginny flared her nostrils. She couldn't lie, not to Flora. 'I know, but it's only the summer. I have a whole half a year left to tick it off my list.'

'Yes, but you may as well go now, when the opportunity is staring you in the face.'

Ginny looked across at Darryl. He looked just as unenthusiastic as she was with the idea. 'No, I don't want to get in the way of him doing his job.'

'Tish-tosh, you wouldn't be. Would she, Darryl? You tell her,' Flora said as she patted his forearm.

'Not at all. You're very welcome to come along. As Flora said, it would be nice to have the company.' Crossing his arms, he smiled, his lips thin, forced.

Ginny glanced from Flora to Darryl again and shrugged. It didn't look as though she had much choice. Or Darryl. Great. She raked her fingers through her hair, last night's knots catching at her knuckles, and said, 'I can't go like this.'

'Go home and get changed. Darryl can pick you up in half an hour when he's finished here,' Flora said, waving her away.

'Okay, I get the message.' Ginny sighed. She knew Flora was only looking out for her, just wanting her to take a break, have a day off, but a whole day with Darryl? It sounded like the opposite of relaxing. Still, she *had* always wanted to visit Looe Island Nature Reserve...

16

Was that the door? Pulling her T-shirt over her head, Ginny grimaced. It was. It must be Darryl. She checked the time on her alarm clock. He was early too, only by five minutes, but when she'd only had half an hour to shower and change, five minutes was a big deal.

Scrunching dry her hair as she pulled open the door, she said, 'Sorry, I just need to grab my bag.'

'No worries.' Darryl looked around the small white hallway.

'Look,' Ginny said, 'are you sure you want me to come along? Are you sure you won't be happier going on your own? You don't really want me hanging around with you all day, do you?' She glanced towards the living room door. Being bored all day seemed like the better option.

'Of course not.'

'Right. Okay, I'll get my bag then.'

Pushing the living room door open, she looked around. Where had she put it? When had she even used it last? She didn't need a handbag for work, and she couldn't remember the last time she went out anywhere which wasn't related to Wagging

Tails. A few months ago, maybe. She shook her head. She didn't care about that. Wagging Tails was her world: her friends were there, the people she thought of as her family. She didn't need anyone else. Besides, she knew many of the people who lived in West Par due to walking the dogs around the area or them volunteering at Wagging Tails. She had more friends here than she'd ever had back in London, especially if you didn't count the people who she'd known through association with Jason only.

She looked behind the sofa. No luck, she'd just have to go as she was. She didn't need a bag anyway.

'Are you almost ready? The tour starts soon, and we've got to get there first.' Darryl peered through the living room door. 'It looks lovely in here.'

'Thanks.' She glanced around the room, a few-days-old pizza box lay on the coffee table, a half-empty glass of orange juice next to it. Sure it did.

Apart from buying furniture and placing a few pot plants around the room, she hadn't done anything since moving in. Luckily, the stark white walls of the cottage had been perfect for her taste – the perfect backdrop for her plants and a stark contrast to the colourful scatter cushions crammed on the sofa. 'I'm ready.'

'Great. Shall we take my car?'

Pulling her trainers on, Ginny agreed and then, after locking the wooden front door, she followed him down the narrow path through the small flower-laden front garden. Closing the wrought-iron gate behind her, she looked back at her little chocolate box cottage and smiled. From the moment Flora had shown her the cottage, she'd felt at home.

* * *

'Are you okay?' Darryl gripped hold of Ginny's arm, his face pale.

'*I* am.' Looking at him, she laughed.

He was sitting next to her in the boat, a bright orange life jacket covering his shirt, one hand gripping her arm while he held on to the edge of the bench with the other.

'Sorry, I didn't mean to laugh,' she continued, 'but I don't think I've ever seen you not so sure of yourself before. I take it you're not a fan of boat rides?'

'Nope. Much to the disgust of my dad who used to be a keen fisherman and was desperate to teach me the tricks he'd picked up—'

He suddenly clasped his hand over his mouth.

'I'd lean over the edge if you're about to be sick.'

As he looked across to the edge of the boat, Darryl's eyes widened. 'I'll be fine.'

'Sure you will.' She took his hand in hers, covering it with her other hand. 'We've not got much further to go now anyway, but tell me about this story you're writing. Why Looe Island?'

Taking his other hand away from his mouth, Darryl took a deep breath. 'Jason wants me to start a column focusing on a different tourist attraction around here each week.'

'That sounds interesting.'

'Yes, it does actually.' He looked out across the ocean, though his hand gripped Ginny's tighter.

She looked down at his hand in hers, his skin warm against hers. She could almost feel the brush of his lips against hers from yesterday. Looking away across the water, she shook her head, pushing all thoughts of that moment away.

'Hey, focus on me. Tell me what other places you've got lined up.' She tapped his hand gently, bringing his attention back to her. Whatever she thought of him, he had helped her that day in the lift. He hadn't needed to. Now was her turn to help him work through his fears.

'Next week I'm booked in for a class on traditional Cornish pasty making, believe it or not.'

'That sounds fun. Are you a good cook then?'

'Not so bad. I can hold my own. I used to cook a fair bit for friends, now I cook for my dad.'

'He's lucky then. I'm a terrible cook.' She'd attended an evening cookery class when she'd lived in London, on Jason's request, but the class had been that busy she'd not really learned anything, not retained much anyway.

'I'm sure you're not that bad.' He smiled.

It was working. The conversation was taking his mind off the fact they were coursing through the ocean, miles from land, at a speed he'd rather not be aware of.

'Oh, not if you enjoy the burnt bits.' She grimaced. She really was terrible. Jason had always cooked. Always. Since they'd met. Had the cooking lessons been a ploy to keep her out of house? She shook her head. It didn't matter. Not now. She watched as another boat passed them, the waves it created bouncing along the sides.

'Burnt bits can be nice.' He shrugged. 'They're the best bits on a roast potato.'

'That's true.' She leaned in closer to him in confession. 'I've never cooked a roast.'

'Never? As in never ever or just not for a while?'

'Never as in never.'

Looking across at her, he raised his eyebrows in mock shock.

'Oi, don't look at me like that. I bet there're millions of so-called normal things you've never done.'

'Umm, like skydiving, you mean?'

She rolled her eyes as Darryl chuckled. 'Look, we're almost here now. And look at the seals.'

As they slowly pulled into the small docking area, Ginny could see at least fifteen seals lounging on the rocks to the side of them with more in the ocean bobbing their heads up and down as if to welcome them to the island.

'Come on, let's get off this thing.' Standing up, Darryl tugged his life jacket over his head before leading the way off the boat.

She picked up his discarded life jacket and followed him. 'I think you're supposed to keep that on until you actually set foot on dry land.'

'I'll take my chances.'

Stepping down onto the landing stage, Ginny threw Darryl's life jacket in a large box to the side before pulling hers off and joining him and the small group of other tourists.

'Welcome to Looe Island Nature Reserve,' said the leader of the tour, tugging her long brown hair into a ponytail. 'I'm Nancy and I'll be taking you on your guided walk today. Can I take this opportunity to remind you that we all have a part to play in the preservation of this wildlife jewel in the ocean and remind you to follow me, your guide, and to stay on the designated paths. We'll head up to the reception area in the Old Tractor Shed where I'll give you each a laminated guide and talk you through the health and safety guidelines.'

'Wow, look at all the seals.' A woman wearing a large-brimmed sunhat looked back towards the boat and the ocean.

'That's right. We're very lucky to have an abundance of grey seals who have made the ocean and rocks around the island their home. Does anyone know how big the seals can grow?'

'That one looks as though it must be at least a metre long.' The woman took her hat off and fanned herself with it, its wide brim flapping with the movement.

'A good estimate. They can actually grow up to three metres long and weigh up to three hundred kilograms, making them Britain's largest mammal.' Nancy nodded behind her. 'Shall we explore and see what other wildlife we can discover?'

'Three metres long?' Ginny fell into step alongside Darryl. 'That's crazy.'

'It sure is big. I don't think I'd like to meet one down a dark alley.'

'I think you'll be okay. I've not heard that seals like hanging about by the pub.' She grinned.

'Ha ha, very funny.'

'I thought so.'

They followed Nancy up a slight incline, the shrubbery bordering the trackway very neat.

Darryl smiled at Ginny. 'Thanks for keeping me calm on the boat. I've always struggled with seasickness.'

'No worries.' She shrugged. 'Let's say we're even now, after you helped me in the lift.'

'Good idea.'

In the time she'd known him she didn't think she'd seen him as sincere as he was being now. Of course, it didn't change anything. He was still the same person who had written those articles, but it was comforting to see a different side to him. 'Is that how you knew how to help me when I was having that panic attack?'

'No. My sister suffered from them when we were growing up. I learned how to help her by watching my mum, and then when my mum passed away, it was me who stepped in to help her.'

'Oh, I'm sorry to hear about your mum.' Reaching out, she touched his forearm. 'How old were you?'

'Fourteen.' Darryl held back a branch, letting Ginny slip past.

'That was the age I lost my dad.' She swallowed. Even though it was over twenty years ago now, she still remembered the day her mum had sat her down to tell her about the car accident. She shuddered. She didn't think she'd ever forget her mum's swollen bloodshot eyes and the expression on her face. She'd been at her gran's house, the smell of flapjack filling the air after they had spent the afternoon baking. Once a favourite pastime of Ginny's, now tainted with the wrenching sadness of finding out she'd lost her dad. Only recently she'd made the connection of her hatred of baking with that afternoon. She'd never shared it with anyone, and always had difficulty explaining to people why she hated cooking so much.

They were approaching a small squat reception building.

'Thank you.' Taking the door from the person in front of them, Darryl stepped back, letting Ginny through first.

'Thanks.' Ginny smiled at him as she slipped into the building.

'That's it, in you all come.' Nancy began to hand out the laminated guides. 'Here's some information about the wildlife and foliage you may come across on our walk. The guided walk will take approximately an hour and a half and then you'll have just over an hour to explore on your own.'

'It's only been a reserve since 2004?' A man with a large camera hanging around his neck tapped at the laminated guide.

'That's right. When Babs Atkins passed away, she bequeathed her former home to Cornwall Wildlife Trust. The two Atkins sisters, Babs and Evelyn, bought Looe Island in 1965 and Evelyn subsequently wrote two books describing their experiences: *We Bought an Island* and *Tales from our Cornish Island*. Since 2004, the Cornwall Wildlife Trust has protected the island.'

Ginny looked down at the leaflet in her hand before glancing at Darryl. 'Shouldn't you be writing this down?'

'I know all of this already. Research.' He tapped the side of his head. 'Through scouring the internet, plus from chatting with my dad. This trip is primarily to get photos and to have the first-hand experience of visiting.'

'Has your dad visited a lot before then?' He must have done, the way he was speaking about him.

'Yes, he's lived here, in Cornwall, all of his life. He used to visit the nature reserve fairly regularly before he retired as part of his job with the trust.'

'He worked for the Cornwall Wildlife Trust?'

'Yes, not exclusively on the island or anything but the times he visited were special to him. He always says there's something magical about this place. Even as a child, years before it was bequeathed to the trust, we'd come to the town, and he'd lift us up, pointing towards the island and promising us that one day he was going to visit. The island of magic, he called it.'

'Oh wow, and now you're here.'

'Now I am.' Grinning, he took out his mobile and began to take photos of the land surrounding the old tractor shed.

'Come on, it's time to go.' She tugged on his shirt as the group moved away.

'Right, coming.'

17

As the group followed the path ahead, Nancy began describing the wildlife they might see – an array of butterflies, the distinct orange and brown gatekeepers, dusty brown ringlets, meadow brown and red admirals.

They walked past a beautiful white cottage, its tables displaying an assortment of jams, chutneys, apple juice and fruit and vegetables.

'Is this for sale?' The woman with the hat pointed to the produce.

'It certainly is,' Nancy replied. 'We'll veer back this way on our return to give everyone the chance to buy something before you head back over the waters. We're proud to say that we're working towards becoming completely food and energy self-sufficient on the island. We're not quite there yet, but close.'

'Don't you worry about attracting rats with all of this out here like this?' The man with the camera began clicking away, taking photographs of the laden tables. 'I can imagine a place like this, with very few predators, that rats would be a big problem.'

'You're right: rats could become a problem, with the lack of predators, and it has been a problem in the past. Brought across on a shipwreck hundreds of years ago, rats invaded the island resulting in the island community coming together to eliminate them. More recently, they came across on boats again causing the population of black-backed gulls to plummet as they'd invade their nests and eat the eggs. Fortunately, our team managed to eradicate them in 2006.' Nancy picked up an apple and inspected it before putting it back down again.

Ginny looked back at the produce as Nancy led them away.

'How long have you worked at Wagging Tails?' Darryl looked across at Ginny.

Pausing, Ginny frowned. Why was he taking an interest now? 'Four years and three months.'

'A fair while then. What made you move down here?'

'I don't know. I've always liked the beach and always thought I'd end up living by the sea.' She looked down at the uneven path in front of her. Maybe she should open up to him a bit. After all, he was trying. 'Honestly, I left London shortly after Jason and I finished, and I didn't really know where I was heading, just that I needed to get out of the city. When I got to Trestow, I saw a poster asking for volunteers at Wagging Tails and so I hopped on a bus to West Par.'

'Just like that?'

'Just like that.' She shrugged. 'I guess some of the best plans aren't actually plans at all.'

'Wow, that's lucky.'

'Very.' She smiled. She knew how lucky she'd been. 'Flora took pity on me and took me in before offering me a job and finding me my cottage. It could have turned out very differently, but my mum had just moved abroad and I didn't really have anything to lose. How about you?'

'Me?'

'Yeah, I'm guessing you've not lived in West Par your whole life. For one, I'm sure I would have seen you around.' Even though she spent most of her waking life at Wagging Tails, she lapped the cove a fair number of times throughout the week walking the dogs and she was certain she would have remembered him if she'd seen him about.

'You're right. I haven't. I lived in London up until recently.'

'Huh, we lived in the same city, and both moved down here.'

'Yes, coincidence hey?' He grinned as they sidestepped around a couple in front of them who had paused to take photos.

'Why did you move back here? I'm guessing it wasn't work?' She laughed. As much as he was trying to make up for the way he'd behaved, it was still at the front of her mind.

'Ha.' Looking down at the path, Darryl shook his head. 'My dad's not been very well so I came down to look after him.'

'Oh, I'm sorry.'

'Don't be. He's on the mend now.' Spotting a red admiral butterfly, he paused and took a picture.

'I'm guessing you worked as a journalist up in London too?' If so – and she assumed he had – then working for the *Trestow Telegraph* must be a stark contrast to his former job.

'Yes, that's right.' Darryl smiled sadly.

Ginny nodded. So, he'd come down here to care for his dad. Had he taken a step back in his career? Was that why he'd been so flippant about Wagging Tails? 'Do you miss it? The hustle and bustle of the city, I mean?'

'In a way. Don't get me wrong, after growing up here, I'm a big fan of West Par, but nothing beats the opportunities London offers, does it?'

'We'll head up to what is known as the Viewpoint.' Nancy's voice rang out around them, stopping their conversation. 'From there we'll be able to spot various local birds and other wildlife.

We may even be lucky and spot a basking shark or a dolphin in the ocean just off the island.' She pointed up a slight incline.

'Ooh sharks. We'd best be careful not to fall in.' Darryl laughed.

'Ha ha, I'm pretty certain we'll be safe even with a couple of basking sharks.' She looked across at him. He missed London. Would he be going back when his dad had recovered?

* * *

'How come we're the only ones heading up here?' Ginny looked down the track to where the rest of the group were either meandering slowly back the way they'd come or were still engrossed watching out for wildlife from the Viewpoint. Now the guided walk was over, Nancy had given them free rein over the island, as long as they kept to the designated tracks.

'I want to see how far up this track goes. There's something I want to show you.' Darryl pointed to a rock protruding into the trackway. 'Mind that.'

'What do you want to show me?' She glanced back down the hill. Should they be going up this far?

'You'll see.'

She shrugged. 'Okay.'

They were on a track and that was allowed, she guessed, as long as they didn't break their promise – not to disturb the wildlife.

'I'll tell you when we get there. It shouldn't be much further.' Turning around, he looked at her and grinned. As he did so, he walked backwards – straight into a hedge of brambles growing across half of the track. 'Ouch!' Reaching his hand behind his back, he tried to brush the brambles from his shirt.

'Careful. Here let me help.' Minding not to touch the thorns, she carefully unhooked the brambles from the fabric of his shirt. 'I have a feeling you may have just ruined your shirt.'

Looking over his shoulder, Darryl shrugged. 'Never mind.'

Carefully holding the brambles between the thorns, Ginny tucked it behind anther branch, securing it in place. Him having worked in London explained a lot, explained his attitude towards covering their story. 'Can I ask you something?'

'Of course.'

'And you'll be honest?'

'Ah, that sounds ominous.' He looked uncertain.

'Not really. I just wondered if you were so... umm... flippant about writing about Wagging Tails because you felt you'd taken a step back after working in London?'

Keeping his eyes focused ahead of him, he paused before carrying on.

'Sorry, I just wondered...'

Why was she apologising? It was a legitimate question.

'I just wanted to know.' She swallowed. 'Don't worry, you don't have to explain. I shouldn't have asked.'

Coming to a stop, Darryl looked at her, creases appearing between his eyebrows. 'You're right. I was so close to a promotion to editor-in-chief when I got the call about my dad. I took a couple of months out and then got the job at the *Trestow Telegraph*. It wasn't cutting edge stuff, we weren't reporting on any big stories as such, but it wasn't so bad. Just, you know, small-town stuff.' He rubbed a hand across the stubble on his chin. 'And then the editor-in-chief's job came up there and I applied for it.'

She nodded. She could almost guess where this story was going.

He laughed, a low hollow laugh. 'Then your lovely ex arrives on the scene, fresh from the city, straight from some glossy magazine or other and they decided he has more recent experience than me. I mean, can you believe that? He's from a magazine, not a paper. Anyway, he takes a dislike to me, and you can probably guess the rest.'

'Jason puts you on all the rubbish jobs? Stories about people decorating their living rooms in the style of a cave, that sort of thing?'

'Yes! Exactly. The darn cave house.' Chuckling, he slapped his forehead. 'I assumed Wagging Tails would just be a dead-end story, like all the previous assignments I'd been given. I'm sorry. It's no excuse but when I started writing about Wagging Tails, Jason was being all high and mighty, taking every opportunity to shoot me down, usually publicly.' He rolled his eyes. 'And things were up in the air with my dad. I'm not excusing how I behaved, I'm just trying to explain.'

Ginny nodded slowly. It felt good that he was being honest. That was all she needed. Honesty. 'And now?'

'Now? Honestly? And I mean zero offence to you, Flora, and everyone else at Wagging Tails, but it's not ground-breaking journalism.' He held his hands up, palms forward. 'It's not. But it's meaningful. Wagging Tails is an important part of the local community, people love the place and are interested in the work you do, but more importantly, this is a chance where I can make a difference. Through my work I can reach people, potential adopters, volunteers, people who will come to Family Fun Day. It might not be the big stories I used to cover in London but it has heart, value.'

Ginny nodded. He meant it. She could see he was telling the truth. The way his face had flushed with colour and his eyes were meeting hers, she knew he was finally being genuine. 'How's your dad now?' she asked.

'As I said, a lot better. Thank you. Truly on the mend.' He smiled, his eyes lighting up.

'That's good then.' She smiled at him. He'd sacrificed his career for his dad.

'Yes, very good. And I *am* sorry. I know I apologised on the walk with Luna too, but I mean it. I really do. I'm sorry if my actions, or my lack of action, affected any of the dogs in your care or jeopardised the running of the Family Fun Day. If I'm honest, everything was just getting on top of me. I realise that now.'

'And the fact that you've gotten to know us and realise how awesome we all are helped I'm assuming?' She laughed.

'Yes, there's that too.' He smiled. 'Am I forgiven?'

'Possibly. It depends on what you're about to show me.'

'Yes, well, I hope it's still visible. Hmm, I say that as though I've been here before, but I haven't. I only know from what my dad has told me.' Veering to the right, he led her up towards a steep ledge. 'Yes! Come and look.'

Holding out his hand, Darryl helped her to step closer to the edge and pointed towards the skyline.

As she held his hand, Ginny felt his fingers wrap around hers, firm and secure yet gentle. She could feel the telltale warmth of a blush flush across her face as she gripped his hand, the memory of yesterday's almost kiss fresh in her mind.

Holding her hand above her eyes, she peered into the distance. From this height she could see right across the island towards the ocean opposite. Trees and greenery covered the sloping hill in front of them, birds flitting from treetop to treetop. She could just imagine the abundance of wildlife hidden beneath the canopy of the trees. Beyond, she could see the clear water of the ocean, a grey cluster of seals huddled on some rocks just off the shoreline.

'It's beautiful.'

'It sure is, isn't it?' Darryl placed his arm around her waist and turned her to the side, so she was now nearly facing him. He pointed to some ruins below. 'Do you see those?'

'The ruins? Yes. What are they?'

'They're the remains of an old twelfth century chapel.'

'Wow.'

'And do you see the dip next to the ruins? It's quite tricky to spot it with so much foliage growing over it.' His arm was still around her waist as he tried to explain where it was.

Squinting against the midday sun, Ginny followed Darryl's gaze. Could she see it? Yes, the foliage was uneven. There was a dip. Something that looked as though it might once have been a crater. 'I do see something.'

'Ahh, I was hoping you would. During the Second World War, Looe Island was mistaken for a warship, HMS *St Georges*, which, actually, is a bit of a coincidence being as the island was known as St Georges Island back then.' He shook his head. 'Anyway, that's where it was hit. Down there behind the ruins of the chapel.'

'That's crazy.'

'Yep.' His arm was still around Ginny's waist, she couldn't help but notice. Surprisingly, it felt natural. 'Is that interesting enough for you to forgive me?'

'Ha ha, yes, I think it is actually.' She smiled, comfortable in his closeness. She looked across at him. His face was inches from hers, his eyes tearing up as he looked down upon the crater his dad must have told him about years ago. 'I'm glad I came today.'

Glancing down, he smiled. 'I'm glad you did too.'

She could feel the warmth of his breath against her cheek.

'Thanks for inviting me.'

'Thanks for coming,' he whispered, reaching out and gently tucking a loose strand of hair behind her ear. His fingertips lingered against her cheek for far longer than necessary.

She could see those golden flecks in his irises again, could smell his earthy-scented aftershave, could feel the pads of his fingers against her cheek, caught in the moment. Bringing her hand up to the nape of his neck, she felt his fingers stroke her cheek. She felt his palms cupping her chin gently towards him.

And then his lips were against hers, gentle, warm, smooth. Hers against his.

18

'Are you coming in?' Twisting around in the passenger seat, Ginny looked at Darryl.

'No, I'd better not. I'd best get back to the office.' Darryl took her hand. 'I had a great time, even if the boat ride back was even choppier than going out.'

'The water was practically still,' she laughed, her hand on the door handle. 'I had a great time too. Thank you.'

'No, thank you, but I'd have to disagree with you about the sea being still.' Chuckling, he leaned forward and kissed her.

Smiling, she shook her head before opening the car door.

'Ginny?'

'Yes?' She looked back at him.

'Do you fancy doing something tonight? Maybe we could go out for dinner or for a drink or something?'

'I'd like that.'

'Okay, great. I'll give you a call after work then.'

Nodding, Ginny closed the car door and walked towards the door of Wagging Tails. She brought the palms of her hands up against her cheeks. Was this really happening? Was she actually going to go on a date with Darryl? The kiss had felt right. It had all felt right, but it was still Darryl. He was still the man who had written those awful things about Wagging Tails. The man who hadn't understood how pivotal the help of the press was for the success of their fundraising, for the running of the dogs' home. Was she really ready for this? Ready to go on a date with him and forget everything. She looked up at the sign above the door to the reception. This was her home, her life, her family, and he hadn't seen the importance of it.

Pushing the door open, she paused. All was quiet. He had apologised, explained and was trying to make up for his mistakes though. But was it enough? Did it mean enough to her? And he'd shown what he could be like, who was to say he wouldn't revert back to the person he'd been when she'd first met him?

'Flora?'

'Hey, Ginny, lovely. I'm through here.'

Ducking behind the counter, she followed Flora's voice into the kitchen. After giving her a quick hug, she asked, 'Did Frank and Dino get off okay?'

'Oh, yes. They were picked up this morning. Not long after you left, actually.' Standing up, Flora grabbed a slice of toast from the toaster and buttered it. 'Their new family just called to say they seem to be settling in well so far. Do you want some?' She nodded towards her plate.

'No thanks. Hopefully that's a good sign then.'

'Hopefully.' Flora tilted her head. 'I see you've enjoyed your day too?'

Ginny shrugged, hoping the flush of embarrassment she could feel racing to her cheeks didn't give her away. 'It was okay.'

'Just okay?' Flora laughed. 'How's Darryl?'

'Good.'

Don't smile. Don't smile.

'Just good?'

Ginny began pulling wet blankets from the washing machine. 'He apologised for the way he's been acting and explained why he had.'

'I see.' Flora nodded knowingly. 'I rather think the poor boy has tried to make up for his failed articles already, don't you? What with helping fix up Luna's kennel and the articles he's published since.'

Ginny shrugged. 'Maybe.'

'We all make mistakes, love. It just takes a bit of forgiveness to be allowed to move on.' Flora looked over at her. 'Although it looks as though you've already forgiven him?'

'Maybe,' she repeated, not wanting to say anything more and risk betraying herself. Especially as she wasn't even sure how she felt herself.

'Maybe! Judging by the colour of your cheeks, you've more than forgiven him.' Flora chuckled. 'Have you got something to tell me, lovely?'

Ginny sat down. What had she expected? This was Flora. She would get it out of her eventually.

'We might have... kissed.'

'I knew it! I knew there was something going on between the pair of you.' Flora reached across the table and patted her hand.

'How could you? I didn't even know. Not until today.' She grimaced. 'Okay, yesterday. We had a moment yesterday on the walk with Luna but...'

Looking back, maybe she'd been a bit harsh on him. He'd only been trying to tell her the truth – what he'd told her today. She shrugged. For someone so good at getting words on paper, he'd done a rubbish job at getting his spoken point across yesterday.

'I have a way of figuring these things out,' Flora said. 'A sixth sense, if you like. So tell me everything.'

'There's not much to tell. We just had a good talk, that's all, and the next moment we were kissing.' She could feel the flush of warmth dancing across her cheeks again.

'You like him?' Pushing her now empty plate away, Flora opened the biscuit tin, took one out and passed the tin across to Ginny. 'Of course you like him. It's written all over your face. Over both your faces.'

'You knew that he liked me?' She pulled out a biscuit, stunned at what Flora was saying.

'It was obvious, wasn't it?'

'No.'

How was it obvious? She'd assumed he'd hated her as much as she had him. Taking a bite from the biscuit, she let the sugary taste melt in her mouth.

'I assumed he hated me as much as I hated him. How did you work out he liked me?'

'Oh, the little looks he gives you, the way he would always pop round with daft excuses like dropping off those dog toys he found in his dad's garage, things like that.'

Ginny frowned. Had there really been signs? Had she just completely missed them? Placing the half-eaten biscuit on the table, she pulled her hairband off her wrist, bundled her hair up into a messy bun and cleared her throat. This was too much to think about; she needed to change the subject. 'Have you got the list of stallholders signed up for the Family Fun Day? I thought I'd go through them and allocate stalls?'

Flora nodded. 'I'll go and get them for you.'

'Thanks.' Ginny smiled. She loved Flora. She loved the way she was happy to talk about everything and anything but also knew when to let a subject lie. She pulled her mobile from her pocket and checked the screen before rolling her eyes at her impatience. Did she really think he'd text her already?

Looking towards the door to the reception area, she frowned. Flora had pulled the door to but Ginny could still hear voices. Flora was talking to someone, someone she didn't much care for, if she was going by the clipped tone in her voice.

The other person was talking now. The other person, she realised, being Jason. What was he doing here? Biting down on her bottom lip, she pushed her chair back. As much as she'd like to hide away until he left, that wouldn't be fair on Flora.

Pulling the door open, she paused.

'Ginny. How lovely to see you.' He grinned.

'Jason was just asking whether we were pleased with Darryl's articles. I've told him we are.' Flora folded her arms.

'Ah okay. Is that all, Jason?' Ginny pursed her lips.

'Yes, but being as I've run into you, Ginny, may I have a quick word?' He smiled at Flora, and then added, 'In private.'

'Okay, but I've got things to do so please make it quick,' Ginny said, crossing her arms.

Run into her? How could he possibly pretend that he'd 'run into her' when he'd gone out of his way to come to her place of work?

'Just a couple of minutes, lovely.' Flora tapped her on the arm before disappearing into the kitchen.

'What can I do for you, Jason? Are you looking for a dog to adopt? Have you seen a particular one on the website?' She smiled. She'd never allow him to adopt one of their dogs, but she didn't want to acknowledge whatever his real reason for being here was. She'd play him at his own game.

'Uh, no. You know I don't like... am allergic to dogs.'

'Of course, how could I forget?' She tapped her forehead. 'You'd best be quick then. I wouldn't want you breaking into hives or anything. Not when you've got to get back to the office and no doubt have lots of important meetings to run.'

'True. I'll cut straight to the chase then. Have you given any more thought to my offer?'

'Your offer?' She frowned.

'Accompanying me to dinner?'

'No, I haven't.' She folded her arms.

'Maybe you could.' He leaned towards her, reaching out across the counter, and gently touched her chin.

She jerked her head back, narrowing her eyes. What was he playing at?

'You have a bit of muesli or something there.'

Muesli? She wiped the back of her hand across her chin before looking at it. Biscuit. It was biscuit.

'So?'

'So, what, Jason?' He was still talking about dinner? 'Do you remember why we split up?'

'I—'

'That's right, you had an affair. Not only did you have an affair, but you also proceeded to kick me out of our shared house – yes, shared – and immediately moved your mistress in.' Ginny could feel her nostrils flaring. 'I'm sorry, do you still need to be reminded of this?'

'I remember, and I appreciate how much I hurt you. What you've got to remember though is that it wasn't all rosy for me either. Natasha and I split up shortly after you left and then I was alone too.'

Had she heard that right? It hadn't been easy for him? She tapped her fingers against the edge of the counter, trying to hold in her anger.

'Besides, it was four years ago now. Over four years, and I've changed since then. And now I'm living so close to you, I thought

it would be nice to catch up. Maybe continue where we left off?'
He raised an eyebrow, a lopsided grin etched across his face.

Ginny took a deep breath. There wasn't any point trying to reason with him or to attempt to get him to understand. Jason was Jason. He was always in the right.

'Jason, I've changed too and there's absolutely, one hundred per cent, no chance that we're going to ever pick up where we left off. Thank you for the offer but I'm sure you need to get back to the office now.'

She walked around the side of the counter and held the door open.

'You're right, I should get back.'

As soon as he'd stepped outside, she shut the door firmly behind him.

'I didn't mean to eavesdrop, but was he being serious?' Flora was carrying two coffee mugs. 'And more importantly, why on earth were you ever with a man like him?'

'Oh, don't. I honestly couldn't tell you what just happened.' Shaking her head, Ginny took the mug. 'Thanks.'

'Good job you've got a nice new man now and you don't need to even contemplate giving the likes of him another chance.'

'Umm.' Slumping her elbows on the counter, Ginny looked into her coffee, watching as the bubbles from the cafetière floated towards the edges of the mug before bursting.

'What's up, lovely?' Flora rubbed Ginny's hand.

'Are they all the same?' She straightened her back. 'Men, I mean. Not all of them. I know your Arthur was one of the good ones, and Percy of course. But the rest, or the men I seem to attract, are they all the same? Am I drawn to those who are destined to break my heart?'

'Ginny! Listen to yourself! You can't tar Darryl and Jason with the same brush!'

'Can't I? Because let's be honest, Darryl was pretty terrible when we first met him, wasn't he? What if that's just my type? I fall for the bad guys. Not that I'm saying I've fallen for Darryl, because I haven't, but—'

'Stop.' Flora placed her hand over Ginny's. 'You're over-thinking things and trying to see similarities where there aren't any. Darryl's a good guy.'

Ginny swirled her mug around, forcing the remaining bubbles to collide and burst.

'I'm a good judge of character, even if I do say so myself,' Flora continued. 'And Darryl is nothing like Jason. Those two are poles apart. Yes, Darryl was foolish when he first began writing about this place – he didn't realise the power of his own words – but that doesn't make him a bad person. Besides, he's told you why, and now it's up to you to decide if what he's told you was a good enough reason.'

Slowly, Ginny nodded. 'You're right.'

'Now, why don't you go into the kitchen and carry on with the plans for the Family Fun Day? Get something to eat and take things easy, you must be shattered after sleeping in with Frank and Dino last night.'

'Yes, you're probably right. I'm just tired.' Picking up her mug, Ginny went through to the kitchen and pulled her notebook from the drawer. She'd feel better after some rest.

'And, Ginny.' Flora peered through the kitchen door.

'Yes?'

'Don't let Jason and your past ruin what you could have with Darryl.'

19

'And then he turns up with a red rose in his jacket pocket, just as we'd discussed, but he only had the biggest bunch of red and white roses hiding behind his back too, didn't he?' Susan passed Ginny a mug of tea.

'Oh wow, that's so sweet! And how was the date? The first of many I assume?'

'Oh, I do hope so. He was such a lovely chap. Even more so in real life than he was online. He hadn't given that much away in his dating profile which had almost put me off but, you know, it made for an interesting first date.' Susan pulled out her mobile and began to scroll. 'Here, do you want to see a pic? We asked the waiter to take one at dinner.'

'Ooh yes, definitely.' Leaning forward, Ginny peered at the photograph, in which Susan had a red rose stuck behind her ear and was sitting next to a balding man with a bow tie. 'He looks fun.'

'He really is. Though when he first turned up in his red bow tie to match the red roses he'd brought me, I must admit, I did almost run a million miles in the opposite direction. I mean, a bow tie was a little much for the local restaurant, but I'm so glad I didn't. I really think he may be a keeper.' Taking her mobile back, Susan gazed at the picture.

'So, you're seeing him again then?'

'Absolutely. We're going to the cinema tonight. He's picking me up straight from work, so he'll be able to meet everyone and then we'll go for dinner before catching the film.' Susan pushed her chair back. 'Right, I'd better get a wriggle on. Tyler's new family are due in an hour, and I want to take him out for a nice long walk first, wear him out a bit. You're planning this morning again, aren't you?'

'Yes, I'm going to try and figure out where to put everyone's stalls and I've got to ring a few stallholders to confirm their pitches.' She pulled out the list Flora had given her yesterday. 'Can you let me know before Tyler goes though, please, so I can come and say bye?'

'Of course I will. Good luck.' Susan gave Ginny's paperwork a cursory nod before leaving.

'Thanks.' Leaning back in her chair, Ginny picked up a pen and tapped it against her chin. How did Susan manage to have it so easy? She'd been on one date with a guy, and she was certain he was The One. Did it really work like that? She shook her head. She wasn't being fair. How many dates had Susan had before meeting this guy? Ten? Fifteen, maybe? And that was only in the last couple of months. Some people must find it easy, sure, but for the people who didn't, should it be as hard as it was? If she was doubting Darryl and comparing him to Jason, then maybe it wasn't even worth trying.

Ginny massaged her temples. If she could get rid of this headache, then she'd be able to think more clearly. Darryl wasn't Jason, she knew that. Darryl didn't even like Jason.

Shaking her head, she looked down at her map of the

paddocks. They had fifteen stallholders interested. Now she just had to work out the best places to put everyone. With only a few weeks left, she needed to get this thing organised.

That was one thing Darryl had done right since his initial blunder: plugging the Family Fun Day in the paper. And the phone calls kept coming. Yes, Darryl had turned things around.

* * *

A knock at the kitchen door tore Ginny from her thoughts. She'd been pondering whether it would be deemed bad taste to pitch a vegan food stall next to a van selling burgers. 'Come in.'

'Morning.' Darryl paused in the doorway. 'Flora said you were in here and to come through.'

'Darryl. Hi.' What was he doing here? She hadn't even decided whether yesterday's kiss had been a good thing or a foolish mistake.

'Can I come in?'

'Yes, of course. Did you want a drink?' Standing up, Ginny picked up her now stone-cold mug of tea and downed the dregs of it.

'No, I'd better not. Jason's been breathing down my neck all morning and I'm supposed to be interviewing someone about a goldfish that can count to three later.'

'A goldfish that can count?' Laughing, Ginny spat her cold tea back into the mug. 'Why to three? If they've taught it to count, why stop there? Why not four? Or five? And how does it count? Has it developed the ability to talk or does it swim in circles to communicate?'

Darryl chuckled. 'There are so many questions.'

'I don't understand why you think Jason's giving you all the dead-end assignments... I mean this one could actually become record-breaking news. Just imagine, it could completely transform even the top scientists' thoughts on evolution, not to mention change the way the world thinks about eating fish.'

'You're right. It could do. Cutting edge stuff my job is.' Taking a couple of steps towards her, Darryl reached out. He wiped her chin. 'Tea.'

'Oh yuck. Sorry. Although to be fair it was you who made me laugh in the first place.' She picked up the tea towel and wiped his finger before patting her chin dry.

Darryl cupped her cheek, looking her in the eye.

Did she want this? Did she want to risk getting hurt again? With Jason's latest visit still fresh in her mind, she stepped back. Ginny walked across to the map spread out on the table. She wasn't ready to make the decision whether or not she should give Darryl a chance yet. Or whether or not she was even ready to think about getting into a relationship with someone. Maybe that was the problem. Maybe Jason had scarred her so much she was unlovable, unworthy or just didn't want to let another man in, didn't want to trust again.

Taking a deep breath, she picked up a pen. 'I'm just trying to arrange the stalls for the Family Fun Day.'

'Oh, yes? What is it... another three weeks now, isn't it?'

'Yes.'

'That'll come around quick.'

'It will.' She bit down on her bottom lip and looked at Darryl. 'Sorry, what was it you needed?'

'I don't need anything.' Smiling, he walked towards the table. 'I was just wondering if you'd like to come for dinner later? I know you couldn't make last night so thought it'd be nice for us to do something after work today?'

'Tonight?'

Should she make an excuse?

'Ginny! Come quick.' Tim pulled the kitchen door open, his voice laced with urgency. 'Something's wrong with Luna and I can't find Flora anywhere.'

Dropping the pen, Ginny ran after him. 'Flora's readying Tyler for his new home. What's happened?'

'I don't know. She was fine about five minutes ago. I walked past as I was taking Bertie back to his kennel and she was fine, but then when I walked back again to take Belle and Tiger up to the paddock, she was just lying there.' He held the reception door open as Ginny and Darryl ran through. 'It's not like her, she's always up and trying to get my attention.'

'Is she hurt?' Ginny raced across the courtyard.

'I don't think so. She's not moving though. She's breathing but just...' Tim fiddled with the lock on Luna's kennel before pulling the door open and letting Ginny through.

'Hey, Luna. Is everything okay?' Speaking softly, she lowered herself to the floor and stroked her head. Just as Tim had said, she was unresponsive, flopped out on her front, her eyes open but glazed. 'Has she been on a walk today yet?'

'Yes, I took her earlier. She was fine then though. I took her to the cove and she was paddling in the sea and seemed really happy. Normal.' He held his baseball cap in his hands, turning it around and around. 'I was allowed to take her out of the grounds, wasn't I? It's the first time I have but—'

'Yes, of course you can.' Ginny smiled. 'It's nothing you've done. Did she eat anything on the walk? Anything from the ground? Anything she shouldn't have?'

'Umm, I don't know. Someone had dropped a sandwich near where we crossed the road. She didn't eat any of it though. Well, I don't think so at least. I tried to keep her away, but she may have done.'

'Okay.' Ginny gently pulled up the side of Luna's mouth to

check her gums. 'Her gums are pale. Too pale. I need to get her to the vets'. Are you okay ringing Flora and letting her know what's going on?'

'Yes, yes. I'll ring her.' Tim shifted from foot to foot.

'Thanks. I'll go and get my car, bring it as close as I can.' Standing up, she pulled her keys from her jeans pocket.

'I'll get mine.' Darryl began walking out of the kennel. 'I'll take you.'

'You don't have to.'

'It makes more sense. That way I can drive and you can sit in the back with Luna.' He nodded.

'Okay. Thanks.' Ginny placed her hand on Tim's forearm. 'This isn't your fault. If it's something she's eaten, you can't have avoided it. She would have done the same with any of us.'

'Is she going to be okay?'

'She'll be fine.' Ginny looked back at Luna, still lying there, oblivious to those around her.

At least she hoped she would be fine.

20

'Darn, there're roadworks this way. Do you know the back route?' As he slowed the car down to a stop in the long line of traffic, Darryl stabbed at the satnav.

'Yes, turn down there and follow the road around. It'll take you through Penworth Bay but it'll still be quicker than waiting here.' Ginny pointed to the narrow road on their left.

'Good thinking. How is she doing?' Darryl glanced back towards them before taking the left turn.

Ginny grimaced. Luna had barely reacted when Darryl had lifted her into his car and throughout the journey she'd stayed in the same position he'd placed her in, flopped across the back seat. 'The same.'

'That's no good, is it?'

'I don't know.'

'We'll be there soon, Luna,' Darryl said as he ran his fingers through his hair. 'Just hold on until we get there.'

The car bumped over the potholes along the narrow road. Luna lifted her head up a fraction as a gurgling noise came from her throat.

'Darryl, quick, pull over.' Pulling against her seat belt, Ginny twisted to face Luna. 'I think she's going to be sick.'

Darryl pulled the car into a lay-by and raced around to the back of the car. 'That might be a good thing, right?' he said as he pulled the door open. 'If she's eaten something she shouldn't have, getting it out of her system might be just what she needs.'

Ginny supported Luna's head as she coughed, a trail of yellow vomit dribbling down to the footwell. Then, laying her head back, Luna looked up at Ginny before closing her eyes.

* * *

'Here, I'll carry her. You get the door.' Darryl scooped Luna up before kicking the car door shut.

Running ahead of him, Ginny raced to the door of the vets' surgery and pulled it open, holding it as Darryl followed with Luna.

'Bring her straight through.' Gavin, the local vet, led them into a practice room. 'Pop her on the table please.'

As soon as Darryl had lowered Luna down, Gavin began examining her gums before holding a stethoscope to her chest. 'Has she eaten anything she shouldn't have?'

'I'm not sure. She went out for a walk this morning and may have eaten a bit of a sandwich, but we don't know. What do you think is wrong with her?'

'It's difficult to tell before further tests, but my guess is she might have an obstruction.' Gavin moved the stethoscope to Luna's stomach. 'Or ingested some kind of mould...'

'Is she going to be okay?' Darryl plunged his hands into his pockets.

'We'll take some bloods and X-ray her abdomen. Once we

have the results, we'll have a clearer picture. If you could wait outside, please?'

'Yes, of course.' Stepping forward, Ginny stroked Luna's back before bending down and whispering to her, 'We'll be right outside. Gavin, here, will take good care of you.'

Darryl stroked Luna's head before following Ginny into the waiting room.

* * *

Wrapping her hands around the cardboard takeaway cup, Ginny looked across at Darryl. 'You okay?'

'I will be when we know more.' He took a slug of his drink.

'Sorry about your car. I'll clean it later.'

'Hey, that's the last thing on my mind. I'm just hoping Luna will be okay.' He reached across and rubbed Ginny's forearm.

'Thanks. Me too.' She looked across to the closed door to the practice room. They must have been waiting at least an hour already. An hour with no news. Was that a bad sign?

A sound began to emanate from Darryl's pocket.

'Sorry.' He reached into his pocket, the shrill ringtone filling the small waiting area. 'Hello?'

Ginny watched as Darryl walked towards the large window overlooking the car park as he spoke quietly into his mobile.

Ginny watched as his shoulders slumped. She couldn't hear what was being said, but if the number of times Darryl began to speak and was interrupted was anything to go by, it wasn't an easy conversation.

After a few minutes, Darryl returned and rubbed his palm across the stubble on his chin before taking his cup again.

'Is everything okay?' Frowning, she watched as he downed the rest of his coffee.

'Yes, all good.' He gave a short smile.

'Are you sure? It didn't sound as though it was.'

'It was just Jason. Asking where I was. The owner of the goldfish rang the office to complain because I didn't turn up.'

'Oh, the counting goldfish? Do you need to get off? I can get a taxi back.'

'No. The goldfish can wait. I wouldn't be able to concentrate anyway, not knowing if Luna was okay.' He held out his hand for Ginny's empty cup before throwing them in the bin next to him.

'You're not going to get into trouble for missing the interview?'

Darryl shrugged. 'I can't seem to please Jason whatever I do so I've just given up.'

'I don't blame you, it's almost impossible to please him.' Ginny shook her head.

'It definitely seems to be for me, that's for sure.'

'Ginny?' Gavin opened the door to the practice room and signalled for her to join him.

'How is she? Do you know what's wrong with her yet?'

'She's stable.' Gavin closed the door behind them. 'We found traces of mycotoxin in her blood which confirms she must have ingested mould. She's been having seizures which we're currently treating her for.'

'Seizures?' Ginny covered her mouth with her hand. That couldn't be a good sign.

'We expect them in cases like these. We've induced vomiting and are trying to rid her body of the toxin.'

'But she's going to be okay?'

'We're doing everything we can and you caught it early so we're optimistic.' Gavin laid his hand on Ginny's arm and nodded. 'All we can do now is wait. Someone will give you a call later to update you.'

'Can we see her?' Ginny tucked a strand of hair behind her ear.

'Not yet, I'm afraid. Once the seizures have stopped, we can make her comfortable and then you can. You are more than welcome to wait.' He looked down at his notes.

'Okay, thank you. I'll wait.' Turning, Ginny stepped back into the waiting room. It was empty now, the clinic closed to routine appointments for lunchtime no doubt. She turned to Darryl. 'You can go. I'm going to wait. I just want to see her before I head back.'

'I'm not going anywhere.' Darryl enveloped her in his arms. 'I'll wait with you.'

'You don't have to.' Her voice was muffled against his shoulder. She closed her eyes, his warmth comforting her.

'I want to.' But there was that sound was again: his mobile ringing. Taking a step back, Darryl rolled his eyes. 'Sorry, I'd better get this.'

Nodding, Ginny sat back down, the edge of the hard blue plastic chairs digging into the back of her legs.

'Jason, I've told you, there's been an emergency. I'll get back to the office when I can... No... I've got to go now. Bye.'

Darryl sunk to the chair next to Ginny with a loud sigh.

'Fun at work still?'

'Lots of fun.' He rubbed his hand over his face before looking across at her. 'It sounds as though Luna should be okay though, that's the main thing.'

'Yes, hopefully.' She looked back towards the practice room door. 'Thank you for staying.'

'I wouldn't do anything else.' Taking her hand, he smiled.

Shifting in her chair, Ginny looked towards the window.

'Is everything all right between us... After yesterday?' Darryl frowned.

Keeping her eyes fixed on the window, Ginny watched as a magpie hopped along the other side of the window ledge. 'I don't know.'

She could feel him shift in his chair.

'In what way? I thought we had a connection, especially after spending the day together. You don't?'

She had to tell him the truth, it wasn't fair otherwise.

Forcing herself to look at him, she met his eyes. 'I just don't think I'm ready for a relationship, that's all. You're great and everything but, I don't know. It's me. I just...' What else was she supposed to say?

'I'm not Jason.' His voice was low, quiet.

'What?'

Letting go of her hand, Darryl leaned forward with his elbows on his knees, his eyes focused on the pale blue lino. 'Did I tell you my ex cheated on me too?'

'Really?' She looked across at him. 'You've not told me anything about your ex.'

'That's because I don't like talking about that time in my life.' He shrugged. 'There's not much to tell anyway. Not really. I was fresh out of uni, fell in love and thought we had a great relationship. Then I walked in on her having a romantic dinner with my so-called mate.'

'Sorry to hear that.'

'It's a long time ago now. After that, I threw myself into my career. I couldn't see myself trusting anyone again.'

'Why didn't you tell me about your ex cheating on you before?' She glanced down before looking back up at him.

He shrugged. 'I don't know. As I said, it happened a long time ago now and I didn't really think it was very important.' He shifted in his chair to face her.

'It never disappears, does it? That feeling of betrayal?'

'No, it doesn't.' He shook his head.

Did that mean he didn't trust her? Wouldn't ever trust her?

'I'd like to see where things lead with us?' He looked across at her, his hands clasped between his knees. 'I understand if you don't though.'

Ginny nodded slowly. It was now or never. She either told him she felt the same or she told him to leave, that she didn't want anything more to do with him. She swallowed. One thing she knew was that however exasperated she'd felt about him to begin with, something inside her had changed over the last couple of days and, in truth, she couldn't imagine him not being there, tomorrow, next week, or next year. Flora was right. She had noticed there was something between them before Ginny herself had, perhaps even before Darryl had. Maybe she should jump, make the leap and see where it got her. Maybe Flora was right to tell her not to let her past with Jason ruin her future. Leaning forward, Ginny closed her eyes as she felt the warmth of Darryl's kiss upon her lips.

From the open doorway, Gavin cleared his throat. 'Luna's ready to see you now.'

21

Grabbing her cardigan from the coat hooks behind the counter, Ginny called out to Flora. 'See you tomorrow.'

'Whoa. You're off? You're going home?' Flora took her reading glasses from her nose and set them next to the clipboard she'd been writing on before looking across to Percy. 'Did you hear that?'

'Yes. It's gone five.' Ginny looked at the clock.

'Oh, I know it is. I've just never known you to willingly walk out of the door a few minutes after your shift ends. I'm normally the one kicking you out before I lock up for the night.' She widened her eyes. 'Is there something you want to tell us?'

Feeling the telltale heat of a blush flushing across her cheeks, Ginny unzipped her lunch bag, checking she'd put her bottle inside. 'No.'

'This wouldn't have something to do with that reporter, would it now?' Percy tilted his head.

'Maybe.' Ginny grinned. She couldn't help herself. She'd managed to keep quiet all day and not mention anything, but it felt good to share the news of her date with someone. Especially

Flora and Percy. 'We're seeing how things go... We're going to a Cornish pasty making course tonight. He has to go for work so I'm going too.'

'You decided to give him a chance?' Flora grinned.

'Yes, I did.' Ginny nodded. Only time would tell if she was making the right decision.

'Just make sure you tell him he'll be answering to me if he does anything to upset you.' With a grin, Percy pointed his mug towards her.

'I will.' She laughed. 'It's super early days though.'

'I won't rush out and buy a hat for the big day just yet.' Flora chuckled as she gave Ginny a quick hug. Then she shooed her out of the door. 'Now go. You don't want to be late.'

* * *

After locking her car, Ginny rushed across the road to where Darryl stood waiting outside Trestow College. 'Sorry, I'm late.'

'Don't worry. You're here now.' Darryl drew her in for a hug before kissing her on the lips. 'How's Luna?'

'She's much better. I spent a bit of time at the vets' with her after lunch, she's still a bit wobbly on her feet but a different dog compared to yesterday.'

'That's a relief. I was going to pop over to look in on her, but Jason's been breathing down my neck all day, plus I had a super important interview.' Darryl grimaced.

'Ha ha, that wouldn't be with the goldfish by any chance, would it?'

'Yes, although sadly it turns out the goldfish isn't quite as chatty as we were led to believe, so the interview was with Orion's very proud human parents.'

'Orion? That's a cute name for a goldfish.' Ginny grinned.

'I thought so too.' Darryl chuckled before turning serious. 'Are you one hundred per cent sure you want to come to this thing with me? I remember what you told me about Jason and the cookery classes.'

'Yes, of course. This is for fun. Or at least I'm hoping you think it is and you're not going to be totally embarrassed when I quite possibly burn everything or set fire to the oven?'

'Not at all. I'm terrible at making pastry so you setting fire to the oven will be my perfect cover.' Chuckling again, he looked towards the college. 'Ready?'

'Ready.' Taking his hand, she led them towards the reception desk.

* * *

'Any ideas?' Darryl picked up a mound of sticky dough and threw it from hand to hand, long stretches of yellow mess clinging to his fingers.

'I thought you were the chef?' Laughing, Ginny poured some more flour into the ceramic mixing bowl. 'Would you like me to take a photo of you holding it up? I think it'd be a great one for the column.'

'Er... no thanks.' He flung the dough back into the bowl, spraying a light film of flour across the work surface. 'I think I'll have to ask to take a photograph of someone else's masterpiece to pop next to my article.'

'That might be a good idea. Everyone else seems to be getting on all right.' She looked around the room. Rows of workstations and ovens filled the space, one or two people at each. 'It'll be less embarrassing that way.' She tried to keep a straight face.

'Oi! I can't believe you said that!' He held out a sticky finger and wiped yellow goo down her cheek. 'Even if it is true.'

Gasping, she wiped her cheek before dipping her finger into the bowl and drawing a line of yellow mess across his nose.

Chuckling, he moved to throw something else at her but happened to look across at the teacher and noticed she was walking towards them. 'Oops, looks like we might be in trouble.'

'Oh dear, it'll be detentions for us.' Laughing, Ginny picked up a damp dishcloth and wiped his nose.

'And how are we getting along here?' Tina, the teacher of the class, pulled her glasses to the end of her nose and looked in their mixing bowl.

'Not very well, I'm afraid. I've never been able to make decent pastry.' Darryl wiped his hands on the tea towel before picking up the laminated recipe card.

Tina gingerly picked up the mound of dough before letting it fall back into the bowl. 'Ahh, there's your problem. It's been over-worked. Start again and I'll come and demonstrate it for you.'

'Right. Okay. Thank you.' Darryl picked up the bowl and shook its contents into the bin. 'Take two.'

'Come on, we can do it this time. Shall I read out the ingredients again?' Ginny picked up the recipe card as Tina walked away.

* * *

'I've really enjoyed tonight. Thank you.' Ginny tore off another piece of Cornish pasty and popped it in her mouth before looking back across the ocean. After the class a detour to West Par Cove to eat their culinary creation had been a great idea of Darryl's.

'Thank you for coming.' Darryl picked up his takeaway coffee cup and took a sip before resting it back on the pebbles again. 'You can't get more perfect than this, can you? Eating a Cornish pasty made by our very own hands and looking out across West Par Cove.'

'Nope. I'd say this has been a pretty perfect first date.' Ginny grinned and pointed to the pasty. 'And this isn't so bad either. I'd say we make a pretty good cooking team.'

'Ha ha, you're right. I think it's turned out pretty good.'

'So will you be giving the class a good review then?' She shuffled closer to him, pulling her cardigan tighter around her.

'Are you cold? Here, do you want my jacket?'

'Nope, I'm happy like this.' Smiling, she looked up at him.

'Here.' He slipped his arms out of his jacket and pulled it across Ginny's shoulders, wrapping his arm around her waist and holding it in place.

'Perfect.' Leaning her head against his shoulder, she closed her eyes, listening to the rhythmic waves of the ocean in front of them.

'I'll take you on a proper date tomorrow, if you like,' he whispered into her hair, his breath tickling her scalp.

'That sounds good.' But then, sitting up, Ginny remembered something. 'Oh, I can't – not tomorrow. Once a month Flora and Susan hold a thank-you type thing for everyone who works at Wagging Tails and all the volunteers. Flora gets pizza and Susan bakes cakes.'

'That sounds fun.'

'Why don't you come? The amount of time you've spent there recently, you're practically a volunteer anyway.'

'Okay. Why not?' Kissing the top of her head, Darryl wrapped his jacket around her again.

22

'I absolutely hate humans sometimes.' Flora closed the door, making the doorframe shudder.

'What's happened?' Ginny grabbed the clipboard and marked that she'd walked Belle and Tiger.

'I've just had a call from someone who's bringing a dog in. Found abandoned in a lay-by on a busy road, would you believe it? Fortunately, the selfish former owners had tied him to a fence but the poor soul must have been terrified with all those cars hurtling past, especially at this time of the day.' Flora pulled out the notebook she used to log the dogs in and out and slammed it onto the counter. 'I'm sorry. Cases like this just really get to me. Anything could have happened to the poor thing. Just imagine if he'd run into the road.'

Ginny wrapped her arms around her. 'Don't apologise. You care for them, that's why it hurts so much.'

'I know, lovely. I just can't wrap my head around how some people can be so cruel, that's all. You'd have thought after thirty-five years in the job I'd have gotten used to it.' She smiled.

'No, you'll never get used to it, because you like to see the best in people so when people behave like that, it's a shock.' Ginny picked up Luna's lead. 'But remember what you always tell me and Alex: look for the good people. It's normal to focus on the bad but there's more good in the world.'

'Yes, you're right. I know you are.' She paused. 'It was a carful of teenagers who found the poor thing. They noticed him from the other side of the carriageway so turned back around at the roundabout, going miles out of their way to pick him up.'

'How long is it going to be until they get here?'

'About twenty minutes, I think.' Flora closed the notebook.

'I'll go and make up a kennel then.' She put Tiger and Belle's leads back.

'No, don't worry. I can do that. You go and spend some time with Luna. She'll be glad of the company after being at the vets'.'

'Are you sure?'

'Positive. Go on.' From the large storage cupboard, Flora pulled out a duvet and blankets.

'Okay. Shout if you need any help.'

Ginny closed the door behind her and made her way to Luna's kennel.

'Hey, do you fancy a walk?' she said when she saw Luna's bright face. It was good to see her looking so well after her stay at the vets'.

'Yes, please,' came a voice.

Jumping, Ginny turned around. 'Darryl, you scared the living daylights out of me!'

'Ha ha, sorry. I'm happy to come on a walk though.' After rolling the sleeves of his shirt up, Darryl opened the door to Luna's kennel and bent down to fuss over her.

'That'd be nice. I was going to take her down to the cove. You're early though, the thank-you dinner doesn't start until half six.'

'No worries. I was rather hoping you wouldn't mind me mucking in and helping beforehand?' Twisting around, he held his hand out for the lead.

'Of course not. The more the merrier.' Grinning, she passed it to him. 'How come you're out from work so early anyway?'

'Oh, you know. I was on important business, following up on a lead for a story, and I happened to finish early. I was going to snap a couple of photos of Belle and Tiger to pop in tomorrow's paper, if that's all right?'

'All right? That'd be great. They've had all their behaviour checks and everything, so are ready to be adopted.' On leaving the kennels, Ginny closed the door behind them and began to walk next to Darryl.

'Great. She looks a lot better.' He nodded to Luna who was straining at the lead, pulling him across the courtyard. 'Looks as though she's eager to get to the beach too.'

'Yes.' She slipped her hand in his free one and squeezed it. 'Thank you.'

'What for?' He frowned.

'For caring about the dogs.'

'Of course I care.' He kissed her on the forehead. 'In fact, I've been doing a lot of thinking recently.'

'Oh, yes?' Ginny grimaced, not sure what he was about to say.

'Now that I'm settled at my dad's place, I've been thinking about adopting a dog myself.'

'Really?'

'Yes. Do you think I'd pass the checks?' He looked across at her, his face serious.

'I should think so. Your dad is there when you're at work anyway.'

'He is, but I'll be able to pop back during the day too. I could always tell Jason I'm visiting Orion, the counting goldfish.' He chuckled.

'That's true. I think you'd be able to offer a wonderful home to one of these lot. Did you have anyone in mind?' She held up her hands. 'In fact, don't answer that. I know exactly who would be perfect for you.'

Darryl grinned and looked down at Luna. 'I wonder if you're thinking of the same dog as me.'

'I think I am.' She smiled and laced her hand back in his. 'I noticed you have a soft spot for her from the first time you met her and I think the same can be said of her. You can pop in and fill out the forms after our walk if you like?'

'I'd like that very much.' He squeezed her hand and smiled.

* * *

'Coming through.' Susan waltzed into the reception, trays in her arms laden with cupcakes.

'Do you need a hand?' Darryl looked up from the forms he was filling out at the counter.

'No, I'm okay thanks.' She grinned as she pushed open the kitchen door with her foot.

Ginny watched as Darryl signed the paperwork. After walking Luna, he'd been eager to make a start on the adoption process straight away.

'All done.' Darryl passed the adoption form to Ginny before taking a sip of his coffee.

'Just this one left.' Ginny laid out another piece of paper.

'Wow, that's a lot of forms.' Darryl wriggled his fingers.

'We're very thorough.' She laughed.

Their laughter was interrupted by Flora who pushed open the door and held it for three teenagers who stepped through.

'Hi, Darryl. Hey, Ginny. I've invited our three heroes to join us for the thank-you dinner,' she said. 'This is Liam, Joe and Declan. If it wasn't for them, poor little Cookie might still be on the side of the road.'

'Thank you so much for rescuing him.' Ginny smiled as the three of them filtered into the small reception area.

'No problem.' Declan nodded.

'How is Cookie? Has he settled into his kennel okay?' she said as Darryl shook hands with each of them in turn.

'He has, yes. He's still very nervous but I think he just needs a bit of time.' Flora opened the door to the kitchen, ushering Declan, Liam and Joe through. 'I've just got a bit of paperwork and then I'll be with you. Our volunteers will be coming shortly but, in the meantime, help yourself to drinks.'

'They seem nice.' Ginny smiled as Flora shut the door.

'Yes, they've asked to volunteer here too.'

'Wow, that's brilliant. Good people, they are.'

'Yes, good people.' Flora nodded before looking down at the papers on the counter. 'What's all this then? You've finally figured out you belong to Luna?'

'Sorry?' Darryl looked up from the form he had returned to, pen in hand.

'You've realised that you're meant to adopt Luna?' she said again. 'Sometimes it's obvious that one dog and one human are meant to be, straight from the word go.' She picked up the completed form and began to read it through.

'How did you guess that?' Darryl frowned.

'Ahh, once you've been working here as long as I have you pick up a thing or two.' Patting him on the shoulder, she chuckled. 'I know she'll be very happy with you.'

'Really? What happens next then?' Darryl finished signing the second form and straightened his back.

'We'll go through the motions, visit your home, make sure your dad's on board, but I can't foresee any problems so you should be able to take her home pretty soon.' She put the form back down and nodded towards the kitchen door. 'I'd better go through.'

'Great. Thank you.' Darryl turned to Ginny and grinned. 'It looks as though you might be meeting my dad sooner rather than later then.'

Turning her back on him, she placed the forms in the filing cabinet and frowned. Meeting his dad? Already? But they had barely begun seeing each other, meeting his dad felt like a huge step. She closed the drawer and shook her head. She'd be meeting him in a professional manner, nothing more.

* * *

Taking a slice of pizza, Ginny looked around the kitchen. It was jam-packed: the chairs were all taken, and people were standing around, leaning or sitting on the work surfaces. She grinned. This was probably her favourite time, each month, when everyone got together for Flora and Susan's thank-you dinner. Not only was it nice just seeing everyone, chatting and laughing, sharing news about their lives or the dogs at Wagging Tails, but it also illustrated how many people gave up their time and volunteered for the good of the dogs.

Carrie twisted around in her chair and looked at Ginny who was standing behind. 'Ginny, how's Luna doing? We heard she was poorly?'

'She's absolutely fine now. Completely back to normal.'

'What was wrong with her?' Daniel, Carrie's partner, turned to join in the conversation.

'The vet thinks she ate something mouldy on her walk.'

'Aw, glad she's better now.' Carrie tapped Daniel on the arm. 'Did Daniel tell you what happened to Scout last week?'

'No, what happened?'

'Who's Scout?' Darryl said through a bite of his pizza.

'Sorry, Darryl this is Daniel and Carrie. They're both volunteers here and both have adopted dogs from Wagging Tails. Carrie has Winston, a little West Highland, and Daniel adopted Scout.' Ginny looked from Darryl to the couple. 'Darryl is a reporter at the *Trestow Telegraph*.'

'Ooh, I saw your piece about Tyler. It was brilliant.' Carrie grinned.

'Thank you. What was wrong with Scout?' He leaned across and picked up another slice of pizza.

'He only ate half a bar of dark chocolate.' Daniel grimaced. 'I accidentally left it on the coffee table before going to work. I didn't think anything of it as he's normally so good at ignoring food. I can leave a full bowl of cereal on the arm of the sofa and get up to pop into the kitchen and he won't bat an eyelid. Anyway, luckily, I only work up the road at the school; I try to pop home at lunchtime so I found the chocolate gone and the wrapper strewn in pieces across the rug.'

'Oh no. Chocolate can be deadly. Especially dark chocolate. I take it he's okay?' Ginny picked up her mug of coffee.

'Yes, he's fine. I rushed him to the vets' and Scout gave me the cold shoulder for the rest of the day after they forced him to vomit it up.' Daniel shrugged. 'It was an expensive and scary lesson to learn but I make sure to double-check I've not left any food around now.'

'I bet.' Darryl shook his head. 'Why do they do this to us?'

'Flora said you're adopting Luna?' Carrie said as she peeled the paper case off of one of Susan's cupcakes.

'All being well,' he said, his eyes bright.

'That'll be brilliant. She's such a cutie.'

'She sure is.' He leaned back against the work surface, looking at Carrie closely. 'I'm sure I recognise you from somewhere. Did you used to work in Penworth Bay?'

'Yes. Well, I still do. I've got a pottery studio up the hill just past the pub and garage, but you probably recognise me from Elsie's bakery?' She scooped a blob of icing onto her finger.

'That's right. The Cornish Bay Bakery. I try to pop in at least twice a week for one of Elsie's cheese and onion pasties.' He turned to Ginny. 'You must have tried Elsie's cheese and onion pasties?'

'Absolutely. Hasn't everyone?' Ginny laughed.

'How are the preparations for the Family Fun Day going?' Daniel looked at Ginny. 'Elsie's hiring a stall, isn't she?'

'Yes, she is.' Ginny nodded. 'I think we're almost there. I just can't believe how quickly it's come around.'

'I'm sure it will be great. I'm really looking forward to it,' Carrie said, licking the icing off her finger. 'I've already packed up the pottery pieces I'm going to bring, and I've made lots of little clay dog ornaments for people to paint if they want to.'

'I love that idea. People will be able to paint them like their dogs.' Ginny grinned.

'That's what I thought. I hope they'll go down okay.'

'I'm sure people will love them.'

Ginny turned away from Carrie to look across at Flora where she stood at the front of the room, tapping a spoon against her mug.

'Sorry to interrupt. I just want to say a huge thank you to each and every one of you for everything you do for Wagging Tails and the wonderful dogs we look after. I also want to say a special thank you to Darryl, who has not only written some amazing articles for the *Trestow Telegraph*, which has led to a lot of interest in our upcoming Family Fun Day and the adoptions of Tyler, Frank and Dino, but has also spent many an hour here volunteering – walking the dogs, helping Susan and Ginny fix up the outdoor kennel and generally helping around the place.'

A loud chorus of 'thanks' and 'well dones' rose around the room.

Smiling, Darryl nodded to the group. 'It's been a pleasure. Thank you.'

Flora cleared her throat. 'Before you get back to the pizza and cakes, I'd just like to say a little more. I'd like to take this opportunity to thank our newcomers, Declan, Joe and Liam, the heroes who rescued our latest pooch, Cookie, who they found in a lay-by on the side of a busy road and who have also just signed up to volunteer with us.'

A huge round of applause erupted in the small room. Liam, Declan and Joe all blushed.

'And, last but not least. As you are all aware it's our annual Family Fun Day in less than three weeks' time and as you've probably guessed we're on the scrounge for people to man the home's stalls, help out with the taster training lessons and generally to be around and ensure things run smoothly. If you'd like to volunteer, please see Ginny to register your interest.' She smiled and indicated to where Ginny was standing.

Ginny raised her hand in acknowledgement before looking behind her on the work surface and realising she'd left her notebook back in the reception area.

After letting the kitchen door swing shut behind her, Ginny rummaged through the shelf behind the counter. She was sure she'd left her notebook somewhere out here.

'Do you need a hand looking?'

Ginny smiled to see that Darryl had followed her out.

'It's orange, isn't it?'

'Yes, with "Family Fun Day" in huge letters on the front.'

'And the words "Ginny 4 Darryl" written in block capitals on the back?'

'What?' Turning around, Ginny blushed only to see Darryl was holding up the notebook. 'For your information I've not written that anywhere.' Is that what he thought? That she'd fallen for him? It hadn't even been her who had made the first move.

With a chuckle, he passed her the notebook.

'Thank you.' Hugging the notebook to her chest, she bit down on her bottom lip and nodded towards the kitchen door. 'We'd better get back.'

23

Hearing a gasp from the kennel next door, Ginny put the floor brush back into the bucket of soapy water and stood up.

'I'll be back in one moment, Cookie, sweetie.' She pushed herself to standing and made her way to the next kennel. 'Susan, is everything all right?'

'No, not really.' Susan was leaning against the wall of Tiger and Belle's kennel. 'Dean has just sent me a message.'

'Dean? Your ex-husband?'

'Yes. The one and only. He's been evicted from his flat and wants to come home.'

'But it's not his home any more. It's yours. Even when you were together it was you paying the bills.' Ginny frowned. In the four years she had known Susan, Dean must have pulled this trick at least three times; the last time Susan had caved, and they'd ended up getting back together for two months. Two months during which Susan had turned up to work every day in tears, desperate to break up with him but not having the heart to do so.

'Yes, it was, but as he says, it was still his home for twenty-one years.' She wiped her sleeve across her eyes.

'You can't be thinking of taking him back? Do you remember how miserable you were last time? And how difficult it was for you to get rid of him?'

Susan nodded. 'But this will be different. We won't be together; he'll just be staying with me until he finds somewhere else.'

'He won't find somewhere else. He won't look for somewhere else. This is Dean we're talking about. Once he gets through your door, you'll struggle to get rid of him, you know you will.' Ginny sighed. 'And how about your new man, Malcolm? What will he think?'

'Oh, Malcolm is one of the good ones, he'd understand.' Susan smiled sadly.

'Susan, as your friend, I'm begging you not to take him in. He's got friends he could ask. It's not down to you.' Ginny rested her hands on Susan's shoulders. 'You deserve better than him.'

Susan looked down at her phone again, rereading the text.

'Look, why don't we go on a double date? Me and Darryl, you and Malcolm. It'll be fun.'

Anything, just please don't get back with Dean.

'Sorry?' Susan frowned, looking up.

'A double date – you and Malcolm with me and Darryl?'

'Tonight?'

Ginny shrugged. 'I'd have to check with Darryl, see if he's free, but, yes.'

'Yes... that's a good idea,' she said, though Ginny could tell she was still thinking about Dean. Tucking her phone in her pocket, Susan forced a smile. 'We've actually got a reservation at The Quayside Inn tonight for six o'clock.'

'Great. I'll check in with Darryl later – I'm popping around his anyway to carry out the adoption inspection – and let you know. Hopefully see you later.'

Susan nodded. 'Thanks, Ginny.'

'No reason to thank me. I'm looking forward to it.'

'No, thank you for reminding me what Dean is like. He always knows how to make me feel sorry for him.' She shook her head. 'I always fall for his games.'

'Hey, you're a good person. He just tries to take advantage of your good nature. That's on him, not you.'

After giving Susan a hug, Ginny turned and made her way back to Cookie's kennel.

* * *

'So, are you ready to meet my dad?' Darryl chuckled as he pulled the car to a stop outside a small stone cottage. 'I wouldn't usually bring a date round to meet my family quite so soon.'

'Hey, we don't have to tell him we're dating. I can be professional, you know.' Ginny grinned.

'Ah, it's a bit late for that, I'm afraid. I've already told him.' Darryl made a face. 'I hope you don't mind.'

'Of course I don't. It's actually quite sweet.' Reaching across, she took his hand.

'Have you mentioned our relationship to any of your family yet?'

'My family down here is Flora, Susan and Alex, so yes, they may have an idea.' She laughed. 'As for my mum, well I've not spoken to her since we met, but I normally ring her at the end of the month. I'll definitely be telling her.'

'Great.' Darryl unclicked his seat belt and looked towards the cottage. 'Shall we?'

'I'm ready.'

After grabbing the clipboard in the footwell, Ginny climbed out of the car. She'd only ever met one partner's family before, unless she counted the parents of her 'boyfriend' in primary school, and that was Jason's, after they'd been together a year and a half. Was she ready to meet Darryl's dad? Was Darryl ready to introduce her already?

Pausing, she looked back at him. 'If you weren't adopting Luna, when do you think you'd introduce me to your dad?'

'I've not really thought about it, but I'd have no qualms introducing you this early.' He clicked his car locked before looking at her. 'Ginny, I'm looking forward to introducing you to my dad.'

'Really?' Was he? Had he introduced his previous partners this early? Was this just what he did? Maybe meeting the family wasn't a big deal to him.

'Really.' Taking hold of her hand, he leaned across and kissed her before pushing open the garden gate.

'Just so you know,' she said, 'if you hadn't already met Flora, I'd happily introduce you too. And, of course, if my mum lived in England still.' She thought she would anyway.

With a smile, Darryl let the gate swing shut behind them before heading to the front door.

As he unlocked the door, Ginny held the clipboard to her chest. What if his dad didn't like her? Didn't approve? She swallowed.

Ushering Ginny inside, Darryl called out into the small hallway of the cottage, 'Hi, Dad.'

He closed the door behind them before leading Ginny into a large living room.

'Hello, Darryl. Hello, dear, you must be Ginny. Darryl's told me so much about you. It's lovely to meet you at last.'

'Ginny, this is my dad, Patrick.' Darryl bent down to hug him quickly before returning to stand next to Ginny again.

'Nice to meet you, Patrick.'

'Call me, Pat.' Pat smiled as he pulled himself out of the armchair and stood up, using a walking frame to balance himself. 'Can I get you a tea or a coffee, maybe?'

'I can get the drinks,' Darryl said as he held his elbow, steadying him.

'No, no. I'm more than capable, Darryl. Thank you though.'

'A tea would be great, please,' Ginny said to his welcoming expression.

'One nice cuppa – coming up. Now, I understand you've come to assess the house, see if we're fit enough to have this Luna come and live with us. Is that right?'

Ginny followed him out into the hallway and into a galley kitchen that ran the length of the cottage. 'That's right. It's just a formality.'

'Don't worry. I understand that.' Pat smiled at her as he filled the kettle. 'All our dogs to date have been rescues. We had our first when Darryl here was just knee high. Honey was her name, a golden lab too. A tiny little thing for her breed. You must remember her, Darryl? She used to sleep at the end of your bed. Every night without fail, me and your mum would hear this pad-pad-pad sound as Honey made her way upstairs, following you to bed.'

Darryl grinned. 'Yes, I remember. You trained her to play hide and seek with us.'

'That's right, yes. I'd forgotten that.' Pat glanced at Ginny. 'Milk? Sugar?'

'Just milk please.'

'Coming up.' Pat pointed to the fridge. 'Darryl, could you pass me the milk please?'

'Sure.' Darryl did as he was asked and then turned to look out of the window. 'Shall we have a look in the garden? I saw you have a couple of questions about the back gate and the fence.'

'Yes, off you two go,' Pat said. 'I tell you what, why don't you both go off and do your checks and I'll find us a packet of cream tea biscuits?'

* * *

'He likes you,' Darryl said, glancing across at Ginny before starting the car.

'Do you think?' She ran her finger across the top of the clipboard.

'Oh yes, he doesn't crack open the cream tea biscuits for anyone. They're his favourite. Even the doctor gets plain biscuits.'

'That's a relief. He seems really nice. Genuine.' She rolled her shoulders back and leaned her head against the headrest. She'd been so worried about meeting Pat, but he'd been nothing but welcoming, telling her stories about Darryl's childhood and even bringing out the old family photo album. Was Darryl right? Did he approve or was he just being polite? She wiped off a bit of dried mud from the leg of her jeans.

'He is. He's a good guy.' Darryl grinned. 'But enough about that. Luna... Have we passed or are you going to keep me in suspense a bit longer?'

'You've passed.' Ginny laughed, trying to push all thoughts of inadequacy to the back of her mind. This visit had been about Luna, not her. 'We both knew you would anyway. I know you and I know you've had dogs before, in the same house, so your chances were good.'

'Ha ha, well it's still a relief.'

'Luna's going to be so happy here.' She glanced back at the cottage. The garden was huge, reaching right back to the fields behind, and judging by how much Luna loved playing on the beach on the extendable lead, Ginny knew she'd feel right at home.

'I hope so.'

'She will be.' She placed her hand over his, where it was resting on the gear stick.

'So, is it The Quayside Inn we're going to, the one on the way to Trestow?'

'Yes, that's right.'

'We're not too far away then.'

'Thanks for doing this,' Ginny said. 'Susan had a call from her ex-husband who's trying to weave himself back into her life again, so I thought it'd be nice to go on a double date. Try and take her mind off it.'

'I'm looking forward to it. I have a lot of respect for Susan; it'll be nice to get to know her partner too.' Darryl glanced across at her and smiled. 'Here we are.'

'We can tell Susan the good news about Luna too.'

'Yes, I'll need to pop along to the pet shop tomorrow and choose a dog bed and some toys and bits.' They both climbed out of the car and, after pocketing the car keys, Darryl held his hand out towards her.

'I'll come with you. If you like, that is...' Should she have offered? She didn't want to give him the impression she didn't think he knew what he was doing, or worse, that she thought she should have a say in his choices.

'I'd like that very much.' He kissed her on the forehead and then held the pub door open.

'Ginny, Darryl, over here!'

Susan was waving at them from a table by the window.

'Fantastic to meet you, Ginny, and Darryl too,' Malcolm said warmly after they'd made their way over. 'Susan has told me so much about you both.' He stood up and shook both their hands before running around and pulling out Ginny's chair.

* * *

'... and just as we thought it was all over, the fire alarm goes off again. Out we all troop, just to be told it's safe to go back in.' Malcolm straightened his bow tie before placing his hands on the table in front of him. 'Anyway, it turns out that it's just a fault with the fire alarm. A spider was running around inside it. Would you believe it?'

Ginny laughed. 'A spider?'

'Yes, yes, I swear. It was a spider.'

'Now, if I may, I need to excuse myself for a call of nature.' Standing up, Malcolm patted his mouth with his napkin and tucked his chair under before turning to Susan and pecking her on the cheek.

'So, what do you think?' Leaning forward, Susan clasped her hands together, looking at Ginny and Darryl intently.

'He seems really nice. Fun to be around,' Ginny offered genuinely.

'Yes, a true gentleman.' Darryl nodded and took a chip from Ginny's plate.

'Oi!' Laughing, Ginny shook her head. 'Yes, a gentleman... unlike you.'

'Ah, yes, but you knew that when you agreed to date me.' He wiped his fingers on his napkin.

'True.'

'Oh no...' Susan's face dropped.

'What is it? Are you okay?' Reaching her hand across the table, Ginny tried to comfort her friend. What could have upset her?

'It's Dean. I don't understand. How did he know I was here?'

'Dean? Where?' Twisting in her seat, Ginny tried to seek him out. And there he was, heading straight over to their table, a bunch of beautiful but slightly drooping carnations in his arms.

'Who's Dean?' Darryl looked from Ginny to Susan and back again. 'The ex?'

'Yes. Not only does he want to get back with her, he's trying to make her let him move in too.' Ginny frowned.

'And I'm assuming you don't want that?' Darryl looked across to Susan.

'No, I'm happy with Malcolm. I've given Dean chance after chance and all he does is use me. I don't think I can cope with it all again.' Covering her face with her hands, Susan began to cry.

'Don't worry, I'll pass the message on.'

And with that, Darryl stood up.

'You're not going to do anything daft, are you?' Ginny looked up at him, worried.

'Ha ha, no. I'm a journalist, I'll talk to him.'

'What do you think he's going to say?' Susan said as he walked away.

'I'm not sure.'

Ginny turned around and watched as Darryl approached Dean and shook his hand. He was still smiling. It even looked as if he might invite him to the table rather than send him packing. But then, putting his arm around Dean's shoulders, Darryl led him outside.

'What's he saying to him?' Susan leaned back, trying to watch through the window.

Ginny shrugged. Whatever he was saying, Dean seemed to be listening.

'Oh, he's coming back in now.'

'All sorted,' Darryl said when he got back to the table.

'What did you say to him?' Susan glanced back outside to check that Dean really had gone. 'I've tried to tell him to leave me alone a million times and yet he still tries to play the guilt trip with me.'

'I just told him the truth. I said you'd moved on and he needed to as well.'

'You did?'

'Yes, was that okay?' Frowning, Darryl picked up his drink.

'Yes, yes. It's great. I've just never been able to get him to take me seriously.' Susan reached across and touched Darryl's hand. 'Thank you.'

'I can't promise that, but I tried my best to explain that it wasn't fair to keep harassing you and he seemed to understand...' Darryl shrugged.

'Oh, even if he gives it a rest for a few weeks, I'm grateful.'

Ginny looked up and saw Malcolm walking back towards them.

Lowering her voice, Susan looked at Darryl and Ginny. 'Do you mind not mentioning anything to Malcolm please? I don't want to send him running before we've really got to know each other.'

'Of course.' Darryl nodded.

'Who wants some dessert?' Malcolm said as he slipped back into his seat, picking up his napkin and draping it over his knees.

'Ooh yes, dessert sounds like a great idea. I might just go and have a look at the specials board behind the bar.'

'I'll accompany you.'

Ginny watched as Malcolm and Susan walked towards the bar, arm in arm, before lowering her voice. 'So tell me, what did you really say to Dean?'

'Just what I told you. I said she'd found someone else,

someone who treated her right and he should be a gentleman and let her live her life.' He shrugged once more.

'And he took that? He understood?'

'I'm not sure, I think he was just shocked that I'd gone to talk to him and not her.'

'Hopefully he's got the message then. At least for a bit. Susan deserves the chance to see how things go with Malcolm before Dean steps in and tries to mess it all up.'

24

'Two weeks to go! How do these look?' Alex pulled a pile of papers from his rucksack and spread them across the kitchen table.

'Wow, these are amazing!' Putting her pen down, Ginny picked up one of the brightly coloured A4 posters Alex had painstakingly drawn. 'You drew these?'

'Of course. I didn't go to art school for nothing.' He held up one of the posters and pointed to the huge words, 'Family Fun Day'. 'Do you think they get the message across?'

'Absolutely.' Ginny looked at the posters again, each one different, some depicting illustrated dogs, others brightly coloured stalls. 'They must have taken you hours.'

'Oh, they did. I've been working on them since last week's staff meeting so thought I'd bring them to this week's.'

'Thank you.' Ginny smiled. 'We can ask shops and cafes to display them here in West Par, in Penworth Bay, Trestow and maybe even further afield.'

'Good idea, Ginny,' Flora said and patted Alex's forearm. 'They are truly fantastic, Alex. Well done.'

'I like to work my creative muscle every now and again.' He slipped the posters back into his rucksack. 'Anyway, enough about my fabulous talent. What's next on the meeting's agenda?'

Ginny looked down at the scribbled list of points in her notebook. 'I've allocated each stallholder their pitches now and I'm working through the list of volunteers to give each of them jobs.'

'It sounds as though you've got everything covered.' Susan smiled.

Ginny shifted in her chair. 'I just keep thinking I've missed something.'

'I don't think you have, Ginny. It sounds as though you've got it all in order,' Percy said.

'I agree. You've done a tremendous job, lovely.' Flora patted Ginny's arm.

'I hope so. I don't want to let anyone down.' Ginny looked down at her list again before flicking through to the beginning of the notebook and checking the master list she'd drawn up when Flora had first asked her to plan the Family Fun Day. Everything was ticked off. She looked to Flora. 'I think that's all I needed to say.'

'Okay, thank you, Ginny.' Flora wrapped her hands around her mug. 'In other news, Cookie is still very nervous and still hasn't ventured out of his kennel for a walk or an explore yet. I know we've all been trying to sit with him and get him used to us, and it's working; he comes closer all the time so he'll get there. It's just going to take a little more time.'

'He'll come round. You remember Breeze? The Great Dane? He refused to step outside his kennel for well over a month, poor thing.' Percy lowered his mug. 'But when he did, he soon became a right social butterfly.'

'Oh, yes, Breeze.' Flora nodded, remembering.

'Didn't he become a therapy dog?' Ginny asked.

'That's right. The lady who adopted him takes him into the care home at Trestow to visit. It just goes to show old dogs *can* learn new tricks.' Flora grinned.

'I can sit with Cookie for a bit now, if you like?' Ginny downed the dregs of her tea and stood.

'That'd be great, thanks. Just before we get on, I just want to bring your attention to something. I had a call earlier from a concerned resident in Trestow. She said that she's been hearing rumours about a puppy farm operating out of abandoned factories and warehouses around Trestow's industrial estates.'

'Oh, not a puppy farm.' Alex slumped back against his chair. 'Have they informed the police?'

'They have, but from what I understand there isn't any concrete evidence so the police are struggling to pinpoint their location.' Flora placed her palms on the table. 'Hopefully, it's just that, a rumour, but I think we all need to keep our ears to the ground in case there's any truth in it.'

'We will.' Susan nodded.

'Great. Thanks, everyone.'

* * *

'That's it. You're so close.' Ginny looked at Cookie out of the corner of her eye. Crouched low, Cookie inched closer, still at least half a metre away but closer than he'd dared step towards Ginny so far. 'It's okay, I'm not going to touch you. I'm not even looking at you. I'm just going to leave this treat a bit closer to me and you see if you're brave enough to come and get it, okay?'

Sitting on his haunches, Cookie looked at her.

Ginny laid a small treat on the floor halfway between them. 'That's it. Just a little bit further. You can do it.'

Sneaking a look, she grinned. Cookie had taken the challenge and was now eating the treat.

The door to the kennel opened and shut quietly and footsteps padded towards her. Ginny peered out of the bars of the kennel.

'Hey, Ginny, lovely.' Flora kept her voice low as she bent down next to the door to Cookie's kennel. 'Oh look, he's got quite close to you today.'

'Yes, he has. It's slow progress but like you said, he's getting there.' As she spoke, she slid another treat across the floor.

'That's great.' But then Flora frowned. 'We've got a bit of a problem. I wondered if you could ask Darryl to help us.'

'What's happened?'

'Clarke has pulled out of the Family Fun Day. In fact, he's no longer offering dog training lessons of any sort.'

'Please tell me you're joking?' Ginny looked at Flora. She wasn't joking. 'Why?'

'His mother is sick back in America, apparently, and he's upped sticks to be with her.'

'Why didn't he tell us before? Or has it just happened?'

'I'm not sure to be honest. He sent an email this lunchtime.' Flora took a deep breath. 'Anyway, there's nothing we can do about it now, we've just got to move on.'

'And fast.'

'Exactly, so I wondered if Darryl would be able to pop an advert in the paper or write a shout-out for us or something.'

'Two weeks to find a local trainer to give lessons and who's willing to showcase their work at the Family Fun Day.' Ginny chewed her bottom lip. 'It would be easy if all the local training classes weren't oversubscribed already. Who's going to want to come and work for a day for free when they know they can't fit any new clients into their classes anyway?'

'I don't know.' Flora shook her head. 'But let's not get to the worrying stage yet. Let's see if Darryl can entice anyone; if not then we'll look at the structure of the day and tweak things a little.'

Tweak things? The whole Family Fun Day practically revolved around the taster dog training lessons – agility, tracking, hoopers. All of them. Without them they'd just be a regular summer fayre with a dog show. No different to loads already scheduled. She looked at Flora; she had that deep crease between her eyes again. She might be trying not to show how worried she was, but she couldn't hide it from Ginny.

'I'll go and ring Darryl now.'

'Why don't you pop up there?' Flora suggested. 'You could take some of Alex's posters, see if some shops or cafes in Trestow can display them?' Pushing herself to standing, Flora held open the kennel door.

'But if we can't get another trainer can we even use the posters? They could be seen as false advertising.' Ginny grimaced, standing up and following Flora to the reception area.

'Oh, tish-tosh, we're a dogs' home, no one's going to be that petty. Chin up, we'll find someone.'

* * *

Tucking the few posters she hadn't managed to pin up anywhere under her arm, Ginny pushed the door to the office building open. She checked Darryl's reply to her message asking if he was in the office again. Yep, he'd definitely said he would be here and to go straight up.

So why did she feel so nervous?

Slipping past the building security, she began to walk up the stairs. Jason probably wouldn't even be here, and if he was, so what? She'd told him exactly what she thought of him the other day; hopefully he'd just keep out of her way. Yes, it would be fine.

At the top of the stairs, she peered through the small window. No sign of Jason, and she could just about make out Darryl sitting at his desk at the far end.

She pushed the door open.

'Morning, how can I help you?' The woman behind the reception desk glared at her.

'I've just come to speak to Darryl.' She pointed towards the back of the office.

'And do you have an appointment?'

'No... Yes. He knows I'm coming.' Turning, Ginny made her way towards Darryl, thankful the receptionist didn't call her back or try to see an appointment card or something to prove she had a right to be there. 'Hi.'

Looking up from his computer, Darryl grinned. 'Hey, aren't I glad to see you. Please save me from writing up a local story about a man who has collected so many pebbles he's covered the floor of his entire house with them.'

'Ouch. That must hurt to walk on.'

'Actually, no. I had the privilege of visiting this morning and he's covered them in resin so they're surprisingly comfortable underfoot. He's laid them out in different patterns using their colours: waves in one room, stripes in another and a kind of weird shape in his front room which I think is supposed to be some sort of self-portrait.'

'Oh.'

'Oh, indeed.' Darryl chuckled. 'Anyway, you said it was urgent. What's happened?'

He jumped up and wheeled a spare chair over to his desk where he indicated her to sit down.

'Our trainer has dropped out of the Family Fun Day, quit his job completely.' Ginny sat down and leaned her elbows on his desk. 'He's moved to America to care for his sick mum so there's no hope of him changing his mind.'

'Ah, aren't the lesson trials a big part of the day?'

'Yes, exactly. Anyway, Flora wondered if you'd be able to squeeze in a shout-out to anyone who wants to take his place. The problem we've got is most dog training classes around here are full and have waiting lists. So they don't need to do any advertising, which is why Clarke liked the trials; they enticed people to go along to lessons. He was relatively new so his classes weren't full. Plus, we need someone who can come in and work with the dogs at Wagging Tails too.'

Darryl nodded.

'So we're left with no live trials or, at best, if we can sign up someone we know, we'll be offering trials but if people enjoy them there'll be no spaces in the regular classes for them to join.'

'Okay.' Pulling his notebook from under a pile of papers on the desk, Darryl picked up his pen. 'I can definitely squeeze something in. Let me jot this down.'

'Thank you. You're a lifesaver!' Reaching across the desk, Ginny squeezed his hand.

'Not yet, I'm not, but I'll do my best.' Looking up at her, he grinned.

'Thank you. Right, well, I'd better leave you to it then.' She stood up and grabbed her bag. 'Really, thank you.'

'No worries. Here, I'll walk you out.' After closing his notebook, he stood up.

As they walked through the desks towards the front of the office, Ginny glanced quickly towards Jason's office, thankful that it looked empty.

'How's the new dog?'

'Cookie? He's nervous but getting a little braver.' She smiled at the memory. 'It's a big day for you tomorrow. Are you all set for picking up Luna in the afternoon?'

'Absolutely.'

'She's going to love her new home.'

'I hope so.'

'Oh, she will.' Taking his hand in hers, she led the way down the stairs. 'Everyone can see how much she dotes on you.'

'You've never thought about adopting one of the dogs?'

'I've been tempted, yes, but if I did, I wouldn't be able to spend as much time up at Wagging Tails as I do.' She shrugged. 'There have been a fair few dogs who have pulled on my heart strings.'

Darryl nodded and pushed the door to the foyer open.

What she saw ahead of her made her pause. Pulling Darryl back quickly, she watched as Jason walked through the double doors and approached the lift.

'What?'

'Sorry, it's Jason. I just don't want to run into him.'

'Oh, okay. Has he said something?' Rubbing the back of his neck, Darryl glanced through the small window in the door.

'Yes and the other day... I may have told him what I thought of him.' She cleared her throat.

Darryl chuckled and raised his eyebrows. 'You spoke your mind to Mr Ego?'

'In my defence, he asked for it.' She tucked her hair behind her ears. 'He came to Wagging Tails insisting I go to dinner with him, and I just saw red.'

'He asked you out to dinner?'

Ginny nodded. 'He's asked me a few times since moving down here. He appeared to have forgotten how badly our relationship ended so I reminded him.'

Darryl grinned. 'Well, I guess I won't be needing to have

words with him like I did Susan's ex at least.' He stepped towards her. 'I wish I'd seen the look on his face though.'

'Umm. He didn't look too happy.' What did he mean by that? By saying 'words' it implied he hadn't just spoken to Dean calmly as he'd said. Had he threatened him?

'I bet he didn't. One thing he hates is being told what to do, or what not to do.' Taking her hands in his, he lowered his face to hers.

'He does not.' Kissing him back, she focused on a mark on the wall. Would Darryl really have threatened Dean or was she reading too much into it?

25

'Is Darryl all ready for Luna?' Flora asked as she leaned against the paddock gate.

Bending down and throwing the tennis ball for the twenty-eighth time in the last ten minutes, Ginny grinned and watched Ralph barrel after it. 'Yes. He can't wait. Nor can Pat, his dad.'

'Oh good. What time is he picking her up?'

'Straight after work, I think.' Ralph dropped the ball at her feet, looking up expectantly. 'Good job, Ralph. You want to go again?'

'That'll work out nicely then.' Bending down, Flora fussed Ralph through the gate as he spotted her and poked his head through the wooden slats, the ball once again in his mouth. 'Percy wanted a quick word.'

'With me?'

'No, with Darryl.'

'Oh, right.' Ginny frowned. 'What about?'

'I'm not sure, some club Percy thought his dad might like to join or something.' Flora shrugged. 'Darryl mentioned his dad liked to play cards, I think.'

'Ah, okay, I'll make sure he speaks to him then.'

'Great.'

'Oh, Flora?'

'Yes, lovely?'

'I'm trying to organise a movie night round mine for Friday. Are you free?' Ginny threw the ball again. It had been too long since she'd had everyone round her house, it would be nice for them all to catch up outside work again.

'That sounds nice. I'm in.' And with that, Flora turned and made her way back to the kennels.

'Right, Ralph, we should probably head back too.' Ginny pocketed the ball. 'Oh, don't look at me like that, not with those gorgeous brown eyes of yours.'

Ralph nudged her leg.

'Okay, okay, another ten minutes and then we'd better get back. We need to get the supplies ordered or you're not going to have any food next week... And you don't want that, do you?'

* * *

'Susan, do we usually order ten or fifteen boxes of the dental sticks? My mind's gone completely blank.' Ginny tapped the pen between her eyebrows before taking a gulp of coffee.

'Fifteen.' From where she was rooting around in the wash basket, Susan held up a purple teddy. 'This is Tiger's, right?'

'Yes, that's right. He's taken a real shine to it. Belle, on the other hand, prefers to drag their blankets around the kennel.'

A knocking came from the kitchen door and Ginny looked up to see Darryl letting himself in.

'Hi, Darryl.' Susan smiled. 'Big day for you today, hey?'

'Yes, yes.' He grinned, and then leaned down and kissed Ginny on the top of her head. 'How's your day been?'

'Good, thanks. How about yours?'

'So-so.'

Ginny glanced up. 'Sorry, one moment. I just need to finish up these orders or I won't get them submitted in time.' Looking back at the order form, she tried to focus again.

'No worries. Susan, do you need a hand?' Darryl glanced at Susan where she was standing by the tumble drier, folding the last blanket.

'Nope, I'm done now. Thank you though.' She picked up the pile of clean laundry and carried it out. 'I'll catch you before you leave to say bye to Luna.'

She nodded as Darryl held the door open for her.

Coming back into the room, Darryl perched on the edge of the table next to Ginny, tapping the toe of his shoe against the kitchen tiles. He picked up a pen, holding it up and inspecting it.

She looked up at him. What had happened? He was usually so relaxed around her, certainly not one to fidget. 'What's up?'

'Nothing. Everything's fine.' Smiling, he put the pen back down.

'No, it's not. You're not usually restless like this. Has something happened at work?' Or was it to do with her? He'd been fine with Susan, but now... Now he wasn't. Had she done something wrong?

Shifting position on the table, Darryl grinned. 'Oh, you know me well.'

'Ha, I do. Now out with it. What's wrong?' Leaning back in her chair, she crossed her arms. Was he breaking up with her? She couldn't very well blame him if he was. She'd been off with him, distant. She knew she had, but it was all so new to her. After having such a long break between relationships, it was to be expected, wasn't it? Normal to keep the walls up a little longer. Looking down, she pinched the bridge of her nose. She'd blown it. She'd doubted him too much and too often. He must have picked up on it, picked up on how unsure she'd been feeling about the whole thing. It was all her fault. She'd ruined it all before it had even truly begun.

'Honestly, it's nothing I can't handle. It's just that Jason was really off with me today.' He grimaced. 'Don't get me wrong, he's been off with me since the moment he arrived, but he, I don't know, it was different today. When you spoke to him, did you tell him that we're dating?'

'No, I didn't.' Ginny shook her head. 'Not because I didn't want to, just because us dating didn't come up in the conversation. It was about our past.' Should she have? Darryl had introduced her to his dad, and she hadn't even admitted to her ex that she was seeing him.

'No, that's okay. I didn't mean that you should have told him, I just wondered if that was the reason behind him acting the way he has today.'

'What's he done?'

Darryl picked up Ginny's empty mug and twisted it in his hands. 'He tried to pull me from the Wagging Tails column for a start.'

'Seriously? He can't do that! What about us getting a new trainer? The Family Fun Day will be a complete disaster.'

How could he?

'I refused. I spoke to him, loudly, in front of the whole of the office. I told him how much was riding on the column and that if someone else took over now they'd be starting from scratch.' Darryl shrugged. 'He backed down.'

She pushed the order forms across the table. Why would Jason do that? Darryl had told her that Jason only gave him the dead-end jobs, had Jason realised that Darryl's column about the home was a success? That the human interest story mixed with tales about the dogs they rehomed was the perfect combination to attract readers? Maybe Jason wanted to take it over himself. Maybe he wanted the success for himself. Pulling the order forms back towards her, she picked at the corner of the paper. Is that why Darryl was dating her? He'd seen a way to get closer to the story? Through her?

'Eventually. It took some debate, that's for sure.' Darryl stood up and began pacing the room.

'Oh, right.' She shook her head. No, Darryl wasn't like that. She was comparing him to Jason. Again. She needed to stop doing that. Every bad thing she thought about Darryl was because she was comparing him. She needed to try to take Darryl at his word, at face value. Knowing Jason as well as she did, and the fact he'd been trying to wedge himself back into her life, it wouldn't surprise her if Jason had found out about them seeing each other and would try to break them up, that, or he was just trying to get closer to her after the way she'd spoken to him. She'd dented his ego, he'd need to try to show her she hadn't won.

'I bet it's because I had a go at him. He's trying to punish me, but by doing so he's going to punish the whole home. We're getting to the bottom of our funds and without the Family Fun Day we might not even be able to continue. Don't get me wrong, we've had a few donations from the *Trestow Telegraph* readers but we need a huge influx of other funding too.'

'I don't think it's about what you said to him.' He placed the mug back on the table carefully. 'I don't know. He was making everything difficult for me this afternoon. Pulling up mistakes that weren't there, basically rewriting my article about the pebbled floor and then telling me it wasn't newsworthy enough to be published in the paper.' Darryl shrugged. 'This is from the guy who specifically told me to write about it.'

'Oh, that is strange.' Ginny took his hand. 'Maybe we've both annoyed him then?'

'Maybe.' Walking across to her, Darryl reached out a hand to help her from her chair. 'Anyway, enough of Jason and his weird ways, let's concentrate on the good things we have coming up.'

'Now, that sounds like a plan.' Ginny wrapped her arms around his waist, pulling him closer. Yes, she needed to start giving him a real chance. 'Are you ready to take Luna home now?'

'I am indeed.'

* * *

Darryl leaned his elbows on his knees, watching Luna sniff around the living room. 'Do you think she understands that she's here to stay? Or is she wondering when she'll be taken back?'

'She knows this is her new home.' Ginny rubbed his shoulder. 'Just look at that tail! If she wagged it any faster, she'd be taking off.'

Darryl smiled. 'She does look happy, doesn't she?'

'Of course she does. She's with you and every single one of us at Wagging Tails knows how much she dotes on you. She's your match.' And if she could just shake off these feelings of unease maybe Ginny could be his match too. Grinning, she shook her head. What was she even thinking? It was far too early in the relationship to be even wondering that.

'Oh, I hope you're right.' Twisting in his seat, he cupped his hands on her cheeks and kissed her.

'Here they are. I knew I'd kept them somewhere.' Pat shuffled into the living room, his walking frame thudding against the polished floorboards as he moved, a wedge of takeaway menus gripped in his hand.

'Ah great, you found them.' Darryl took them while his dad

settled back in his chair. 'What do you both fancy for dinner? My treat to celebrate Luna settling in.'

'I don't mind. You know I'll eat anything.' Pat slumped back into the armchair. 'I'll let you two lovebirds choose.'

"What would you like?' Darryl shared the menus between them.

'Umm, pizza maybe? But I don't really mind.' Ginny shrugged. Darryl hadn't commented on the fact his dad had called them lovebirds. Was he embarrassed of her? One moment he was acting as though she meant something to him, the next he didn't even react to a comment like that, joke or not.

'Pizza sounds good.' Pulling out the pizza menus from the pile, Darryl looked across at Luna. 'Oh, I think she might need to go out.'

'I'll come with you. We can show her the garden.' Standing up, Ginny tapped the side of her leg. Luna followed immediately.

'Good idea. Do you want to see your new garden, Luna? You might even find a tennis ball or two.'

'Did you hide some tennis balls out there?'

'I may have done.' Darryl chuckled as they stepped through the back doorway. 'She should find them easy enough though, they're not very well hidden.'

Ginny laughed before looking down at the grass beneath them. 'I'm having Flora, Percy, Susan and Alex over tomorrow evening for a movie night. Do you want to come? Susan's probably going to ask Malcolm too, so there'll be a few of us.'

'I'd love to.' Wrapping his arms around her, he leaned his chin on her head and for a moment they quietly watched as Luna snuffled around in the flowerbeds.

When Luna came back and dropped a tennis ball by her feet, Ginny bent down and fussed her head. 'Well done, Luna! You found one of the balls.' She turned back to Darryl. 'Do you know what? I think she'd be really good at tracking.'

'Oh, I bet she would.' Kneeling down, Darryl also began to fuss Luna.

'You could bring her along to the Family Fun Day and take a trial lesson. If we manage to get a new trainer, of course.'

'That's an idea.' Taking the ball from Ginny, he called out to Luna, who excitedly jumped around in anticipation of a game of fetch. Darryl threw it across the garden and Luna raced in its direction, before delicately picking her way through the flowerbed it had landed in. 'After the argument with Jason, I managed to get the plea for a new trainer in so all being well, it should be in tomorrow's paper.'

'Fantastic. Thank you.'

26

After setting a bowl of crisps on the coffee table, Ginny hurried to the door. 'Flora, Percy,' she greeted as she beckoned them in. 'Thanks for coming.'

'Thanks for inviting us.' Flora stepped inside and drew Ginny in for a hug.

'Yes, ditto. I wouldn't miss one of your movie nights for tickets to the football.' Percy then walked across to the coffee table and scooped up a handful of crisps.

'Percy! Wait until the others get here at least.' Flora shook her head, but Ginny could see she was smiling.

'It's okay. I've got another packet,' she said. 'Have as many as you like.'

'Thanks, Ginny.'

'Oh, Ginny. I meant to say, we had another call from a dog trainer interested in the Family Fun Day!' Flora clapped her hands.

'Really? That's three people now.' Ginny called over her shoulder as she walked into the kitchen to grab another packet of crisps.

'Yes, I've rung them back and asked them all to come in tomorrow for an informal chat. I thought that way we can see who's the best fit. I know it's short notice, but the Family Fun Day is creeping up on us.'

Ginny agreed. 'The sooner we get a new trainer started with our dogs the better.' She refilled the bowl with the fresh packet of crisps as the doorbell rang again.

'I'll pop the kettle on,' Flora said as she made her way to the kitchen.

Ginny pulled the front door open. 'Susan, Malcolm, hi. So pleased you could both make it.'

'Evening, Ginny. Thank you for the invite.' Malcolm stepped inside.

'You're welcome.' Hugging Susan, Ginny grinned at Malcolm. 'Go on through, Flora's got the kettle on.'

'Ooh, lovely, I could do with a nice cuppa,' Malcolm said as he helped Susan out of her summer jacket.

'The coat hooks are just behind you.' Ginny began shutting the door, when another voice piped up.

'Hey, don't forget about me!' Alex was sprinting up the garden path.

'Alex! I was thinking you'd ditched us for a better invite.' She threw her arms around him.

'Am I the last one? Do I get to make the grand entrance?' He looked behind him at the empty pathway.

'Ha ha, we're still waiting for Darryl, but you're more than welcome to make a grand entrance anyway.'

'Has *he* ditched you?' Alex said as he shut the door behind him.

'Maybe.' She pulled her mobile from her back pocket and frowned. 'Yes, he has. It seems he's got a work thing.' She reread the short text. He'd just said 'a work thing', no description beyond that. Jason had never given her any real description when he'd been cheating. His excuses had always been short. She supposed because he hadn't been bothered to even make up a proper lie, spend any time on his excuses to her, or else maybe he'd kept his lies as vague as possible so if she'd questioned him he wouldn't have tripped up. Darryl wouldn't cheat though, would he? They'd only just started seeing each other. What would be the point? Wouldn't he just finish things if he wanted to see someone else? Pushing all thoughts of Jason and Darryl out of her mind, she hung up Alex's coat. She was going to enjoy tonight whether Darryl had stood her up or not.

'Oh, that's rubbish. Never mind, we can still have a good night.' Putting his arm around her shoulders, he led her into the living room.

'Alex, lovely. Good to see you've made it.' Flora placed a tray laden with mugs on the coffee table and began to pass them around. 'Tea all round. I wasn't sure if Darryl was joining us, so I've made him one too.'

'He's not, I'm afraid.' Ginny held up her phone. 'He's been held up at work.'

'Oh, that's a shame.' Flora passed Ginny a mug.

'Does that mean I get to have his tea too then?' Picking up the spare mug, Alex settled himself on the floor as Flora and Percy took the sofa.

'Help yourself.' Ginny laughed as she grabbed a cushion before sitting crossed-legged on the floor next to him.

Alex clapped his hands. 'Ooh, guess what Cookie did today?'

'What?'

'He came and took a treat from my hand. Actually from my hand, can you believe it?' he said and pointed to his palm.

'Wow, that's great news. Well done, Alex.' Susan grinned as

she sat down in the armchair, with Malcolm settling next to Percy on the sofa. 'That must have taken some patience.'

'Thank you.' Alex smiled. 'I've been trying to spend at least an hour in his kennel with him each day, and today, it paid off.'

'He's got a soft spot for you, Alex.' Flora smiled and she took a sip of her tea.

'Yes, great work.' Ginny nudged him in the side. 'Shall we pop the film on now? The pizza should be here any moment.'

'I'll do it. I'm sure I saw the remote somewhere,' Percy said.

As the screen flickered to life, the doorbell rang. Ginny pushed herself to standing. 'That must be the pizza.'

'Yum, I'm starving.' Alex leaned back against the wall and downed his first mug before making a start on the spare.

Pulling the front door open, Ginny was expecting to see the delivery guy and grinned as she greeted them. 'Hi...' Her voice wavered as she realised it wasn't the pizza being delivered.

'Hello. I must say I wasn't expecting quite such a warm welcome after our conversation the other day.' Jason smiled slowly.

'Jason? What are you doing here?' Gripping the edge of the door, Ginny looked him up and down. With his hands in the pockets of his suit trousers, he looked as sure of himself as he always did.

'I wanted to talk—'

'Wait, just stop. I thought I'd told you: I don't want to talk to you. I don't want to go to dinner with you. We literally had this conversation the other day, as you clearly recall.' She started to close the door but he jutted his foot in the way. Flaring her nostrils, she glared at him. 'Move.'

'Oh, I will, but first I need to say something.' He held his hands up, palms forward. 'Before you say any more this isn't about us, our past relationship or our future.'

'Our *future*?' Ginny scoffed at the word. 'You cheated on me. There is no "our future".'

With a loud dramatic sigh, Jason folded his arms. 'This is about Darryl. I know you two have been seeing each other.'

Darryl? So he did know about them then? This was why he'd tried to take Darryl off the Wagging Tails column. She opened and closed her mouth. There wasn't any point in accusing him. He wouldn't tell the truth anyway. 'So what? Who I see or don't see has nothing to do with you.'

'It does if he's going to end up hurting you. He's bad news, Ginny.'

'Darryl? Bad news?' She scoffed. How did Jason have the audacity to say anything of the sort. 'Compared to you, he's an angel. You? You need to carry a warning sign around your neck for every woman you meet.'

'Ginny, I'm being serious.' His voice was low and steady.

Ginny rolled her eyes. 'Right, well, thank you. I'll bear that in mind.'

'I'd suggest you do.'

'Thanks.' Glaring at his foot, she waited for him to move out of the way before shutting the door. And then, leaning back against it, she sighed. How had he found out about them? Had he seen them together at the office?

'Ginny, is everything okay?' Percy peered around the living room door.

'Not really. It was Jason. He came to warn me off Darryl.' She shook her head.

'Did you say Jason?' Susan joined Percy in the doorway.

Ginny nodded. How had he even known where she lived? Frowning, she felt instinct take over, and very quickly, she was back opening the front door and running down the path.

'Jason, stop.'

He turned around slowly, a slow grin spreading across his face. 'You want to hear more?'

'I want to know how you found out where I live.' Coming to a stop in front of him, she shoved her hands in her pockets.

'Sorry?'

'My address. How do you know where I live?' She met his gaze.

'I don't think that matters. Not more than what I'm trying to tell you, do you?'

'Yes, I do actually. How do you know where I live? I have a right to know how you've found out my personal details.'

'Phone book.' He shrugged.

'I'm ex-directory.'

Did anyone even still use the phone book? Were there still physical copies of the phone book being printed?

She shook her head. 'Jason, tell me.'

'I've told you.' With a cold shrug, he turned around.

'Don't you walk away from me.' She narrowed her eyes. She had a right to know. She had a right to know how he knew where she lived. 'Tell me.'

'Fine. You really want to know? Anna told me.'

'Anna? She wouldn't have.'

Anna, one of only two true friends she'd had back in London. Anna, who had promised not to tell anyone, least of all Jason where she had moved to.

'I don't believe you.'

'Don't believe me then.' Jason smirked. 'It's up to you.'

'Why would she have told you?'

'We were an item. She told me everything.'

'An item?'

Anna had hated Jason. She'd begged Ginny to walk away long before he'd cheated on her. Two years before, in fact.

'She wouldn't have dated you.'

'Who said we dated.' Looking back at her, Jason shrugged. 'We spent the night with each other a few times a couple of years before we broke up. And when things finished with Natasha, she got in contact with me again.'

'You cheated on me with Anna? My Anna?' Tucking her hair behind her ears, she let her arms fall to her sides. None of this made any sense. 'She hated you. She *hates* you.'

'She's never hated me. She wanted you to finish with me. There's the difference.'

Ginny looked at the pavement. 'No.'

'Yes.' Jason crossed his arms.

'Why? Why did you follow me down here? You cheated on me at least twice. You clearly didn't want to be with me. Why on earth would you track me down and follow me here?'

'Don't flatter yourself. I moved to Trestow for the job. I just thought I'd look you up and say hi, that's all.'

And with no further comment – on either Anna or why he was down here chasing her – he walked away.

Ginny closed her eyes. Jason cheated on her with Anna?

'Come on, lovely. Let's get you inside.' Flora's voice was quiet, reassuring.

Feeling the weight of her friend's arm around her shoulders, Ginny turned around and let herself be led inside.

'He had an affair with my best friend behind my back.'

'Oh, Ginny. That must have been tough to hear.' Closing the front door behind them, Flora drew her in for a hug. Ginny could smell Flora's coconut shampoo on her hair.

'I know it happened a long time ago now, but she was my best friend. She was supposed to have my back – not cheat on me behind my back.'

27

Rolling over in bed, Ginny reached for her mobile again. Still nothing. Darryl still hadn't messaged her. Not one message since the one standing her up last night. Pushing herself to sitting, she pulled her pillow up and leaned against the headrest. She was letting him win – Jason – she was letting him wheedle into her relationship with Darryl.

She raked her fingers through her hair. She'd forgotten to plait it before she'd gone to bed. That's what he wanted. That's what Jason wanted. He wanted her to question Darryl. He wanted her to doubt him. He was planting the seeds of doubts, trying to break them apart.

She winced as her fingers caught a knot, yanking her hair from her scalp. What Jason didn't know was that she had been planting the seeds of doubt herself. She'd been comparing Darryl to Jason since she'd first met him, looking for signs, reasons why she shouldn't trust him. She saw that now.

Were the signs really there though, or was she picking apart a normal, perfectly good relationship? She guessed that remained to be seen.

Bringing her knees to her chest, she lowered her forehead to them. Who could blame her? Jason had well and truly messed her around, probably destroyed any hope of her being able to trust another man completely again. It had been lie after lie and even now, four years on, she was still unravelling the lies.

Anna though. Why Anna? What had Jason been thinking? He'd known they were best friends.

She sobbed. What had Anna been thinking? All the talk of her hating Jason, all the times Anna had tried to get Ginny to leave him, had that only been so she could have Jason for herself?

A flash of anger rose from her stomach, and she sat up and picked up her phone. There was only one person who could give her the answers, and that was Anna herself. She scrolled through to Anna's name and hit the 'call' button.

Holding her mobile against her ear, she listened to rings before the voicemail kicked in, Anna's voice happily, innocently, telling her to leave a message.

She ended the call and flung the phone to the end of the bed. What would she say to her anyway? She wouldn't be able to believe anything Anna told her, not now. There wasn't any point in speaking to her. Not now, not ever.

She looked across at her alarm clock. She was late.

* * *

'There you are, Ginny. I was about to send a search party.' Hanging Ralph's lead back on the hooks behind the counter, Flora looked across as Ginny opened the door.

'Sorry I'm so late. I overslept. I'll make up the time later.'

'Don't be so daft. The amount of extra time you put into this place, you could have a whole year off and not have to explain.'

Walking around the counter, she drew her in for a hug. 'And how are you feeling today?'

Ginny shrugged. 'Honestly?'

'Of course, honestly.' Flora tucked a loose strand of Ginny's hair gently behind her ear.

'I just keep trying to figure out if there had been any clues. Jason or Anna must have said something or done something to make me suspicious. How didn't I notice?'

Taking a deep breath, Flora looked at her with kind eyes. 'Sometimes there aren't any signs.'

'Or else I was just too trusting to see them.'

'Ah, no, you're not too trusting. They were just untrustworthy people.'

'I should have seen. How could I not have?'

'Look, people let us down sometimes. It's human nature to be flawed. Heck, we see the results of such human flaws enough here, don't we?' She took her handkerchief from her pocket and wiped Ginny's eyes. 'Jason and Anna, and whoever else he may or may not have had an affair with in the past, aren't worth wasting any more of your time over. You've got Darryl now and that's who you need to focus on.'

'But...'

Flora held her palm up, stopping her mid-sentence. 'I know what you're going to ask; how can you trust Darryl when you trusted Jason and he let you down?'

Ginny nodded. It was a reasonable question. A question Ginny had been trying to answer herself ever since she and Darryl had begun seeing each other.

'Well, in response to that, I'll ask you to answer my question. Did you ever truly trust Jason? One hundred per cent?'

Ginny shook her head. 'No.'

'And Darryl? Do you trust him?'

'I think so. I don't know.' She'd been trying to trust him but with Jason around, she knew she hadn't really given Darryl a proper chance, she knew she'd been looking for the flaws Jason had. 'Jason said he had something to warn me about him.'

'But you can't trust Jason, right? He's proven that time and time again he can't be trusted?'

'No, he can't be trusted.'

'Then why trust him on this? Why believe him over what you feel?' Flora used her index finger to nudge Ginny's chin upwards, to look up at her. 'Believe in your own intuition.'

Taking a slow steady breath, Ginny nodded. Flora was right. She couldn't trust Jason, he'd proved that himself, so why was she even still thinking about his warning? She shouldn't be. 'You're right.'

'Good. Now, why don't you go and freshen up and I'll pop some coffee in the cafetière before the interviews – sorry, *informal chats* – begin?'

Without waiting for an answer, Flora disappeared into the kitchen.

Going into the small bathroom, Ginny massaged her temples and looked in the mirror. This was it. She wouldn't let herself think about Jason's so-called warning any more, and as for his confession? That was in the past. In the way way past.

* * *

'Thank you so much for coming, Sally.' Patting the notes she'd made during the interview, Flora stood up from the kitchen table and held out her hand.

'No, thank you. It's been a real pleasure. You all do such a fantastic job here, I really would love to be part of it.' Sally smiled. 'Thank you both for taking the time to see me.'

'Thanks for coming in.' Ginny led the way through to the reception area and waved her out before joining Flora again. 'I think it's fair to say that you saved the best until last. She was great, wasn't she? Brilliant with the dogs when we showed her round and so patient with Tiger and Belle during her training demonstration too.'

'Yes, she certainly was.' Flora took the empty mugs over to the sink and then turned back around to Ginny. 'Are you thinking what I'm thinking?'

'That we should hire her?'

'The other candidates were good, but they were missing the passion Sally has.'

'Definitely.' Ginny grinned. She could picture Sally fitting right into their team. 'I'll have a look and see if I can find the timetable for last year's tasters; at least that will give her an idea of how to structure the demonstrations and sessions for the Family Fun Day.'

'Great. And I'll give her a call. Let her know she's got the job. There's no point in keeping her in suspense.'

Ginny dragged a chair across to the work surface. She was pretty sure Clarke had kept his notes in the top corner cupboard. Climbing up, Ginny opened the door and began to rummage through the paperwork – detailed notes depicting one-to-one sessions with previous residents at the home, behaviour and training reports and, something else, a yellow folder. Yes, that must be it. She remembered Clarke commenting that he liked bright colours; he said he'd chosen yellow because he was one hundred per cent certain the sun would be shining down on them on the Family Fun Day. And it did; it had been one of the hottest days of the year. Now, if she could just pull it out from between the two folders either side of it.

Prising away the two folders, Ginny tried to wriggle it out.

There was some movement. Just a little more this way. The folder freed, sending papers cascading to the floor.

'Is this a bad time?'

Catching as many of the papers as she could, while holding on to the elusive yellow folder, Ginny turned on the chair. 'Darryl. No, this is probably a great time. Can you just...?' She held up the armful of papers.

'Of course.' Striding towards her, he reached out his arm and grabbed another folder just as it slid from the shelf above her head. 'Now, that was close.'

'Ha ha, thank you. I think you just saved my life.'

'Yes, you don't really want that on your death certificate, do you? Crushed by flying paperwork.' Darryl chuckled as he scooped the papers out of her arms and dropped them to the table before holding out his hand for her.

'Thank you.' Taking his hand, she jumped down from the chair.

'Did you find what you were looking for?' He nodded at the yellow folder.

'Yes, I think so. I'm hoping it's the plans and itinerary for the taster training sessions and demonstrations for the Family Fun Day from last year.' She flicked through the pages. Yes, it was. Hugging it to her chest, she grinned. 'Guess what? We've got another trainer, all thanks to your plea in the paper yesterday. We had three candidates and, to be honest, they were all good, but Flora's on the phone offering the job to one of them right now.'

'That's fantastic news. So the Family Fun Day is saved?'

She nodded. 'Yes, once again you've saved the day.'

'Ha ha, that's not what I meant.'

'I know, but it's true. Without you raising awareness we wouldn't even be having the Family Fun Day at all, or at least only with a couple of stalls, no trainer and probably only half a dozen or so visitors.'

Looking at the floor, Darryl ran his fingers through his hair. 'Yes, well, I'm sure you'd have been fine.'

Ginny frowned. Why would he say that? Why wasn't he taking the praise? He'd done a good thing. Unless... unless he was embarrassed because his motivation behind the success of the column had more to do with his personal success rather than theirs. She rubbed her eyes. She was tired. She couldn't think straight, not with everything whirring around in her mind. 'We really wouldn't. Anyway, how's Luna settling in?'

Grinning, he pulled out his mobile and showed Ginny some photos; Luna sprawled across the sofa; Luna in the garden with her tongue hanging out; Luna jumping in the air after a tennis ball. 'Great. It feels as though she's always been there and she's already swanning around the house thinking she owns the place.' He chuckled. 'Who am I kidding? She knows she owns the place.'

'Aw, that's so good to hear.'

'Do you want a hand with that?' He nodded behind her.

Ginny looked behind her at the heap of folders, notebooks and loose papers strewn across the work surface, the floor and the chair she'd climbed on to reach the top shelf. 'Haven't you got work?'

'Yeah, but I'm already here for work – in a sense. I wanted to pop in to speak to Percy about a bridge club he goes to. He mentioned they were looking for players and my dad is eager to go along. I was also going to offer to write about it in my column next week, see if there's anyone else out there to make up the numbers.'

'Ah, so you *are* on work business?' She grinned. 'Does that mean you can stay for a quick cuppa?'

'I mean, I suppose I should ask the opinion of Percy's trusted colleague about the bridge club.' He wrapped his arms around her before looking at the mess and stepping away. 'First though, I'll help you tidy that heap up.'

'Thanks.'

'Anything to keep me out of the office a little longer.'

'Oi, is that all I am to you? Someone to assist you playing hooky from work?' She laughed as she bundled up a heap of loose papers.

Chuckling, Darryl shrugged. 'That and so much more.'

Ginny looked at him, the smile had gone, replaced with a frown. Jason was still giving him a hard time then. 'It's no better then?'

'If you mean Jason, then no, if anything he's worse. Whenever he's in, I feel as though I'm back at school, waiting to be called to his office to have my work ripped up in front of me.' Looking down, he shook his head before looking at her and smiling. 'It could be worse though; I could have to sit with him at the lunch table.'

'Darryl, I feel so bad. I'm sorry.' She reached out and touched his hand.

'Hey, it's not your fault.'

'Well, it is really, isn't it? If we weren't seeing each other none of this would be happening.'

'I'm not sure he knows. We've always rubbed each other up the wrong way, ever since he got the job.' Shrugging, he lifted a pile of folders to the shelf.

Sitting back on her haunches, she watched as he rearranged the papers so they wouldn't fall back down. 'Oh, he knows.'

'Really?' He clenched his jaw as the papers fluttered from his grip. 'Darn.'

'Oh, hi, Darryl.' Susan, carrying a pile of blankets in her arms, appeared and was heading towards the washing machine.

'Morning, Susan. How's Malcolm?'

'Oh, he's doing just great, thank you. We've booked to go away for the weekend at the end of the month.' She grinned as she loaded the blankets in the machine and closed the door.

'Lovely. Anywhere nice?'

'Up to Norfolk. He's originally from there so I'll be meeting the family too.' She reached for the box of washing powder. 'And, by the way, thank you again for what you said to Dean; whatever it was it's done the trick. He's not messaged me once since.'

'That's great news.'

Ginny held the papers in her hand tighter. So whatever he'd said to Dean *must* have been more than the friendly chat Darryl had made out it had been.

'It sure is a relief, I can tell you.' She looked across to Ginny and Darryl. 'Anyway, I'll let you two get on. I won't be a moment.'

Nodding, Darryl turned towards Ginny, picking up where they left off. 'How can you be sure Jason knows about us?'

'Oh, you've told him about last night then?' Susan asked, stabbing the buttons on the machine. 'Nasty business, it is. But you'll be all right, love. Well, that's me done here. See you later.'

Ginny bit down on her bottom lip. She hadn't meant for Darryl to find out about last night. Not like that, through Susan, anyway.

Darryl frowned. 'What happened last night? I thought you were having a movie night?'

'I did.' She shook her head. She couldn't talk about this now. 'How was your work thing, anyway? Sorry, I should have asked before.'

'Oh that, that was nothing. Literally.' He bent back down and continued piling up the notebooks. 'It was really odd actually. Jason insisted I go and meet this man to discuss a complaint he has with the council, but when I got there, the bloke didn't have a clue what I was on about. If I didn't know better, I'd have thought he'd sent me on a wild goose chase.' He rolled his eyes.

Ginny nodded, pushing the papers back onto the shelf.

'What did Susan mean?' he asked again. There was no getting away from the question. 'What happened last night?'

Shoving her hands in her pockets, she watched as Darryl placed the last of the notebooks away before shutting the cupboard door. It was now or never.

'Jason came round.'

'To your house?'

She nodded. 'I didn't even realise he knew where I lived.'

'Oh.' Darryl frowned. 'So you didn't invite him then?'

'What? No, of course not! You know how I feel about the bloke. He turned up and tried to warn me off you.' Looking down at the floor, she picked up a pencil which must have fallen out of the cupboard with the papers. 'We ended up having an argument in the street. Not sure how impressed my neighbours were.'

Darryl looked at her, taking a seat at the table. 'He does know about us then. That explains a fair bit. But he cheated on you, didn't he? Why would he feel he has a right to interfere with us?'

'Because it's Jason and he feels he has a right to do anything he pleases.' Ginny sat down opposite him.

Reaching across the table, he took her hand. 'Are you okay?'

'Yes, I'm fine. I was a bit shaken up at the time, but I'm just angry at him more than anything else. I asked him where he'd got my address from, and it turns out that he'd got it from someone he cheated on me with – my so-called best friend. So that's one more person he cheated on me with on top of the woman I already knew about. He's been seeing my now ex-best friend again recently, after breaking up with his mistress. And for whatever reason she told him my address.' She pinched the bridge of her nose. 'Does that even make sense or am I just rambling?'

Looking down at the table, staring at an abandoned teaspoon, Darryl didn't say anything for a moment, before he stood up.

'Where are you going? I thought you were staying for a drink?'

'I need to speak to him. Find out what he's playing at.'

'What?' Pushing her chair back, Ginny stood up. 'Don't do that.' He'd just get himself into trouble.

28

She was going to be too late. If it hadn't been for that tractor she'd got stuck behind, she'd have got here in time, she thought to herself, as she pushed open the door to the office building and hurried through the foyer towards the stairwell.

After a feeble attempt to run all the way up the stairs, she paused on the landing and tried to ring Darryl again. No answer. On opening the door to the offices, she ignored the offers of help from the receptionist and rushed towards Jason's office. Even though the door was closed, she could hear Darryl's raised voice and that of Jason responding.

She pushed open the door. Jason was sitting down, legs stretched out and feet on his desk, a pen in his right hand. Darryl was standing opposite him.

Pausing mid-rant, Darryl looked at her. 'Ginny.'

'I asked you not to do this, I asked you not to confront him.' She closed the door quietly behind her.

'Ooh, trouble in paradise I see. I hope I've not caused a rift between the two of you.' Jason pointed the pen from Darryl to Ginny and back again.

Slipping her hand into Darryl's, Ginny stood next to him. 'There's no rift between us. I just didn't want Darryl wasting his time.'

'Huh.' Swinging his legs to the floor, Jason wheeled his chair closer to his desk. 'I see.'

'Come on, let's go.' She tugged on Darryl's hand.

Narrowing his eyes at Jason, Darryl shook his head. 'No, there're things that need to be said. Things I should have said before.'

'Darryl, please. He's not worth it. He's not worth losing your job over.' Ginny tugged on his hand. 'Whatever he says can't touch us. Please, Darryl. Listen to me.'

Taking a deep breath, Darryl looked at her. Properly for the first time since she'd arrived. As if realising she was right, he nodded and began following Ginny to the door.

'I figure you've told her then?' Leaning his elbows on his desk, Jason clasped his hands together.

Pausing, she turned to face him again. Told her what? She looked back towards Darryl. She knew she had to be strong. Had to quash the questions if Jason was ever going to give up trying to destroy her and Darryl's relationship. 'I'm not rising to this, Jason,' she said as calmly as she could. 'I don't care what you have to say. I don't even want to lay eyes on you again.' Despite being able to hear her heart hammering, she managed to keep her voice steady before turning back towards the door.

'It's a good job your boyfriend won't be working here much longer then, isn't it?'

Looking back, Ginny glared at him. 'You can't fire him. This is your fault. You've done this.' Jason was angry at *her*; Darryl was just trapped in the middle. He couldn't fire him. There were rules, laws.

'I don't need to, do I, Darryl?'

Shaking his head, Darryl didn't respond. All he did was open the office door and beckon Ginny to leave. 'Come on, let's go.'

Ginny looked back at him. 'You haven't resigned, have you? You can't let him win.'

'No, I haven't.' He glanced at Jason and shook his head.

Looking from Jason to Darryl and back again, Ginny frowned. 'What do you mean?'

'So, I'm right then.' Jason laughed, a low gravelly sound filling the room. 'You haven't told her.'

'Let's go.' Darryl opened the door wider, nodding to Ginny to go through first.

'Wait, what's he talking about?'

'You really haven't told her about your new job applications?' Jason covered his mouth dramatically with his hand. 'Oops, wasn't I meant to say anything?'

'Nice try, Jason.' Darryl met Ginny's eye and lowered his voice. 'Let's talk about this later.'

'What job applications?' Was Jason just making things up? Trying to drive a wedge between them?

'Come on, let's go.' Darryl narrowed his eyes at Jason before guiding Ginny out, closing the door firmly behind them and leading the way towards the stairwell.

Ginny kept her head down, the fierce heat of self-consciousness sweeping across her face as she felt every pair of eyes in the room staring at her.

Out in the stairwell, she leaned against the wall.

'Ginny, let me explain.'

'Explain what?' She couldn't really blame him for confronting Jason. She'd have done exactly the same. She shook her head. She shouldn't be surprised that Jason would pull any excuse, any made-up reason from the air to try to pull them apart.

'About the applications.'

'What? They're real? I just assumed Jason was trying to rile me.' Straightening her back, she pushed herself away from the wall. Darryl *had* been lying to her.

'No, they're real. I applied for some jobs in London and asked Jason to write references. It was before I met you though.'

'You're moving back to London?' She tucked her hair behind her ears. He was leaving?

'No, I was thinking about it but it's not for me. And then, of course, I met you.'

'But I thought you were here for your dad anyway?' She wiped at a pen mark on her left wrist.

'I am. I was. He's a lot better than he was.' Standing in front of her, he cupped her elbows, trying to show her he was still there for her. 'Yes, I applied for a couple of jobs in London, but I'm not interested in them any more. I'm here and I'm staying here even if I have to put up with a boss like him.' He nodded his head in the direction of the office. 'I'm here for you. Plus, I've got Luna now. West Par is home.'

She looked down at the floor before meeting his gaze. 'Are you sure you're not interested in the London jobs any more?'

'One hundred per cent sure. I'm not interested.'

'Okay.' Avoiding his eye, she pointed down the stairs. 'I'd better get back.'

'Ginny?'

'Yes?' She looked back at him.

'Are we okay?'

'Yes, yes, we're fine.' Or they would be, might be. She focused on her breathing as they walked down the stairs. She needed to figure all of this out. She needed to think. To try to work out if Darryl was being genuine and all of the doubts were in her mind or if there really was something to worry about.

* * *

Ginny stared at the sea, the waves lulling against the sand and the water frothing as the ocean crept forwards. Down by her feet, Ralph was enjoying the view too, the sand warming his belly and his eyes transfixed on the rhythmic to and fro of the waves as they made their way up the sand. This was his happy place. Away from the other dogs, taking in the peace of the beach on a weekday afternoon. Ginny knew the quiet times, the hours they were likely to have the beach to themselves, and with his fluorescent yellow jacket warning others to steer clear and the local residents knowing to give him a wide berth, it was a chance for him to relax, the traumas of his past to be stilled.

With a chunk of his ear missing and his fear of other dogs, Ralph had been through a lot – Ginny could only guess at much of it. Yes, he might never be adopted, might always be their resident dog, but that didn't mean he couldn't have a happy life still. Besides, miracles did happen. She traced her finger in the sand. Frank and Dino had lived at Wagging Tails for six years and they were now enjoying their new home. Ralph's perfect match might still appear.

She gently stroked the top of his head, soothing him as she did. They'd have to go back to night-time walks to the beach from next week, Ginny sneaking back into Wagging Tails at midnight, so she and Ralph could avoid the crowds of the summer holiday tourists. Fortunately, because there wasn't much in the way of shops or tourist attractions at West Par, the village didn't get overly busy, but still it was too busy for Ralph.

'I thought I'd find you here.'

Turning, Ginny saw Flora approaching, picking her way across the pebbles towards the sand. 'Flora, what are you doing here?'

'I was just taking a break and decided to come and see how you were both getting on.' She lowered herself down next to Ralph, and began to fuss him.

'We're okay. Just enjoying the peace and quiet.'

'Yes, not much longer left of this.' Flora smiled as she looked out to sea. 'The village will come alive again just in time for the Family Fun Day.'

'Yes, that's the one good thing about it.'

'And back to you sneaking in in the middle of the night to take this one out, I assume?' She glanced down at Ralph.

'I didn't realise you knew.' Ginny grimaced.

'Of course I do. This is me; you can't get anything past me.' Chuckling, she leaned over and rubbed Ginny's shoulder. 'Another thing you can't get past me is the way all this business with Jason has been getting you down.'

Ginny stroked Ralph's paws. 'I'm hoping he'll drop it all now he's confessed about Anna.'

'Yes, hopefully. There's nothing else he can say, is there?'

'No, I don't think so. I think he's trying to split me and Darryl up. When I followed Darryl to the office earlier Jason told me Darryl had applied for jobs in London.'

'Oh, really?'

'Yes, but that was before we met so I'm not really sure what Jason was trying to gain.' She shrugged. 'Did Sally accept the job?'

'Yes, yes, she did. She sounded over the moon. She's recently moved down here from Yorkshire, you remember, so she's thrilled to be able to build her dog training business up with some help from us.'

'That's great news.'

'I told her you were looking for last year's itinerary so she's going to pop in tomorrow, pick it up and meet the dogs properly.'

Flora turned her attention to Ralph, stroking his soft head. 'I think you and Sally will get on well, Ralph, my darling.'

29

Holding the gate to the top paddock open, Ginny stood back as Percy rode through on the ride-on mower.

Percy waved in thanks before heading to the far corner to start mowing the grass.

With her gardening gloves on again, Ginny continued to pull the weeds that were growing between the fence posts. Five days to go until the Family Fun Day and everything had to be perfect. She was determined people would walk through the gates and be glad they'd chosen to spend their Saturday afternoon at Wagging Tails.

'How's it going? Do you need a hand?' Susan walked towards her, gardening gloves hanging out of the pockets of her jeans.

'That'd be great, if you don't mind? I just thought it'd look a bit tidier with all the weeds gone.'

'Good idea. And I see Percy's doing his favourite job.' She grinned as Percy rode by waving.

'Ha ha, any excuse,' Ginny said as she pulled out a huge dandelion.

'I'll have those, please. Malcolm's daughter has a guinea pig.'

She took the dandelion from Ginny and dropped it at the edge of the path. 'Remind me to pick those up later.'

'So, things are going well between you two then?' Ginny smiled.

'Yes, I think so. No, I don't think so, I *know* so.'

'That's great...' Pausing, Ginny shielded her eyes from the sun and looked towards the courtyard. 'Is that a *lorry*?'

Straightening her back, Susan looked over too. 'Yes, it sure looks like it.'

Frowning, Ginny got up and began to walk down the path. 'We've not ordered anything, have we?'

'Not that I know of.' Susan jogged to catch her up before falling into step beside her. 'Flora normally warns us when we're having a big delivery.'

'Very odd.'

Once through the bottom paddock, she opened the gate into the courtyard just as the cab door opened.

'Excuse me, can we help you?'

'Morning, I'm looking for a Ginny Stevenson?' The driver tapped a clipboard.

'That's me.'

'Right, where do you want these?' He climbed out of the cab and slapped the side of the lorry.

'What are they?' Ginny tried to think what she could have ordered which would need a lorry to be transported.

The driver looked up from his clipboard once more. 'Wooden stalls.'

'The stalls? You have the stalls?' Ginny opened and closed her mouth. 'I ordered them to be delivered Friday. We don't need them yet.'

Shrugging, the driver walked around the back of the lorry and began to lower the tailgate. 'You've got them early then.'

'Yes, but we've got nowhere to store them.' She followed him around the back. 'Why are they being delivered today?'

'Look on the order form, it states Monday to Sunday.' He passed across the clipboard.

Taking it, Ginny riffled through the paperwork. 'Where does it say that? I booked them for Friday.'

'Here.' Leaning over Ginny's shoulder, Susan pointed to the order details.

Running the pad of her index finger down the small print, Ginny groaned. 'Oh no. Surely I didn't. Why would I have hired them for the week?'

'I don't know.' Susan frowned. 'Maybe you were just distracted.'

'Excuse me,' she said, trying to attract the driver's attention. 'I'm sorry but I must have put the wrong details in. We only need them for Saturday. I meant to order them to be delivered on Friday not Monday.' She held up the clipboard.

The driver pulled a stack of folded wooden stalls down the ramp of the lorry, the large sack truck they were held together on swinging precariously from side to side. 'Think yourself lucky, you've got them for longer now.'

'But we don't need them, and we can't afford the extra to hire them for longer.' Ginny stared at the order form. She was usually so careful, double-checked everything. How had this escaped her?

'It's only a nominal extra for the week, it's the weekends that are more expensive.' Returning into the lorry, he pulled another laden sack truck down the ramp.

Tapping the clipboard against her forehead, Ginny closed her eyes.

'There you go. I just need a signature from you, and I'll be on my way.' He held out his hand to take the clipboard back.

'And you definitely can't take them now?' Ginny paused, pen in hand.

'I can, but if I do that, I can't guarantee you'll get them back. My colleagues might assume they've been returned and send them on to someone else.'

Sighing, Ginny signed the form and passed the clipboard back to the driver.

'This one's for your records.' He tore off a page and handed it over.

'Thanks.' Ginny folded the paper and slipped it into the back pocket of her jeans. As she watched the lorry pull out onto the main road, she turned to Susan and said, 'What have I done?'

'Ordered stalls for the Family Fun Day.' Susan raised her eyebrows.

'Yep, five days early. Where on earth are we going to store them?' She glanced around. 'Do you think they'll be okay being left out in the open? I don't think it's forecast to rain this week.'

'I should think so. They are designed to be outside after all.'

'That's true.'

Yes, Susan was right. Of course she was.

'I think we should try to wheel them around the back by the shed. Store them away from the courtyard, maybe?'

'Good idea.' Putting her hands on her hips, Ginny looked at the floor. 'I just hope I've not messed up any of the other plans.'

'Hey, I'm sure you haven't. This was just an easy mistake. Anyone could have inputted the wrong dates. Anyway, it's done now.'

'Yes, it's done now.' Ginny nodded.

She watched as Percy rode the ride-on mower into the court-yard and stopped it in front of them.

'What's this then? Someone's organised.' Percy pointed to the stalls.

'Don't.' Ginny sighed. 'I must have put the wrong date on the order form.'

'Ah. Least we know we've got them. Oh, by the way, look what I found.' Percy reached behind him and held up a small yellow teddy. 'This is Luna's, isn't it? I found it in the top paddock, under the tree.'

'Oh, wow, yes, it is. Thank you.' She took the teddy and hugged it to her chest, enjoying the brief moment of comfort it gave her after finding out about her blunder.

'Look, why don't you go over to Darryl's and give that back to Luna? Meantime, me and Susan can move these out of the way.' He nodded to the stalls.

'No, don't worry. I'll do it. It was my mistake.' Ginny shook her head.

'Be off with you. Me and Susan are more than capable and poor Luna will be missing that thing.' Percy parked up the mower and jumped down.

'Okay, thank you.'

* * *

Knocking on the front door, Ginny stood there, the yellow teddy bear hooked under her arm.

After a few minutes, the door opened and Pat stood in the doorway, leaning on his walking frame.

'Ginny. What a surprise to see you. I'm afraid Darryl's at work still.'

'That's okay, I'm not actually here to see Darryl. I've got something for Luna.' She held up the teddy bear. 'Percy found it in the top paddock. When Luna came to us she was carrying it with her so I wanted her to have it back.'

'Oh, thank you.' Pat stood back. 'Come on in and give it to her yourself if you like.'

'Are you sure? I don't want to interrupt anything.'

'The only thing you'll be interrupting is me finishing a cuppa. A cold cuppa by all accounts.' He indicated for Ginny to come in. 'Go on through, she's in the living room. She's found a little spot beneath the window perfect for sunbathing. You go ahead or you'll be waiting all day.'

Nodding, Ginny slipped past him and made her way through to the living room. Just as Pat had said, Luna was sprawled out by the window, legs in the air and belly up.

'Luna!'

As soon as Ginny called her name, Luna was on her feet, running across to her.

'Look what Percy found for you.' She gave an enthusiastic Luna the teddy and fussed her ears. Luna was delighted to be reunited with her toy, wagging her tail from side to side.

'Ah, she likes that.' Pat nodded as Luna flung the teddy into the air before darting forward and catching it in her mouth again.

'She seems to have settled in really well here.'

'The truth be told it feels as though she's always been here.' Pat slumped into his chair.

'I'm really pleased. Luna deserves a loving home.'

'We're grateful for her too.' Pat smiled before pulling his walking frame in front of him again. 'I'm sorry, I should have offered you a drink. Tea? Coffee?'

'Coffee please.' Ginny nodded in the direction of the kitchen. 'I'm happy to get them though.'

'Oh, that would be lovely. Thank you.' Pushing his frame out of the way again, he held out his mug.

Ginny made her way through to the kitchen and clicked the kettle on. As she waited for it to boil, leaning against the work surface, she closed her eyes. She was glad to have a bit of a break after the fiasco with the stalls. But she shouldn't be thinking about that now. As Susan had said, it was done now. She just needed to focus on the next step in the plans for Saturday.

Opening her eyes, she shook her head, and forced herself into action. Right now, she was making coffee. But pulling the fridge door open, Ginny's attention was caught by a newspaper clipping that was attached by a magnet. Was that Darryl? She carefully pulled it off the fridge, and holding it up, she tilted her head. It was Darryl. Darryl dressed in a suit and tie and holding an award.

'Help yourself to a couple of custard creams if you like, Ginny.' Pat's voice wafted through from the living room.

'Okay, thanks.' She glanced towards the living room, then looked back at the photo. What had the award been for? The kettle's switch flicked, reminding her why she was in here. After carefully securing the newspaper cutting back on the fridge door, Ginny finished making the drinks, tucked the biscuit barrel beneath her arm and carried the mugs through to the living room.

'You star. Thank you.'

On the sofa, Ginny took a sip of her coffee before wrapping her hands around the hot mug and clearing her throat. 'I spotted a newspaper clipping of Darryl on the fridge door.'

'Oh, that one.' Pat leaned back against the chair cushions. 'That was a very proud moment of mine, him getting that award. I went up to London then, I did. They put us up in a fancy hotel for the weekend and you should have seen the venue for the awards ceremony.' Patrick whistled.

'Award ceremony? What was the award for?'

'For comment journalism, would you believe? One of the most prestigious awards a journalist can be given.' He grinned.

'Wow, that's amazing.' Ginny's eyes widened. By the sounds of it the award was a huge deal. She wondered if there was a reason why he hadn't mentioned it to her. 'When did that happen?'

'The summer before last. Just before my health began to degrade. Look in that sideboard over there, would you?'

Ginny did as she was asked, placing her mug on the coffee table, and moved over to the sideboard.

'That's it, in the cupboard to the left there's a blue box. Could you bring it here?'

Ginny opened the cupboard door and slid out the box before taking it across the room to Pat.

'Thank you. Here, look, I've kept every one of Darryl's articles he's had published. Of course, there are lots of boxes stashed away in there, but it's this one I want to show you.' He opened the box and flicked through the newspaper clippings. 'Ah, yes, here it is.' He picked up an article and held it out to Ginny. 'You read that one. It's the one he won the award for.'

Ginny carefully took the clipping.

'Here, take the box, have a little look through if you want.'

Sitting back down on the sofa, Ginny placed the box on her lap and began to read the piece in her hand. It was an account of an interview with the then prime minister. The wording was clever, concise, full of emotion. Laying it on the coffee table in front of her, she picked up another clipping, another interview, this time with the head of a rainforest conservation charity. Another interview. Interview after interview, all cutting-edge journalism, all beautifully written.

'He was really successful back in London, wasn't he?'

'Yes, that's my boy. He was.' Pat nodded sadly. 'I just think where he could be now if he'd carried on climbing the career ladder, if he hadn't felt duty-bound to return home to look after me.'

Replacing the articles, Ginny closed the lid. 'He talks so highly of you. He's happy to be able to help you.'

'Yes, well, it doesn't make me feel any better.' He shook his head. 'To think what he had going for him in London and now he's writing about goldfish that can count and reports of painting fake zebra crossings on the road for the ducks.'

Ginny nodded. That was Jason's fault. Ultimately her fault.

'And now I'm much better, he still won't move back. I worry he's given up on his career, using me as an excuse not to put his head above the water again, so to speak.'

'I'm sure he doesn't think that way.'

'Whether he thinks it or not, it's me that's killed his career.' Slumping back against the cushions, Pat made a deep exhale.

'It's not. It's Darryl's choice.' The words sounded empty even to Ginny's ears.

'Anyway, enough of me bringing the mood down, Darryl tells me you're organising a big event at the dogs' home for the weekend?'

30

With the large storage container pulled down from the shelf in the dogs' washroom, Ginny kneeled beside it and began rooting through the contents: a box of oversized foam dominoes, garden chess and a large game of Four-in-a-Row. All good. All could be left out in the paddock near the food stalls, but they weren't what she was looking for.

Standing up, she pushed the container to the side of the room and pulled down another storage box. She stumbled back, corrected her footing and lowered it to the floor. This one was heavier, more promising. Lifting off the lid, she grinned. Yes, just as she remembered, perfectly folded fabric banners, each with photographs of previous dogs they'd found homes for, their tongues lolling as they gazed up happily.

She pushed her hand to the bottom of the container. Perfect. Here was the bunting they'd used last year and the year before that too. Now, what else was in here?

Ginny looked up as Flora came in.

'Did you find the bunting, lovely?'

'Yes, and even better I found these too.' She unfolded a

banner and held it up. 'Look, it's Bobby, the little Jack Russell rescued after getting stuck in a badger's set. Do you remember him? The lovely couple from Looe adopted him.'

'Of course I remember him.' Flora came to join Ginny on the floor. 'He'd come to us with cigarette burns and cuts, bless him. Timid little thing until you got to know him.'

'Yes, that was him. I wonder how he's doing now?'

'We had a Christmas card from his new family, didn't we?'

'Oh yes. That's right.' Ginny folded the banner up again. 'I thought I might fasten these to the paddock fences for Saturday.'

'Good idea.' Flora rubbed at her temples.

Clipping the lid of the container in place, Ginny frowned. 'Are you okay? You look as though something's bothering you?'

'We've had another call about the illegal puppy farm. Do you remember? The one operating out of a derelict factory on the industrial estate in Trestow?'

'I remember. It can't just be a rumour then. Not if we've had another call.'

'That's what I'm afraid of. It's all been reported, and the police have driven by again but still haven't found anything as yet.'

'How come they still haven't found anything?'

'I'm not sure. There's talk of it being a small operation and of them moving the dogs around to avoid being discovered.' Flora shook her head. 'All we can do is hope the allegations are false, or if they're not, and I'm now thinking they're not, that the location is found soon.'

'I guess so.' Ginny nodded.

Flora tapped the lid of the box. 'These are good. I've got a good feeling about Saturday.'

'I'm keeping my fingers crossed.'

'It'll all be fine, just you wait and see.' Flora patted Ginny's hand.

As they stood up, Ginny brushed down her jeans before unclipping the lid again and pulling out the banners. She might as well get them up while she had the spare time.

* * *

'Hi,' Darryl said. 'Flora said you'd be up here.'

Turning around, Ginny searched his face. Had his dad told him that they'd spoken yesterday? Did he know that she'd found out about his big award? His old life? 'Darryl, I wasn't expecting you.'

'Yes, well, I thought I'd bring you some lunch.' He held up a paper bag. 'Cheese and onion pasties straight from Elsie's bakery.'

'You're kidding?' She finished fastening the banner she was working on to the fence and turned around. He didn't know, did he? He'd kept it quiet for a reason.

'Nope, not kidding. She threw in a couple of chocolate chip shortbreads too when I said I was bringing them up here.'

Ginny picked up the remaining banners and draped them over the wooden fence. 'Shall we eat them up here?' They'd have less chance of being interrupted than they would if they ate in the kitchen, and she wanted to speak to him properly. She needed to find out why he hadn't mentioned the award, hadn't explained how well he'd been doing careerwise in the city.

'Why not? It's the perfect day for a picnic.' Darryl walked across to a large log in the centre of the paddock and sat down. 'Those banners look brilliant. I take it they're for the Family Fun Day?'

'Yes, I wanted to get a head start.' Sitting beside him, Ginny took one of the pasties before looking at him. She hadn't seen him yesterday evening. It had been her turn for the late shift and after mulling everything she'd learned about his career over in her mind all night, she knew she really needed to hear his side of the story. 'I popped round to your house yesterday, did your dad tell you?'

'Yes, he did. He said you dropped off a toy for Luna. Thank you.'

'No problem.' She shifted position. 'We got talking about you actually.'

'Oh really? All good I hope?' Grimacing, he took a bite of the pasty, the pastry flaking down his shirt.

'Yes, all very good. He told me how proud of you he was and showed me his box of clippings.'

'Not the articles?'

'Yes. I saw your photo on the fridge too. The one of you collecting your award.'

'Ha ha, I was pulling such a face in that photo. What with all the bright lights on the stage, I couldn't see two feet in front of me.'

'Why didn't you tell me you'd won that award?' There must have been a reason. Was it so she wouldn't encourage him to return to London?

'I didn't think it was important. It's not a big deal.'

'Not a big deal? You won one of the most prestigious awards in the journalism world. Of course it's a big deal.' It was a huge deal.

'I wouldn't go that far.' Darryl held out the paper bag. 'Do you want your shortbread now?'

Shaking her head, Ginny took a deep breath. 'Why aren't you moving back to London to continue with your career? Your dad said he's able to cope on his own now.'

Lowering his shortbread, Darryl glanced at her before

looking into the distance. 'Why would I want to go back to London?'

'Because you used to write cutting edge stuff and now, you're—'

'Writing about what would inspire two perfectly normal, professional people to transform their house into a cave?' He chuckled.

'Well, yes.' Ginny took his hand. 'I'm being serious, Darryl. You applied for those jobs; maybe you should follow them up.'

Looking at their intertwined hands, Darryl frowned. 'Are you trying to get rid of me?'

'What? No, of course not. You know how I feel about you and that's why I'm saying it. I think you should go back to London.'

Sighing, Darryl turned to face her. 'There's nothing I want more than to stay here, in West Par with you, my dad and now Luna. I like my life here.'

Her? She was one of the reasons he wasn't going back? One of the reasons he was giving up on his career. No, that wasn't what she wanted. She didn't want to hold him back. They'd only just started seeing each other, who knew how long it would last, but even if it did, even if they stayed together, she wouldn't want to be the reason, or even one of many reasons, why he was sacrificing his career. She couldn't be. She wouldn't be. 'But you could have everything you ever wanted in London. You could have your amazing career back.'

'I've got everything I want here. And more.'

Ginny sighed. 'I don't want to hold you back. I don't want you to resent me for holding you back.'

'Ginny, look at me. I'm a grown man, I can make my own decisions, and this is where I want to be. Yes, the job might not be the best and I might have an impossibly arrogant boss, but it's convenient.'

'No, you're not thinking it through. Not properly.' She shifted on the log.

'I've never been surer of anything in my life.' Darryl grinned before eating the rest of his shortbread. 'Are we still on for go-karting with Susan and Malcolm this evening?'

Ginny nodded. This wouldn't be the end of the conversation. She wasn't going to be the reason anyone ruined their career chances.

'Great.'

31

'Right, the gloves are off this time.' Darryl grinned. 'Prepare to lose!'

'Ha ha, you just keep telling yourself that.' Laughing, Ginny held up the medal she'd won from the previous race, her face dropping as she remembered the award Darryl had won for his journalism. They hadn't mentioned it since she'd confronted him about it earlier but it was there, like a dark cloud hanging between them. Them both knowing it needed to be discussed, neither of them wanting to bring it up.

'You must have been go-karting before, Ginny, have you?' Malcolm pulled his helmet back on.

'Nope, it's my first time. I must just be a natural.' Ginny flicked her hair over her shoulder and grinned. She needed to put it out of her mind: Darryl's career, his award, the job applications. Just for now. She needed to enjoy the time she had with him because as much as it would hurt to see him leave, it would crush her knowing that one of the reasons he stayed was because of her. Particularly with so many other questions hanging over their relationship.

'It must be all the practice you've had on Percy's ride-on mower.' Susan smiled.

'Yes, it must be, but don't let on to Percy that I use it. He'd be devastated if he knew I've been taking away his mowing time.' She took a quick sip of her lemonade. Two races down, Malcolm and Ginny drawing first place with Darryl second and three more races around the track left.

'I tell you what.' Darryl leaned in closer. 'Let me win this game and I won't tell Percy your secret.'

'Ooh you wouldn't.' Susan laughed.

'Ha ha, nice try but I don't bow down to threats.' Laughing too, Ginny pecked Darryl on the lips before pulling her helmet back on. She couldn't let herself be drawn any more into this relationship. She couldn't be hurt again. 'Let's go.'

'Hold on.' Darryl stepped towards her and tightened her strap before putting on his own helmet. 'As much as I promise I'm going to win, I want you to be around to watch me gloat.'

'You're such a gentleman.'

'Why thank you.' He kissed his index finger and then pressed it against her nose.

'To your karts!' The instructor blew his whistle.

'Oops.' Chuckling, Darryl took her hand and led the way from under the terrace to the track.

'Come on or neither of us will stand a chance of winning.'

Getting in her kart, Ginny looked across at Darryl next to her. The problem was he might be being honest about not wanting those jobs in London now but how could he predict how he'd feel in six months' time, a year's time, ten years' time if they were still together and he'd given up his career for her? He couldn't tell her, hand on his heart, that he definitely wouldn't feel resentment. Or worse, what if he left it too long to get back to his career but they broke up? He'd definitely resent her then and she'd feel guilty too.

'Three, two, one.' The whistle blew.

There were so many ifs, so many uncertainties... Was it even the right time for Darryl to make such a big decision? He must have been planning to move back to London before he met her, or he wouldn't have applied for those jobs.

She shook her head. She'd have to speak to him again later.

Blinking, Ginny looked around her. She'd been so wrapped up in her own thoughts that she hadn't realised the race had already started. Pushing the accelerator flat to the floor, she released the brake, and the kart sprang to life. She sped forward, though she was a whole half-lap behind Darryl and Malcolm, and a quarter of a lap behind Susan.

Taking the corner wide, she passed by Susan before building up speed on the straight run. Darryl and Malcolm were just ahead of her now. Pumping the brake, she powered around the next corner and sped up, weaving around Malcolm with ease. She could sense Darryl to her right, the finishing line mere metres in front.

Ginny hit her accelerator just as Darryl was drawing close to victory. With his guard down, he began to slow and Ginny took the opportunity, taking the lead. After crossing the line, she looked across to Darryl who held his thumbs up to her, the hint of a grin barely visible above the chin of his helmet.

* * *

'I can't believe you won three games out of five! Especially as you've never raced before.' Susan leaned forward from the back seat of Darryl's car and patted Ginny on the shoulder.

'Ha ha. Nor can I, but I did.' She held up the small plastic trophy and certificate as evidence.

'You were scarily fast. The way you undertook me on the last corner of the last race...' Darryl whistled and shook his head '... you were fearless.'

'Yes, you're a deserving winner.' Malcolm cheered from where he was sitting next to Susan.

'Thank you.' Ginny looked down at the trophy. 'This is actually the first thing I've won in my entire life.'

'No, you must have won something before?' Susan said.

'Nope nothing.'

'Not a bar of chocolate for a colouring competition or a certificate for having the highest attendance at school?' Darryl glanced at her from the driver's seat. 'I can imagine you getting one hundred per cent attendance.'

'Really? No, I hated school. If I could have won anything it would have been for being able to make up the most excuses for skipping my lessons, not to mention being a first-rate signature fraud.' Ginny laughed.

'Oh, you signed your sick notes yourself?' Darryl chuckled.

'Yep, wrote them, signed them, even stuck them in an envelope.' She tucked her certificate in the car door pocket and leaned her head back against the headrest. 'I don't know about you three but I'm sure looking forward to this meal.'

'Oh, me too.' Malcolm rubbed his stomach.

'What was the name of the instructor again? My dad used to take me and my sister there every month when we were teenagers and I'm sure I recognised him.' Darryl turned into the pub car park and pulled into a space.

'Was it Mike Green?' Malcolm asked as he opened the door.

'I thought it was Mick, not Mike?' Susan yawned. 'Excuse me, those races must have tired me out.'

'I can't remember, to be honest. Hold on, I'll check on my

certificate.' She grabbed it from the door pocket but as she looked down, Ginny realised she'd picked something else up by mistake. Just as she was about to put it back, some of the text caught her eye – the word 'congratulations'. It was a letter, addressed to Darryl. She knew she shouldn't but her curiosity took over and she scanned the contents. It confirmed what she'd guessed; he'd been offered a job as an editor-in-chief in London.

Editor-in-chief.

Swallowing, she pushed the letter back down and pulled out the certificate again. Anything to give her enough time to control her emotions before returning to the group.

'Did you check?' Susan glanced at her.

'Yes, it was Mick Green.'

'You were right, Mick Green.' Linking arms with Susan, Malcolm led the way into the pub.

'What do you fancy tonight?' Darryl asked. 'They make a mean moussaka here. Me and my dad used to come here when I visited from London.' He wrapped his arm around her shoulders and gave her a squeeze. 'And the chocolate cake was always amazing. Especially with cream.'

'Sounds nice.'

Why hadn't he told her about the job offer?

'It really is.' Holding the door open, Darryl let Ginny walk through first.

'Is this table okay?' Susan pointed to one by the window.

'Perfect.'

Sat down, Ginny tried to focus on the menu Malcolm had passed to her but she couldn't. Had Darryl not told her because he'd chosen not to take it? But even if that were the case, how had he got so far into the process to be being offered jobs? When had the interview been? Had he been to an interview while they were together? And even if it was before, he hadn't mentioned it. Not in all this time they'd be talking about his decision to stay... Why hadn't he told her? Did that mean he *did* still want to move to London? Or at least had a week or two ago?

'You okay?' Darryl rubbed her arm, putting his menu down.

'Yes, fine.' She tried to force a smile.

'That's your phone, Malcolm.' Susan tapped his arm as a shrill ringtone pierced through the hubbub of the pub.

'Sorry, I'll just get this.' He stood up, walked a few steps away but very quickly returned looking apologetic.

'Is everything all right?' Susan asked.

'No, I'm going to have to leave. I'm terribly sorry but my daughter's guinea pig needs to be taken to the vets' and her mum has to go to work.'

'Come on, let's go.' Susan stood up. 'Sorry, you two. You should stay though. Enjoy your meal.'

'Yes, apologies,' Malcolm said, holding up his hand.

'Hold on, I'll give you a lift.' Darryl pulled his car keys from his pocket.

'No, no. We're only a fifteen-minute walk from West Par. We'll get Susan's car from there.'

'Are you sure?'

'Yes, thank you though.'

After Susan and Malcolm had left, Darryl frowned. 'I feel bad not giving them a lift.'

Ginny shrugged. 'You offered. They'll be fine.'

'Yes, you're right.' Darryl turned to look at her and smiled.

Looking down at her menu, she tried to focus as the words swam in front of her eyes. Should she bring it up or see if he tells her about the offer. She pulled her chair closer to the table.

'What are you going for? Have you decided yet?' Darryl scanned his menu before closing it.

Ginny shook her head. She didn't trust herself to answer, to not mention that she'd spotted the letter.

'Ginny?'

The concern in Darryl's voice made her look up.

'Is everything okay?' He rearranged the cardboard coasters on the table, placing one in front of Ginny and one in front of himself.

'Why wouldn't it be?' She folded the menu, flattening the creases.

'I don't know. You were really happy on the way here, but now you seem different. Have I done anything to upset you?'

Ginny took a slow breath in. Should she speak to him, ask him about the job offer now?

'I put my certificate in the passenger side door, but when I went to grab it again, I accidentally pulled something else out.'

'Oh, sorry, I've been meaning to clear the car out, I've got rubbish everywhere.' He grimaced.

'It wasn't rubbish. It was a job offer.' Her words were quiet, her tone low.

'Job offer?' Darryl slumped against the back of the bench. 'Oh, that.'

'Yes, *that*.' Ginny looked at him. 'Why didn't you tell me you'd been offered a job?'

'I didn't really think anything of it, to be honest. It came a couple of days ago and I'd already decided I wasn't going to take it.'

'Have you declined it then?'

Leaning forward, Darryl rubbed the back of his neck. 'Not yet. I've not got around to it.'

'Right.'

He'd not got around to it, of course he hadn't. And if the letter only arrived a couple of days ago, the interview must have been recent.

'When was the interview?'

Darryl picked up the menu and tapped it against the surface of the table. 'Last week.'

'Last week?' Ginny swallowed.

'Yes, but it's not as it seems. I arranged the interview weeks ago, before you and me were really a thing...'

'Yes, but last week? You went for the interview last week?'

How hadn't she noticed? They'd been spending every spare moment together – or so she'd thought.

'When?'

'It was during the day, a video interview online. I would have told you, but I knew I probably wouldn't want to take it anyway.'

'Then why did you do it? If you didn't want the job, why take the interview?' She watched as a waiter walked towards them.

'Are you ready to order?' His pen poised above his notepad, the waiter looked from Ginny to Darryl and back again.

'No, we won't be ordering tonight. Thank you.' She placed her menu back in the holder at the edge of the table.

'We won't?'

'No. Darryl, you told me you didn't want to move to London, you said you were happy here, and yet you took an interview for a job last week?'

It didn't make any sense. As much as it had hurt her, she'd tried to encourage him to jump back on the career ladder, to return to London and he'd assured her he didn't want to. But now... Now, she didn't know what to think. She couldn't think. She was more confused than ever.

'Okay, cards on the table so to speak,' Darryl said, mimicking the idea with his hands, palms down on the tablecloth. 'I did the interview because it was at the paper I'd always aspired to work at, my dream job. I know it sounds daft, but I wanted to see if I could get it.'

'Well, you did.'

'Yes, I know, but I didn't do the interview because I wanted to accept the job. I just wanted to see if I could get it. If I was good enough.'

'But if it's your dream job, maybe you should take it. Maybe you should think about it.'

'Why? I thought things were going well between us? It's here I want to be. It's you I want to be with.'

Ginny looked at him sitting there, his eyes focused on his hands. She knew what she needed to do. She knew she was the one standing in his way. She knew he wouldn't leave West Par, wouldn't put his career choices ahead of them.

Slowly, she stood up. She needed to do this now before she had the chance to back out. 'I'm sorry, Darryl, but this isn't going anywhere.'

'What?' Turning to look at her, he frowned, a deep crease forming between his eyebrows. 'Ginny, please, Ginny, don't. Don't do this.'

'I already have.' Leaning down, she cupped her hands around his cheeks and kissed him firmly on the lips. 'I'm sorry.'

'No, don't.'

She could hear his voice cracking, but she kept her eyes focused on the floor in front of her, on the door, on the tarmac outside.

'Wait, at least let me give you a lift. Don't walk.'

'I'll be fine.'

'Ginny, please. It's dark. Let me at least give you a lift home.'

She stopped, standing still, but she kept her back to him. If she looked in his eyes, she knew she'd cave, she knew she'd run back into his arms. But she couldn't. She saw that now.

'No.' Her voice was firm, final.

32

Pulling the duvet back over her head, Ginny closed her eyes, the beeping from her alarm snoozed once more. She wasn't sure how many times she'd pressed the button. She hadn't been counting, but judging by the sunlight streaming through her curtains, she knew it was late.

Closing her eyes, she tried to push all thoughts away of Darryl, the job offer and what might have been. She'd done the right thing. She had. The image of his face – shocked, hurt, disappointed – tugged at the edge of her mind, always there, always preventing sleep.

It was no good. What was the point in lying there for another hour, another two hours, longer, without sleeping? That's all she'd done since walking through the door last night. She'd slipped into bed, curled her legs up, still in her jeans. She hadn't changed, she wasn't even sure if she'd locked the front door behind her.

Slowly, she peeled off the duvet, scrunching it up at the bottom of her bed with her feet. Without looking at the alarm clock, she forced herself to change out of last night's clothes, she forced herself to go through the motions. Picking up her mobile, she bit down on her bottom lip as she saw how many messages were stacked up from Darryl, how many missed calls – also from Darryl, but also Flora, Susan and Alex. She placed the phone on her bedside table again, next to the equally redundant alarm clock, and left the room.

* * *

Looking down into her coffee mug, Ginny let the voices outside the kitchen door waft over her head. She knew it was Susan and Flora and she knew they were talking about her. Susan had been standing at the counter when Ginny had walked in. Ginny had heard her ask her what was wrong, she'd heard the concern in her voice, but she hadn't been able to answer. She hadn't been able to form the words. Darryl was gone. She'd released him. He was probably already on his way to London. And that was fine. It was what she wanted.

She wanted, *needed*, him to be happy.

'Ginny, lovely. Can I come and sit with you?'

She felt Flora's hand on her shoulder, heard the chair next to her scrape against the floor tiles as she sat down. She listened to Flora's breath as she sat there, patiently, waiting for Ginny to speak.

Closing her eyes, Ginny took a deep, shuddering breath. 'Sorry, I was late.'

'Oh, Ginny. No one's worried that you're late. We're worried about *you*.'

Nodding, Ginny clasped her hands on the table in front of her. She wasn't even sure if she could squeeze the words out, admit them. Did she want to?

'I finished things with Darryl.'

'Oh, right. Can I ask you why?'

Ginny scratched at her index finger with her thumb. 'He got offered a job in London. His dream job.'

'Okay. But I thought he told you he wanted to stay here in West Par? I thought you said he didn't want to go to London?' Flora's voice was quiet, but Ginny could hear the confusion.

'He said he did, but he didn't.'

'Are you sure?' Flora placed her hand on her forearm.

'Yes, I'm sure.' Turning, Ginny buried her face against Flora's shoulder and Flora pulled her closer, hugging her tightly.

'Why don't you go home and try to get some rest?'

Shaking her head, Ginny drew in a long shuddering breath. 'No, I want to be here. I need to look through those plans Sally dropped off for the taster training sessions.'

'Okay, well, if you change your mind, just go home.' Standing up, Flora rubbed Ginny's shoulder one last time before leaving the kitchen and closing the door behind her.

Ginny pulled the green folder Sally had dropped round yesterday and began flicking through the pages. She'd included detailed plan after detailed plan, lists of equipment, risk assessments. Everything. Flora had done the right thing in choosing Sally. Their dogs would be in good hands with her.

Turning to a fresh page in her notebook, Ginny began to write in the timings Sally had specified for each session. She'd need to know them; she'd need to give them to Flora to announce over the tannoy. This was what she needed. She needed to feel needed. She needed to work.

She picked up her coffee mug, took a sip and spat out the cold bitter liquid.

A sharp tap on the kitchen door pulled her from her thoughts and she looked up just as, of all people, Jason sauntered in.

Leaning back in her chair, Ginny peered out into the reception area. There was no sign of Flora or Susan.

'I'm so sorry to hear your news.' He leaned against the table and stared at her. 'You can't tell me I didn't try to warn you though.'

Ginny tried to focus on the words in front of her.

'You're better off without him.' Jason shifted position, the table budging a little as he moved.

Laying her pen down, she looked up at him, her eyes narrowing. 'Please leave.'

'I will. I just wanted to offer you my condolences and see how you were.'

She couldn't do this. She couldn't deal with him. Not right now. Pushing her chair back, she picked up her notebook and Sally's folder, and walked out of the kitchen.

'Hold up. Wait for me.'

She could feel his presence behind her as she made her way towards the door leading to the kennels. Pulling it open, she stepped through before closing it firmly behind her. When she'd reached halfway down the corridor, she sank to the floor, and hugged her knees to her chest, letting the notebook and folder fall to the floor next to her.

Jason wouldn't follow her. He wouldn't come in. She knew that. If there was one thing he detested more than being ignored, it was dogs. Especially dogs who barked, dogs he didn't know and dogs who didn't know him.

Leaning her head back against the cold wall, she closed her eyes.

* * *

When she opened her eyes again, she saw Ralph, across the corridor in the kennel in front of her, staring back at her, his eyes wide, his mouth drooped. She rubbed her eyes; she must have fallen asleep. She could hear muffled voices from the reception area. That was what had woken her up; she remembered voices penetrating her distorted dreams. They must have been real.

She tilted her head, listening. Flora was talking, someone was responding. She couldn't work out what was being said but she recognised the other voice. It was Darryl. What was he doing here?

She closed her eyes again, waiting, willing for him to leave, unsure how long she could stay sitting on the cold concrete floor without wanting to rush through to him, tell him she'd made a terrible mistake – the worst mistake.

It felt as though hours had passed before she heard the familiar click of the reception door as it shut. She counted to one hundred before pushing herself to standing, picking up the notebook and folder and walking into the reception area.

'Ginny, lovely. There you are! I thought you'd gone home. Darryl was here asking after you.' Flora moved out from behind the counter, pulled open the door and searched the courtyard for him but came back in and shook her head. 'He must have gone. I'll give him a call, tell him you're here.'

'No, please don't. This is for the best.' Ginny put the notebook and folder on the counter.

'Look at you, Ginny. You're miserable. *He's* miserable. How can this possibly be in anyone's best interests?'

'Please, Flora. Please don't ring him. He needs to move on with his life.'

'He doesn't want to go to London. He just said so himself. He told me.' Flora shook her head.

'He does. Really, he does, he just thinks he doesn't.' Ginny slumped her elbows on the counter and rested her head in her hands. 'He needs this. I need this. I can't encourage him to stay and have him resent me. Please.'

'I don't agree with you, not for one second, Ginny. He's a grown man and he's more than capable of making his own choices in life.'

'But you won't ring him?'

'Of course I won't. Not if you don't want me to, but I think you should.'

'I know.' Ginny straightened her back, a sharp headache stabbing her forehead. 'Do you mind if I go home?'

Flora sighed. 'No, of course not, lovely. Go and get some sleep and then maybe you'll be able to think more clearly.'

33

'That's it, Ginny. Just a little to the left. Perfect.' Percy brushed his hands together and tilted his head. 'Yes, I think that's about right, don't you?'

Ginny looked at the stall in front of her, the deep red painted wood and the cream canopy overhead to protect the seller from the summer sun. 'Yes, I think that's in the best spot.'

With her hands on her hips, she looked around the bottom paddock. Stalls surrounded a central fenced-off pen area which Sally would use for the training exercises. She nodded. It was all coming together now, taking shape.

'Now only the top paddock to do.' Percy nodded.

Ginny stretched her arms above her head, leaning to one side and then to the other.

'Do you need a rest?'

'No, I'll be fine. I'm just tired, that's all,' she said.

'Ah, yes. Flora did mention your falling out with Darryl.' He held his hands up. 'She wasn't gossiping, mind. Just chatting over her worries to a friend.'

'Don't worry, I know she wouldn't gossip.'

'May I say something about the matter?' He pulled the front leg of the stall nearest to them out a little.

'Yes, if you want.'

She'd had Susan and Alex tell her in no uncertain terms that she was pushing Darryl away, so she might as well listen to Percy's opinion on the matter too.

Clearing his throat, Percy looked at her. 'Now, obviously take this as what it is, ramblings from an old man who's not been in a relationship for a couple of decades, but I'll say it anyway, just in case you can take something from it.'

'Okay.' The only reason he hadn't been in a relationship for a couple of decades was because he refused to confess to Flora how he felt about her.

'Right. Well, love doesn't come along very often, not true love, when you get that aching in your heart when you're apart from them. Maybe once, sometimes twice, in a lifetime. More often than not one person may feel love towards another and for whatever reason the other person doesn't reciprocate those feelings, or else may never know how the other feels for them. And that's fine, there are many circumstances that might cause that to be the case; one may believe that by not expressing their love to the other they're protecting them – maybe they feel they're letting them choose the career path they want which takes them away, for example. Like you're feeling with Darryl, but with you and Darryl it's different. You are both aware of each other's feelings for one another. You're in love, not just you loving him. And when that happens, when both parties are in love with one another, breaking up for a reason should be a joint decision.'

Ginny frowned. She hadn't said she was in love. Was she? Was that why she felt like this?

'Now, I don't mean if one person falls out of love with the other, or if the relationship, for whatever reason, is not in the best interests for both of them. No, I mean if it's a good meaningful relationship, just as yours and Darryl's was. Then breaking up should be a joint decision. You've made the choice for Darryl and that's not fair on him.'

Ginny leaned against the fence and rubbed at her eyes. 'But I broke up with him for his own good. He had such an amazing career before he came here to look after his dad, interviews with some of the most influential people in the world, award ceremonies. And now his dad is better, he should be going back to that life. I can't make him stay here. I'd be selfish if I did.'

'Hey, I understand why you did it. And it's coming from the right place.' Percy patted her shoulder. 'But shouldn't it be his decision too?'

'Yes, but no, he was ready to give it all up to live here.'

'Didn't you have a good career before you moved here? You lived in London too, no? Surrounded by opportunity and paths to success?'

'Yes, I did but—'

'But you decided to move down here because it was what you wanted, right?'

'Yes.'

Percy nodded. 'Well then. Think about whose decision it is for Darryl to stay put or to leave.'

Looking down, Ginny pinched the bridge of her nose. She understood what Percy was saying, but her and Darryl's situation was different.

Wasn't it?

She looked up. 'When you spoke about loving someone else but not telling them, you were referring to yourself, weren't you?'

Looking into the distance, Percy shook his head. 'This is about you and Darryl. Think on it, at least.'

Ginny nodded slowly.

At that moment, Flora pushed the gate to the paddock open, bringing their conversation to a stop.

'Right, you two, I've brought you up some lunch – a flask of tea and some sandwiches.' She paused, looking around. 'Wow, this is looking great.'

Percy smiled at her. 'Thank you, love.'

'You're welcome.' Flora rubbed his forearm. 'Right, I'll leave you to it and get back.'

'Thanks, Flora.' Ginny nodded to the tray of food.

'No worries. It's nice to see you out enjoying the sunshine again.' She frowned. 'Did you get my message earlier?'

'No, sorry, I've not got my phone on me. The battery died and I didn't have time to charge it.' Ginny swallowed. It was true the battery had run out but there were chargers here. She just needed a break from the messages and calls.

'Okay, lovely. I just sent you a message to say that Sally was pleased you liked her plans for tomorrow.' Flora closed the gate behind her.

'Thanks for letting me know.' Turning back to Percy, she raised an eyebrow.

He shook his head and looked towards the end of the paddock. 'This conversation is about you and Darryl.'

'Of course.'

* * *

Rubbing her shoulder, Ginny pulled the stool up to the counter. She must have pulled a muscle when she'd been lifting the stalls. Taking a sip of coffee, she looked outside. The sun was setting, an orange glow hanging over the courtyard.

'Now, are you sure you're up to doing the late shift? I can stay instead, or I can stay with you.' Flora laid her handbag on the counter.

'No, I'm fine. Aren't you trying out Percy's bridge club this evening?'

'Yes, but I can easily cancel. They have other new players joining tonight anyway. Patrick—'

Flora fell silent.

'It's okay. I know you're all going round Pat's to play today. It's his first game too, isn't it?' Ginny picked up a pen from the counter and popped it in the pencil pot.

'Yes. Yes, it is.'

'Well, have fun.' She smiled.

'Are you sure you'll be okay?' Flora laid her hand on Ginny's forearm.

'I'll be absolutely fine.'

'Okay, well, I'll pop back after the club finishes, it should only be on for a couple of hours.'

'You don't need to.'

'I'd feel better if I did.'

Ginny watched Flora leave. She'd be fine. The late shift was normally quite peaceful anyway. She'd check her list of things left to do before the Family Fun Day tomorrow and then she'd take the dogs out before shutting up for the night.

Pulling her notebook towards her, she stared at the list she'd made and rubbed her eyes. She hadn't slept properly since splitting up with Darryl. In fact, the best sleep she'd had since was probably when she'd fallen asleep by the kennels when she'd been hiding from Jason.

Yawning, she tried to push Percy's words out of her mind. They had been all she'd been able to focus on since they'd had that conversation. It wasn't the same though; she was doing this for Darryl, she was only making the decision for them both because he wouldn't. She needed to.

The familiar ringtone of the landline filled the room and Ginny rummaged through the paperwork to find it. 'Hello?'

A muffled voice.

'Sorry, I didn't catch that. This is Wagging Tails Dogs Home; can I help you?'

'... farm... dogs... breeding. Old shoe factory...'

'What? Can you say it again please? It's a really bad connection.' She looked down at the phone as the buzz signalling the call had ended reached her ear.

She scribbled 'shoe factory' and 'breeding' on a Post-it note and circled it. Flora had said there were suspicions a puppy farm was operating somewhere on the industrial estate, but which one? Flora had said Trestow, she was sure of it. Reaching to her back pocket for her mobile, Ginny sighed. Of course, her phone was at home.

She turned to the laptop and typed in 'old shoe factory, Trestow'.

Bingo! The screen filled with results. It was on Green Acre Industrial Estate. She knew where that was. Picking up the home's van keys, she took one last glance around the reception area and then locked up and left.

* * *

Pulling the van up at the end of the road leading to the old shoe factory, Ginny thought through her options. She'd just find the illegal puppy farm and ring the police. At least that way, they'd know exactly where it was and, with the help of the police, she could get the dogs to safety tonight.

She turned the engine off, and after climbing out and clicking the van locked, she made her way towards the factory. She'd expected the industrial estate to be busier than it was, especially with all the haulage companies working out of there, but the shoe factory was down a side road with only a disused warehouse opposite.

There it was. Right up ahead. Trestow Shoes Ltd. She walked around the wire fence of the perimeter. The wire had been cut in numerous places, the thin metal pulled back. She shrugged. At least she'd be able to get in easy enough. Ducking down, she slipped through one of the gaps before running towards the building. As she neared, she noticed most of the windows had been broken, probably smashed by youths throwing rocks or similar.

She froze as she heard a noise to the left. Voices. She ran behind an old wheelie bin and leaned against it, trying to steady her breathing. She didn't dare look out to see who was talking, but before long she could hear laughter and the sound of the wire fence shaking as whoever it was left.

After waiting for a few minutes, she stepped out hesitantly and ran across to where the people had come from. Trying the door, she grinned as it opened easily. She'd still have to be careful in case there was anyone else in there, but she felt better knowing at least two people had left the premises.

After closing the door behind her, she rummaged in her pocket for her house keys and turned on the small keyring torch she'd got in a cracker last year.

She was in a corridor, a long corridor, with at least five doors coming off of it. She made her way over to the first door and leaned her ear against it. Nothing. As she walked deeper into the factory, she listened at each door, before finally pausing again in front of the last one. She was sure she'd heard something. Yes, there it was again, a high-pitched whine. She'd found them; she'd found the puppy farm.

Reaching into her back pocket, she closed her eyes. Her phone was at home, she remembered. She couldn't ring the police.

Holding her breath, she listened again. All she could hear was whining. No other movement. Nothing to suggest any more people were inside.

Taking a deep breath, she slowly pulled the handle down and inched the door open. Yes, she was alone. The people she'd heard leaving must have been the only ones. Slipping through the door, she paused. A fluorescent overhead light had been rigged up, illuminating three dog crates, and coming from them, the sound of dog cries.

As she walked across to them, she spoke quietly as the whining increased. 'It's okay. I'm not going to hurt you. I'm here to take you somewhere else, somewhere safe.'

Kneeling beside the first crate, she took a deep breath in. Before her was a young English bulldog, crouched in the far side of the crate, as far away from Ginny as possible.

'It's okay.' She glanced around and spotted a roll of electrical wire, probably what had been used to rig the light up. She cut a length off with a Stanley knife which was helpfully lying next to it and went back to the crate. 'I'm going to open this now and pop this through your collar. I'm not going to hurt you.'

The young bulldog backed away and began baring its teeth.

Reaching into her pocket, Ginny's fingers grasped on to something and she grinned. She may have left her phone but one thing she never walked out of the house without was a bag of dog treats. She took one, held out her hand and watched as the young dog inched forward. As it took the treat, Ginny looped the electrical wire through its collar in one quick motion. 'Well done, come on out and there'll be plenty more where that came from.'

Holding out another treat to lure it closer, Ginny scooped up the dog, thankful that the promise of treats seemed to be working.

'Come on, let's go and see who else we have.'

In the next crate, a similarly aged toy poodle sat shaking in the corner. Ginny could see how swollen her belly was even without having to open the crate. She shook her head. The poor dog was too young to breed. Both of them were. Again, she used treats to lure the dog into trusting her.

Ginny kneeled down at the final crate. This one was bigger. A golden retriever was clawing at the metal bars.

'Hello, beautiful. It's your turn now. Come on out.'

Just as she slipped the electrical wire through the dog's collar, a loud bang sounded from outside the room. Ginny froze. They were back. The bang must have been the outside door. The sound of laughter and chattering became louder and louder as they neared the room.

'No!'

Gently pulling the heavily pregnant golden retriever from the crate, Ginny looked around the room.

Please be another door. Or a window. Anything.

There was. There was a door in the far corner.

Ginny ran towards it, the three dogs at her heels. Sending up a silent hope, she turned the handle, and relief flooded through her when the door gave way.

Once the dogs were through, she closed the door behind her quietly before turning on her little torch again.

They were in another corridor. This one littered with rusting tools and bits of broken furniture. Not waiting for the people to realise the dogs were missing, she began leading the dogs through, weaving in and out of the remnants of a bustling factory.

She heard shouts coming from the room. They'd realised. She just had to hope they'd assume she'd gone back out the way they'd come in instead of following her this way. Glancing back, she checked the door was still closed. It was.

Picking up her speed, she ushered the dogs forward. In the dim light of the torch, she could just about make out another door ahead, a slither of pale light around the edges, promising the outside security lights on the other side. She shook her head. The irony of having security lighting but no system or plan for keeping people out didn't evade her.

She slowed as she passed an old desk, on which tools and old lamps were piled high. Squeezing past first, she tried to file the dogs through the small gap. But as the retriever passed, too big for the gap, she nudged the desk. Ginny darted her free hand out as the tools wobbled and teetered. She watched, frozen to the spot, as the pile fell to the floor. She barely registered the pain as something sliced through her arm as it fell.

A loud clatter filled the corridor and she held her breath. One, two, three. Just as she turned to carry on, the corridor was suddenly flooded with light.

'Oi, stop there.' A low gruff voice ricocheted through the old factory and Ginny propelled herself forward. She could hear two men behind her now, two men pushing their way through the debris in the corridor. Glass smashed onto the concrete floor, wood splintered, and metal bounced off walls. They were gaining on them.

She bit into her bottom lip and blood filled her mouth, though she barely noticed it. She was almost there. They were almost at the door now. Glancing behind her, she could see the men getting ever closer. Propelling herself forward, she flung herself at the door, her shoulder barging into the wood as it swung open.

They were outside now. The stark white of the security lighting illuminating them and the emptiness of the former car park. They wouldn't stand a chance. Even if by some miracle she was able to get the dogs through a hole in the fence, she was disorientated. She had no idea where she'd parked the van. They'd be caught long before she could even get her bearings.

'Get them!'

Despite her heart hammering in her ears, she could hear the men approaching. But distracted, she stumbled over some rubble and fell, shooting out her hands to save herself. On the floor, she gripped the makeshift leads in her hand and braced herself. It was over. It had to be.

Headlights swung across the car park and she heard a car horn beeping. Was it the police? No, she couldn't see any blue. Without wasting another second wondering who had driven by or why, she pushed herself to standing, regained her balance and continued running. As she neared the fence, she glanced behind her. They were gone. The men were no longer following her. The car must have scared them off.

* * *

As quietly as she could, Ginny loaded the dogs into the back of the van. She slipped into the driver's seat and finally felt as though she could take a breath. She looked down at her hands; she couldn't stop shaking.

Taking a deep breath, she gripped the steering wheel. Whoever had been in that car had saved them from being caught. Darting her hand out, she double-checked she'd locked the doors. She had, but she didn't want to hang around to find out to what lengths the men would go to in order to get the dogs back if they found them.

She started the engine and pulled away, and sped through the rabbit run of roads making up the industrial estate before joining the main road out of Trestow.

As she pulled out onto the narrow country road towards West Par, she began to feel as though the danger was behind them and slowed down to the speed limit. She just needed to focus on the road ahead and getting the three dogs to Wagging Tails. That's all she needed to do: focus.

Shocked out of her resolve, a loud beeping sounded from behind her. She looked in her wing mirror and was shocked to see who it was.

Darryl. It was his BMW.

Indicating, she pulled over and turned the engine off. Without thinking, she jumped out of the van and ran towards his car, ran towards him.

She could see him. He was walking towards her. And in the light of his headlights, she felt his arms envelop her, drawing her towards him. She nestled against his chest, the tears of shock and relief rolling down her cheeks and onto his shirt. Closing her eyes, she heard Flora's soft voice and felt her hug the both of them.

* * *

'That's the three of them settled in for the night. I'll take them to the vets' and get them checked over and their pregnancies dated in the morning.' Flora closed the kitchen door behind her before resting her hands on Ginny's shoulders. 'Do you want another blanket, lovely?'

Ginny shook her head. Next to her, Darryl clasped her hand.

'I think we need to clean up that cut on your arm now. Check it over. You might need stitches.' Scraping his chair back, Darryl pulled the first aid kit from the window ledge and sat back down next to her.

'I'll be okay.'

'You almost weren't,' Darryl said.

Looking at the table, Ginny closed her eyes. She knew that.

'Let Darryl take a look.' Flora lowered the blanket from Ginny's shoulders and hung it over the back of her chair before switching the kettle on.

Darryl gently held Ginny's arm and began to clean the gash. 'When I saw those men chasing you, I thought...' His voice cracked.

'You saw them?' Ginny frowned. 'It was you in the car?'

'Yes,' Flora said as she poured the kettle, filling up the three mugs. 'We saw them running back inside. We looped the factory a couple of times to make sure they didn't venture back out before we caught you up.'

'How did you know?' Ginny took the mug with her free arm, wrapping her hand around it, the heat warming her skin.

'Darryl insisted on coming back here to talk to you after bridge club and we spotted the Post-it note on the counter. We put two and two together.' Sitting down, Flora shook her head. 'Why? Why would you have gone there alone? And then to try to rescue the dogs by yourself? Why didn't you ring the police?'

'I'd left my phone at home.' Ginny took a sip of the drink, the overly sugary sweetness of the tea hitting the back of her throat.

'No wonder you haven't been getting my messages.' Darryl said, and Ginny winced as he began to apply butterfly stitches to the wound. 'I had assumed you were just ignoring me.'

She shifted in her chair. 'I kind of was. That was the reason I'd left my phone at home.'

'Oh, okay.' Darryl sighed. 'I think you need to go and get a tetanus injection. There could have been all sorts in that factory and if you don't know what you cut it on...' He shrugged.

'She had one last year, so she should be covered.' Flora rubbed Ginny's arm. 'Don't you ever *ever* do anything daft like that again, do you hear me?'

'Don't worry. I'm not in any hurry to do so.'

'Good, glad to hear it. We've had enough excitement for at least the next decade.' Flora pushed back her chair before kissing Ginny on the head. 'Right, I'm going to go and check on our newcomers. Get that sweet tea down yourself.'

Ginny nodded as she watched Flora close the kitchen door behind her. She looked at Darryl. 'Thank you for rescuing me.'

'Huh, you rescued yourself. We just gave those men something to think about.' He chuckled softly. 'You should have seen their faces. To say they were scared would be the understatement of the century.'

'We need to ring the police. Tell them where they can find the breeders.' Ginny straightened her back. 'They might have more puppy farms somewhere else.'

'It's done. The police arrested them just after we left. They're going to pop round tomorrow to collect our statements.'

'Right.' Ginny slumped back against the chair again. That was one good thing then.

'There you go. All done.' Darryl stood up and put the first aid kit away before pulling the blanket over Ginny's shoulders again.

Ginny clasped his hand, leaning her head to the side and resting it against his arm. 'I'm sorry.'

'Did you listen to any of the messages I left you?' His voice was quiet.

'No.' She shook her head. 'I knew I might cave if I did, which is why I left my phone at home.'

'Cave?'

'Ask you to forgive me.'

'Would that be such a bad idea?' He slipped into the seat beside her, not letting go of her hand.

'You've got that job offer.' Ginny turned his hand in hers, tracing the lines on his palm. 'Your dream job.'

'Yes, I got the job offer but I'm not going. I enjoy living here in West Par too much. Plus, even though my dad doesn't need me to care so much for him, I still want to be close.' He cleared his throat and looked at her. 'Besides, I've met someone. She's beautiful, funny, my perfect match.'

'Oh?'

'Yes, and she's a crazy dog lady who rescues dogs from derelict factories and speeds away in a getaway van.'

Ginny laughed. 'For a moment, you had me worried then.'

'So, what do you say? Shall we give us another try?'

'You're staying anyway?'

'I'm staying. Although if you say no, I might move to an island off the Scottish coast, but I still wouldn't be taking that job or moving back to London.'

Squeezing his hand, Ginny grinned. 'Then yes, I'd love to give us another go.'

'Thank you.' Leaning towards her, he kissed her, his lips warm and strong against hers.

She sunk into his embrace as he wrapped his arms around her. Resting her head against his chest, she listened to his heart beating, all of her worries and insecurities melted away and she knew in that moment that they were meant to be together. She knew that all her doubts about him had been because she'd been comparing him to Jason, trying to find a likeness between them, but they were as different to each other as they could be. Darryl was nothing like Jason. He'd proven that on so many occasions, but it had taken something like this to happen to make her realise, to open her eyes to who he truly was and to how she really felt about him. 'Percy was right after all.'

'What's that?' As he pulled away, Darryl frowned.

'Oh, he was trying to tell me that... It doesn't matter.'

'Okay. Time for bed, you two.' Flora opened the kitchen door before picking up her car keys. 'We've got a big day with the Family Fun Day tomorrow, so we all need our sleep.'

Ginny nodded and pulled her car keys out of her back pocket.

'Oh no, you don't. You're not going home alone tonight, Ginny. You can sleep at mine.' Flora stepped aside, before shutting the door behind them.

34

'Sorry.' Sally glanced behind her as she hurried past, her arms full of agility hurdles.

'No worries.' Ginny ran to catch up with her. 'Do you need a hand setting up the pen?'

'Ooh, that would be amazing. Everything's just taking twice as long as I thought it would. I think I'm just nervous about getting anything wrong as it's my first time. My first time here, at least, showing you what I can do.' She stepped over the short wooden fence of the area Percy had set up for the taster sessions.

'You'll be just fine. There's no need to be nervous.' Taking some hurdles from Sally, Ginny helped her stand them up on the ground.

'Thanks. This all looks fantastic. I can imagine you'll get a good crowd coming.' She smiled.

'I hope so.' Ginny looked around the paddock. The stall-holders were busy setting up, their wares an abundance of hand-crafted items, crystals, second-hand books and knitted cardies, creating a kaleidoscope of colour across the stalls. 'Do you need anything else?'

'No, I don't think so.' Sally adjusted the line of hurdles. 'Thank you.'

Smiling, Ginny walked towards the top paddock.

She leaned against the open gate and watched as Susan and Alex finished laying the wooden tiles for the disco area in front of the small stage where Tim and his band mates would perform. She could hear the band warming up already as well as the sound of Tim's voice as he checked the mic. Food vans and stalls circled the paddock, and Percy had penned another area for the dog show. Bunting danced in the slight breeze and happy dogs and their owners grinned from the banners she had fixed to the fences.

It didn't feel like yesterday when she and Percy had been setting up the stall. After everything that had happened between then and now, it might as well have been a year ago, the memories fuzzy and dreamlike.

'It's looking great, isn't it?'

Turning, Ginny spotted Darryl walking towards her, mobile in hand and Luna at his heel.

When they reached her, she crouched down and stroked Luna's ears. 'Hello, Luna,' she said sweetly and then turned back to Darryl. 'Yes, everything seems to be going to plan. So far at least. Have you got some good pics for the paper?'

'Yep.' He grinned as he looked down at his phone, the last photo he'd taken still filling the screen. 'I've popped them in a few local social media groups too.'

'Thank you.' She smiled at him.

'How are you bearing up?' Taking her hand, he laced his fingers between hers.

She shrugged. 'I'm trying not to think about it, especially after going over everything with the police earlier.'

'I've found out something I think you need to hear, but it is about the puppy farm, so I can tell you later if you'd prefer?' Darryl ran the pad of his thumb across the back of her hand.

'No, tell me now.' She took a deep breath. She'd rather hear it now and enjoy the day without wondering what it was.

'Someone had rung into the *Trestow Telegraph* with information about the whereabouts of the puppy farm.'

'Seriously? When? Who had they rung? Jason?' She gripped his other hand.

'Yes, Jason. Sometime yesterday before the offices closed for the day. I popped by there this morning before coming here to grab my portable phone charger, thought I'd submit an article I had written and there it was, a note on Jason's desk with the details of the puppy farm scribbled down.'

'Why hadn't he rung the police?'

'I don't know.' Darryl looked away, clenching his jaw. 'If he had though, yesterday evening wouldn't have happened. You wouldn't have risked your life to save those dogs.'

Reaching across, she cupped his chin, gently turning him to face her. 'Hey, I'm okay.'

'I know. I know. I just...' Darryl ran his fingers through his hair. 'I reported him to the owner of the paper. I didn't know what else to do.'

'There's nothing else you can do. Anyone can do. It's done.'

Darryl nodded slowly. 'I just can't believe he'd have kept that information to himself just so he could be the one to break the story. Every journalist knows that information which might put someone or an animal's life in danger gets reported to the police. Forget the story! It's common sense.'

Leaning forward, she touched his lips with hers. 'Darryl, I'm okay. The dogs are okay. We're all okay.'

'Yes.' Darryl glanced away.

'Now let's try not to think about any of it again. Not today. Let's enjoy the Family Fun Day.'

'You're right.' Nodding, Darryl drew her in for a hug, his arms enveloping her completely. 'In that case, shall we go and see if Elsie has a couple of spare cheese and onion pasties to keep our energy up before the gates open?'

'Now, I like that idea.' Grinning, she took hold of his hand and led the way. A small banner with the words 'The Cornish Bay Bakery' and a picture of a lighthouse hung from the front of the stall and an array of cakes, doughnuts and pasties filled the trays. 'Hi, Elsie.'

'Hello, Ginny, love. Hello, Darryl. How are you both doing today? Flora told me about your scare last night.'

'We're okay, thanks.'

'Oh, good. This is all looking great.' Elsie indicated the paddocks. 'All I've been hearing in the bakery this week is people talking about coming today.'

'Really?' Ginny smiled.

'Yes, love. You've done an amazing job. I have a feeling you're going to do very well today.'

'I hope so. Especially now we have all those puppies coming, we're going to need all the money we can raise.'

'Ginny, Darryl. Wow, I can't believe what you did last night.' Diane, who worked with Elsie at the bakery, slid two trays onto the stall's countertop before drawing Ginny in for a hug. 'So glad you're okay.'

'Diane, how are things with you?'

'Oh, I'm good. Happy to be helping Elsie out here today. The bakery will likely be super quiet this afternoon, going by all the interest Alex's posters have had anyway. Plus, I get to see all the dogs.' She looked behind her. 'Anyway, I'd best go and fetch the rest. We've still got the cookies, shortbreads and brownies to put out yet.'

'Thanks, Diane.' Elsie smiled at her before turning back to Ginny and Darryl. 'Can I get you two something? I don't suppose you've had much of a chance to eat today, not with all the setting up to do.'

'Yes, please. A couple of your famous cheese and onion pasties would go down a treat,' Darryl said.

As Elsie prepared their food for them, using tongs to select their pasties and popping them into little paper bags, Darryl snapped some photos of the stall.

'Here, you both go. Get those down you and enjoy the day.'

'Thanks.' Ginny turned and before taking even one bite of the pasty, another person had come over to see her.

'Ginny, there you are.' Flora came to a stop, breathless. 'Have you seen the courtyard? It's full of people!'

'What? Really?'

'Yes, really!' Flora grinned. 'I don't think I've ever seen it so busy. Come on, lovely.'

Placing the pasty back in the bag, Ginny began to walk back through the paddocks.

'I'll let you open the bottom gate into the paddocks and open the event.'

'Oh, I don't know.' Ginny frowned.

'Hold on, wait for me.' Darryl jogged towards them. 'I'll take some photos.'

'Oh no, you won't. Not of me, anyway.' Ginny laughed. 'Take photos of the visitors.'

As they walked through the bottom paddock, Ginny could hear excited voices carrying on the slight breeze. Flora must be right, there must be quite a lot of people waiting to come in. As she turned the corner, Ginny saw just how right she was. The courtyard was heaving with people, and their dogs. So many people.

Rubbing Ginny's shoulder, Flora indicated her to open the gate.

'Go on. Let them in,' Darryl said, leaning across and pecking her on the cheek. 'You deserve this after all the work you've put in.'

'Okay.' Taking a deep breath, Ginny stepped forward and pulled the gate open. 'Hi, everyone. Come on in. Thanks for coming.'

The crowd began to filter through the gate, the sound of excited murmuring filling the air.

'Hello, Ginny.' Stepping away from the gate, Mr Euston waved at her. By his feet was Gray, the little French bulldog. 'Me and Gray have been looking forward to this. I might even pop him in for a tracking taster lesson. If how quickly he finds the hiding place for his treats is anything to go by, he should be pretty good at it!'

'I think that's a brilliant idea, Mr Euston.' Bending down, Ginny fussed over Gray who immediately began sniffing her pocket. Laughing, Ginny pulled out a dog treat. 'I see what you mean. You, Gray, might give Luna a bit of competition.'

'Hold that pose right there!' Darryl laughed as he held up his phone to use the camera. 'Smile.'

Rolling her eyes, Ginny drew Luna and Gray towards her and grinned.

* * *

'How's it going?' Stepping over the small fence penning in the training area, Ginny passed Sally a bottle of water.

'Great. I think. We've had the hoopers and agility sessions and they were all full. I've almost run out of business cards too, so I'm hoping that's a good sign. And thanks.' Taking the bottle, Sally downed half of it. 'I'm just about to begin the first of our tracking lessons.'

Looking across at the gathering crowd, Ginny spotted Darryl and Luna in the queue as well as Mr Euston and Gray. 'That's definitely a good sign about the business cards. I might hang around for this one, if that's okay?'

'Yes, of course.'

A spring in her step, Ginny went over to the queue where Darryl, Luna, Mr Euston and Gray were standing. 'I hope you two aren't going to get too competitive?'

'Ha ha, of course not. Well, maybe a little.' Darryl held his index finger and thumb slightly apart.

'Yes, just a little. Although I'm not sure how well Gray will hold up unless there's food involved.' Laughing, Mr Euston leaned down and petted Gray.

'Ha ha, I think Luna's little habit of falling to the floor and demanding attention may just let us down so we'll both be in the same position.' Darryl looked down at Luna, who had immediately flopped to the floor as soon as Ginny had walked over.

Ginny looked up from where she'd been fussing over the dogs. 'They might surprise you both, you never know.'

'Maybe. As long as we all have fun that's the main thing.' Darryl chuckled.

Sally indicated to Darryl and Luna to join her. 'Can you come forward and we'll make a start?'

Stepping back, Ginny shoved her hands in her pockets and watched as Sally instructed Darryl before showing Luna a small pot of treats. She smiled. Maybe Gray would give Luna a run for her money after all.

'Hello, you.'

Ginny turned and grinned as Flora hugged her around the shoulders. 'Hey.'

'I can't quite believe how many people have come today.' Flora gestured around the paddock. 'We've had so many people enquiring about adoptions. Susan reckons she's had about ten people ask about Tiger and Belle. People who want to adopt them as a pair!'

'Wow, that's amazing.'

'It sure is. Oh, look, Luna found that straight away!' Flora pointed over to Luna who was quickly wolfing down the treat she'd found, before immediately returning to the task, on the search for the next one.

Ginny grinned at Darryl who was standing at the side watching. She gave him a thumbs up.

'I've got to say, I'm so glad you and Darryl managed to sort out your differences,' Flora said, rubbing Ginny's arm affectionately.

'Me too.'

* * *

'Aw, Carrie, I can't believe you make these. They're beautiful.' Ginny picked up the large, curved vase, which was imprinted with wildflowers.

'Thanks.' Carrie grinned before turning to serve a customer.

'Did you see her?' Placing an arm around her waist, Darryl kissed her on the cheek. 'Luna was fantastic at the tracking, wasn't she?'

'Yes, I did. She was brilliant, weren't you, Luna?' She knelt and held out a dog treat for her.

'Hey what about me?' Darryl raised his eyebrows.

'Oh, sorry.' Standing, Ginny pulled a treat from her pocket again and held it towards Darryl.

Chuckling, he drew her in for a hug.

Feeling a nudging on her leg, Ginny turned around. 'Tyler, hello, sweetie. How are you?' She laughed as Tyler's whole body weaved from side to side as he wagged his tail, before looking up at the Smiths. 'How's he settling in?'

'Oh, he's been brilliant. Everyone who's been round our house has commented that he seems right at home. It feels as though he's been with us forever too.' Mrs Smith looked down at Tyler as he sniffed Luna.

'Yes, we can't thank you enough for all you and the rest of the staff and volunteers have done for him.' Mr Smith nodded at Ginny.

'Oh, it's nothing.' She shrugged, the familiar heat of embarrassment creeping up her neck.

'It really isn't.' Mrs Smith shook her head. 'This place is literally a lifeline for so many dogs.'

'Thank you.' Ginny glanced towards the top paddock as Flora's voice announced the imminent start of the Wagging Tails Dog Show.

'Oops, we'd better get going,' Mrs Smith said. 'We've signed this one up for the dog show.'

She waved as they made their way towards Flora's voice.

'It's so lovely to see him happy and settled,' Ginny said as she watched Tyler trot alongside his new family, his chin up and his tail constantly swinging to and fro.

Looking around, she realised the bottom paddock was emptying quickly as everyone was making their way towards where the dog show was being hosted. They quickly joined the back of the crowds filtering into the top paddock.

'I think you can safely say this day has been a success.' Darryl grinned as he placed his arm around her waist.

'It's not been so bad, has it?' She looked into his eyes. 'Thank you for all you've done in advertising it.'

'You're welcome, but it's you who's made it a success. All the hours you put into the planning and organising, they've paid off.'

* * *

* * *

Ginny clapped, standing on her tiptoes, her hands above her head, straining her neck to see above the crowds circling the arena to the dog show. She could just about see as Flora passed a large silver trophy to the Smiths. Tyler received an equally large dog treat.

'Aw, that's lovely, isn't it? What a lovely ending to Tyler's journey at Wagging Tails.'

'Are you crying?' Darryl raised an eyebrow.

'No, my eyes are just leaking.' She swiped at her eyes.

Chuckling, Darryl wrapped his arm around her, pulling her closer. 'You're amazing, you know that, don't you?'

'Ha ha, very funny.'

'I'm being serious. Everything you do for these dogs, the hours you work, the love you show them. There're not many people in the world who care that much.'

'Oh, there is. As Flora always says, there's more good in the world than bad, it's just that we only hear about the bad. We just need to search the good out ourselves.'

Darryl cleared his throat. 'Fair enough. There are others who care, but not many who actually act on that, and even fewer who dedicate their lives to what they so passionately care about. You work tirelessly for them. For all of the dogs you look after.'

Ginny shrugged, a warm blush flashing across her cheeks. 'They give back more than I can ever give them.'

Shaking his head, Darryl gently pulled her towards him before kissing her forehead.

'So, what's next?' he asked. 'I'm guessing although this is your biggest event of the year, there'll be something else to plan?'

'Oh, yes, there's no rest in raising funds, that's for sure.' Shaking her head, Ginny laughed. 'All of us are full of ideas. Like Alex... After creating those amazing posters for today, he's been bitten by the creative bug again and is hoping to draw and sell portraits of people's dogs and give the profit to the home.'

'Really? That's amazing. I can imagine him doing that though, the drawings on the posters were fantastic.'

'Exactly, I think he'll do very well out of it. Flora's been speaking about—' Ginny stopped, as Dylan, a young boy from West Par ran across to them. 'Hey, Dylan, is everything okay?'

'Yes. Guess what?' The young boy grinned as his Jack Russell sniffed around Ginny.

'What?' Bending down, Ginny fussed over the dog before standing and looking at Dylan again.

'Me and Pixie got to do the agility lesson this year!' Dylan's eyes shone with excitement as he hopped from foot to foot. 'And my mum's said I might be able to join Sally's classes when she starts them.'

'Wow, that's amazing.' Ginny smiled. She remembered Susan saying that Dylan had been disappointed last year when he hadn't been able to try the taster.

'See you later.' Dylan turned. 'I think I'm going to go and buy one of Elsie's cupcakes.'

'Hold on, Dylan. I think I may have taken a photo of Pixie during the agility session.' Darryl scrolled through his photos before holding up his phone, a picture of Pixie jumping over a hurdle filling the screen. 'I can print it off for you if you like? Maybe leave it here at Wagging Tails so you and your mum can collect it?'

'Really? That would be awesome! Thank you.'

'You're welcome.' Darryl waved as Dylan and Pixie ran off towards Elsie's stall before turning his attention back to Ginny. 'I have something for you too.'

'Oh? What?'

'Come with me to the bottom paddock and I'll show you.' Smiling, he took her hand and led the way through the crowds of people.

'What have you got me?'

'Ah, over here.'

Frowning, Ginny followed him towards Carrie's pottery stall.

'Hi, you two.' Carrie grinned at them both. She placed a bag on top of her stall before looking at Darryl. 'Have you come to collect?'

'I sure have.'

Smiling, Darryl thanked Carrie before gently pulling out a vase from the bag and passing it to Ginny.

'It's the vase I was looking at earlier!' She smiled as she turned it around in her hands, the beautifully pressed wildflowers a splash of colour against the white curved ceramic. 'You bought it for me?'

'I sure did.' He shrugged. 'I saw you admiring it earlier.'

She slipped the vase back in the bag and then cupped his face in her hands, drawing him towards her, their lips millimetres apart.

'Thank you.'

As their lips touched, Ginny closed her eyes.

EPILOGUE

'That's it, sweetheart. You can do it.' Ginny gently stroked Lily's nose as she panted against the pain. She looked over at Darryl who was sitting on the kennel floor, his legs crossed, rubbing a tiny bundle of a puppy in his hands. Ginny frowned. 'How's he doing? Is he breathing yet?'

Darryl looked at the newborn golden retriever in his hands, the tiny body floppy against his palm, and a deep crease formed between his eyebrows. In that moment, the small pup began writhing against Darryl's hold and a huge grin replaced the concern etched across his face. 'He's okay.'

'What a dramatic entrance, that was, little one.' She gently stroked the small pup before taking him and laying him next to his litter mates at his mum's side. Turning back to Lily, Ginny whispered, 'Come on, Mama, one more pup to go. Just one more.'

'That's it, Lily. You can do it.' Darryl reached out, stroking her across the back.

Ginny watched as the eighth and final puppy entered the world, the sac intact around the tiny body. Reaching forward, she broke the membrane before picking up the pup and blowing in its face. 'You're going to be a lucky little thing, aren't you?'

'That's supposed to be good luck, being born in the sac still, isn't it?' Darryl shook his head, his eyes glistening.

'It sure is.' Grinning, she placed the puppy under Lily's nose and then watched as Lily cleaned her youngest pup.

'I can't believe you're going to have to find eight more new homes.' Darryl made a face.

'I know. Plus, when the other two dogs from the puppy farm give birth, there'll be those pups too.' Looking at Darryl, Ginny smiled. 'We may have to talk nicely to some cute, kind and dog-loving journalist who might be willing to write a piece in the local paper. Bring in some interest.'

'Cute? Don't you mean handsome?' Darryl raised his eyebrows.

'Ha ha, of course. Cute, handsome and everything in between.' Leaning across, she pecked him on the lips.

'Glad to hear it.' Darryl stood up and stretched his arms above his head. 'And, yes, of course, I'd be more than honoured to write an article about the puppies.' Pausing, he looked at her. 'Or maybe we could continue with our column about Wagging Tails? That way we could follow the puppies' stories, let readers get to know the pups and their little characters even before they're ready to be adopted.'

'That's a great idea!' Ginny smiled. 'That could work so well.'

'Yes, I'd have to run it past Mr Ego of course though.'

'Umm, yes.' Ginny sighed. 'Still, you never know, he might agree, even if there's only a slim chance.'

'Yep, there's always hope.'

Wiping her hands down her jeans, Ginny glanced back at Lily and her newborn puppies. 'Look what she's done. Eight perfect babies.'

Placing his arms around her waist, Darryl pulled her in. 'And just think of the wonderful future they'll all have, including precious Lily. All because of you.'

Looking back at the golden retriever, she smiled. In the short few days Lily had been with them, all she'd shown them was kindness, perception, and love.

'Not that for one moment I'm condoning what you did, putting yourself in danger like that to rescue them. There were better, safer ways of going about it.'

'I know, but it's done now.' She turned back to him. 'I still can't believe Flora has managed to track down Lily's owners, her original owners before those—' She shook her head. 'Before she was stolen.'

'It sure does feel like a miracle.'

'Flora always says miracles do happen.' She grinned. 'And I think we've had a fair few recently, what with the Family Fun Day going well.'

'Going well? You mean being a roaring success and bringing in a record amount of funds for the home?'

She shrugged.

'And that's down to you and all the hours you put into planning it.' Darryl smiled.

Ginny raised her eyebrows. 'Don't you mean you raising the awareness of it?'

'Honestly? No, I don't. The Family Fun Day turned out as well as it did because of you. Because of your dedication. People would have come in droves anyway. Word gets around. All I did was to speed up the process.'

'Umm, and you say I can't take praise.' Ginny laughed.

Darryl shrugged and squeezed her tighter to him, kissing her on the forehead just as the shrill ringtone of his mobile interrupted the quietness in the air. 'Drat. Sorry.'

Ginny waited until Darryl had stepped out of the kennel to take the call before sitting back down on the concrete floor, turning back to Lily and her beautiful pups. Smoothing the edge of the duvet Lily was lying on, she whispered quietly, 'Well done, Lily. You're a picture-perfect family now.'

As the kennel door clicked quietly shut behind her, she looked back towards Darryl, his face ashen, his mobile still in hand. Standing up, she rushed across to him.

'Is everything okay? Has something happened? Is it your dad?'

'No, it was the owner of the *Trestow Telegraph*. Jason's been fired , and they've offered me his job.' Darryl shook his head, the colour slowly returning to his cheeks.

'What? Seriously?' Ginny opened and closed her mouth, not knowing what else to say.

He nodded slowly. 'Apparently, he's gone back to London. Left a note on his desk.'

'What did you say about the job?'

'I accepted it.' He grinned.

Grinning back, Ginny took his hands in hers, his mobile caught in the middle. 'That's amazing!'

'Thank you.' He shook his head. 'I don't really know what to think about it all. I can't quite believe what's just happened.'

'You better start believing it.' Standing on her tiptoes, she kissed him gently, his lips soft beneath hers.

'I'm not sure I can. I think it's going to take a good few days for the news to sink in.'

'You know what this means, don't you?' Ginny looked at him and smiled.

'That I've got the best of both worlds? I get the promotion I've worked my working life towards while staying in West Par, being there for my dad and being surrounded by people I can happily call my friends?'

'Yes, all that. And something else too.'

'The love of my life actually believing me that I want to stay and that I'm not missing out careerwise by not returning to the city?'

'Aw, you called me the love of your life.' Ginny held his gaze.

'Of course I did.' Leaning forward, he kissed her.

Ginny laughed. 'You're forgetting something.'

Rubbing his stubble, Darryl frowned. 'I can't think. Well, I can. There are so many positives I can think of, but I have a feeling I'm not going to be able to guess yours too easily.'

'Okay, do you want me to tell you?'

'I do.' He nodded.

'It was that now the buck stops with you at the *Trestow Telegraph*, you'll be able to run whatever stories you want.'

'Of course. In that case, I can officially tell you that, yes, I have decided to write a column on Wagging Tails, and no one can stop me.' He grinned.

'Glad to hear it.' She leaned closer. 'Seriously, thank you.'

Pulling away, Darryl slipped his phone into the back pocket of his jeans and took her hands again, clasping them tightly. 'I love you, Ginny Stevenson.'

Her eyes widening, Ginny felt a warmth rush through her body. 'I love you too, Darryl.'

'Ginny, Darryl.' Flora's voice wafted through from the kennel next door. 'Tinkerbell's started labouring.'

'You've got to be kidding.'

Still holding Darryl's hands, Ginny glanced quickly at Lily and her pups before running through to the kennel next door, Darryl right by her side.

AUTHOR'S NOTE

I'd like to take this opportunity to give a huge shout-out to Wellidogs, a no-kill shelter based in Grendon, Northamptonshire. The dedicated team rescue dogs from the pound and those abandoned or handed in to them. They work tirelessly to provide the gorgeous dogs in their care a safe home, full bellies and, above all, love and kindness.

At Wellidogs, dogs are given a second chance. They are shown patience, training and affection. The wonderful dogs are assessed, trained and given the opportunity to find their forever home, the home they deserve.

As with Ralph at Wagging Tails, they have resident dogs who, for various reasons, have made their home at Wellidogs. These beautiful dogs will spend the rest of their days secure in the knowledge they will forever be loved and cared for at Wellidogs.

Please, if you are considering re-homing a dog, then check out the deserving dogs at Wellidogs, waiting hopefully to be welcomed into a home just like yours. https://wellidog.org/

As a local charity they rely on the generosity of their supporters and the general public to continue rescuing and rehoming the dogs so if you can support them by liking their Facebook page, joining their group, or liking and sharing their posts, or donating, I know they'd be ever so grateful. Facebook page: https://www.facebook.com/wellidogs Facebook group: https://www.facebook.com/groups/wellingboroughdogwelfare

ACKNOWLEDGMENTS

Thank you, readers, so much for reading *The Wagging Tails Dogs'
Home*. I hope you've enjoyed reading about Ginny, Darryl, Flora,
Ralph and all of the Wagging Tails family, humans and dogs, as
much as I have enjoyed writing their story.

A huge thank you to my wonderful children, Ciara and Leon,
who motivate me to keep writing and working towards 'changing
our stars' each and every day. Also to my lovely family for always
being there, through the good times and the trickier ones.

I'd like to thank my sister, Jasmine, her partner, Aidan, and
my niece, Amy, who have given me an insight into volunteering at
a dogs' home.

I'd also like to take this opportunity to thank each and every
person who works or volunteers at a dogs' home or rescue centre.
Thank you for caring for the dogs in your care, and for relent-
lessly fighting for their future and happiness. You are wonderful
beyond words.

And a massive thank you to my amazing editor, Emily Yau,
who reached out and believed in me – thank you. Thank you also
to Sandra Ferguson for copyediting Wagging Tails, and Shirley
Khan for proofreading. And, of course, Clare Stacey for creating
the beautiful cover. Thank you to all at Team Boldwood!

Of course, I need to thank a chance encounter with a golden
lab called Lily and her owner. Lily being the inspiration for
Luna's cute habit of throwing herself at the feet of strangers and
friends alike and refusing to move unless fussed.

MORE FROM SARAH HOPE

We hope you enjoyed reading *The Wagging Tails Dogs' Home*. If you did, please leave a review.

If you'd like to gift a copy, this book is also available as an ebook, large print, hardback, digital audio download and audiobook CD.

Sign up to Sarah Hope's mailing list for news, competitions and updates on future books.

https://bit.ly/SarahHopeNews

ABOUT THE AUTHOR

Sarah Hope is the author of many successful romance novels, including the bestselling Cornish Bakery series. She lives in Central England with her two children and an array of pets, and enjoys escaping to the seaside at any opportunity.

Follow Sarah Hope on social media:

twitter.com/sarahhope35

facebook.com/HappinessHopeDreams

instagram.com/sarah_hope_writes

Boldw⚭d

Printed in Great Britain
by Amazon